**JESSICA GOEKEN**

**Evernight Teen ®**

**www.evernightteen.com**

**Copyright© 2025**

**Jessica Goeken**

ISBN: 978-0-3695-1136-2

Cover Artist: Jay Aheer

Editor: Melissa Hosack

**JESSICA GOEKEN**

# DEDICATION

For Jeffrey, my first successful sequel.

## ACKNOWLEDGEMENTS

I would like to take a moment to thank the people who helped me make this book a reality. My husband, who continues to support me even when things don't always go according to plan. My boys, who inspire me every day to keep chasing my dreams because I want to show them what dream-chasing looks like. My beta readers, Jake and Katy, who never fail to give me invaluable feedback and make my story better every time. And Evernight Teen, for helping to make this indie author's dreams come true.

**JESSICA GOEKEN**

# DOMINANCE BEHAVIORS

## *The Keystone Species Trilogy, 2*

**Jessica Goeken**

**Copyright © 2025**

### Chapter One

Fae want to live. That truth, buried deep inside, is what keeps my feet flat on the floor instead of the open windowsill as I watch General Halasuwa's procession move across the courtyard below. It would be so easy to tip too far forward and end this imprisonment once and for all.

'Courtyard' may be a stretch, but it's the closest word I have to describe the area surrounding the fortress. Nothing grows here. My world is darkness and stone, as devoid of the warmth of life as the Fomorians are of compassion and mercy. A resounding thud echoes up as the first guards reach my tower and throw open the heavy wooden door. Must be time.

A deep breath steadies my nerves. *He hasn't killed you yet. What makes you think he'll do it today?* Truthfully, I'm only alive to stoke Halasuwa's ego. The moment he feels like I no longer serve that purpose he won't hesitate to reunite me with my slaughtered people.

The Realm ceased smoking long ago, yet the Fomorians still feast as though on the eve of their victory. My every hair is in place, that is, in a state of utter dishevelment, when the horn sounds outside my door. The same clothes I wore in that fateful battle slip and flap on my gaunt frame, still dirty, still bearing the blood of those who died protecting me. I'm not allowed to wash them, these symbols of my absolute defeat.

I know my place. Under Halasuwa's heel. My life hangs on this performance, and every performance stretching endlessly into the future. The more debased I appear, the happier the Fomorian leader is, and the closer my escape becomes.

"Your Majesty?" The question is a sneer as the guard opens my door without bothering to knock. I don't warrant such a basic courtesy. The flickering torches in the otherwise dark hallway throw his ram's horns into menacing shadows.

"I am ready," I answer with a steady voice. The guards close in as I enter their midst, as if I pose any kind of threat to them. Without my magic I'm as defenseless as I appear. Sixteen, skinny, weak. Alone. Through the hallway. Down the stairs. Nothing new to see, but I keep my eyes at the ready just in case. Halasuwa doesn't summon me often, so when he does, I have to make full use of the opportunity. The dark, cold stone yields no secrets, and my guards are silent as always.

The guards lead me deep underground, although the fortress of Canowin Hollow already exists in the bowels of the earth. I am kept in a tower, but that tower is merely the highest point of the deepest cave I've ever seen. The weight of the rock above pushes against me, reminding my very being that I do not belong down here.

I am Fae, and Fae belong beneath the sky, not buried under the ground.

Halasuwa's banquet hall lies deeper still, and the effort to walk down hundreds of stairs does nothing to keep the chill from settling in my bones. By the time we reach the bottom I'm shivering, and I only keep my teeth from chattering through sheer force of will.

As I descend the final staircase a hoof the size of a dinner plate slides into my path, catching my foot and sending me tumbling headfirst down the remaining steps. I should have seen it coming. My guards snicker but don't outright laugh, and no one offers to help me up. I say nothing, pushing myself upright and wincing as my badly healed broken ankle falters. I wipe the slime off my hands and wait.

When the hall doors open, the noise of revelry spills out, dinner already in full swing. More horns announce my arrival, and the guards prod me forward as a hush falls over the guests. I am led through the center of the hall, between rows of gawking strangers, until finally stopping before the elevated table at the far end.

Halasuwa notices the fresh grime but says nothing. His standing order says I am not to be harmed; however, there is a general understanding that a little bullying is okay. My guards melt away as Halasuwa stands, commanding every eye in the room. Even for a Fomorian, he's massive, the stump of his arm where Danen took his hand only serving to make him look more formidable. Battle-hardened. Undefeatable.

"Honored guests!" Halasuwa bellows the words, even though silence has reigned in the hall since my grand entrance. No amount of dirt can hide my golden skin and silver hair, an unmistakable sign of my royalty. "May I present Her Majesty, Eve La Stella, Queen of the Fae!"

A roar follows this announcement. On cue, I drop to one knee and bow my head. "General."

"Please, join me, Your Majesty." Snickers race around the room. No one believes his use of my title is sincere, but I rise and ascend the dais anyway. We've each delivered our lines, and the satisfied look on Halasuwa's face tells me my life, for tonight, is secure. I take my place as dinner resumes, a Fomorian-sized chair that swallows my frame and leaves my feet dangling slightly behind and to Halasuwa's left. I'm not permitted to eat, so I don't even look at the food. Instead, I sweep my eyes over the crowd, trying to see who Halasuwa is shmoozing tonight.

Riding high on his victory over the Realm, General Halasuwa was not content to merely return home and live out his days. No. Now that his vengeance is complete it is time for the Fomorians to once again claim their place in the workings of the world. I am his tool, his proof that he is everything the rumors claim him to be. And every time he shows off his new pet, he gains allies fearful of having his might turned on them next.

I don't have names for many of the creatures I've seen in this hall, but I'm pretty sure I know who his guests are tonight. *Goblins*. They smell even worse than the Fomorians, and since they stand only hip-high to the warriors watching them mingle together is almost laughable. I don't laugh. I keep a careful mask of misery plastered on my face, even as their beady eyes rove over me and their hairy fingers make rude gestures in my direction. The Fae have historically had little contact with goblins, as they have no magic and had nothing we desired. There's no denying their interest in me, though. Their hungry gazes make me feel like a lamb paraded in front of a pride of lions.

A small band of goblins approaches the high table

and snag Halasuwa's attention. Their torsos are adorned with blood-red sashes glinting with silver pins, setting them apart from the ordinary rabble occupying the rest of the tables. The delegates, I assume. I can't hear their words over the general ruckus, but their intention becomes clear when Halasuwa nods his head in my direction.

Wicked smiles cross their twisted faces as they approach my chair. I let my fear show, knowing any assertion of pride will reflect badly on Halasuwa.

The goblins mutter amongst themselves in their native tongue, rasps and growls that set my teeth on edge.

Then one of them touches me.

Lightly at first, running its fingers through my silver hair. It cackles, and the others join in, poking and prodding, picking at my skin and clothes.

Their touch makes my skin itch, like tiny insects are crawling all over me. I can't help but squirm, and their picking becomes harsher, more aggressive. Then one of them licks me, leaving a trail of fire across my cheek, and I scream.

"Enough." For the first time, I'm thankful to hear Halasuwa's booming voice. The goblins back off, then grumpily slink away. Halasuwa doesn't look at me, and I'm glad. What would happen if he saw the relief and gratitude in my eyes?

The goblins are still looking at me and muttering, so I search for somewhere else to look. *Keep learning. There's always something new for you to see, you just have to find it.* My eyes land on another table, off to the side but not so far from Halasuwa as to be an insult to their rank.

A rowdy cluster of Fomorians occupies this table, deep in the throes of obvious drunkenness. It doesn't appear to be a happy drunkenness, however. Scowls mar their faces, and more than one sends a disgusted look my way. In the center is a face I recognize, leaning in close and talking fast. His brown skin and budded horns stir a level of emotion in me I can't afford to let anyone see. *Caspian.*

As if drawn by my gaze, his head abruptly swivels, eyes locking onto mine. The scar on his cheek, courtesy of Danen, lies too pale against his brown skin. His expression falters for a heartbeat before he gets swept up in the conversation again. I've lost track of the number of times he's saved my life. And of the number of times he's betrayed me.

His presence here tonight, the only Fae besides me among a sea of enemies, tells me everything I need to know about his loyalty. I tear my gaze away, riveting my eyes to the floor for the rest of the meal.

Still, even with my eyes down I'm not unaware of the precariousness of my situation. I can still feel their eyes on me. Caspian's. The goblins'. Even Halasuwa's. Watching every twitch of my face for a hint of anything more than total subservience. It's a dangerous game I play. Yet, play it I must. My life depends on it. My people depend on it.

## Chapter Two

Eventually, I'm dismissed. I've played my part, and when Fomorians get drunk, they get violent. Can't have them in the same room as the very breakable Fae Queen. Not Halasuwa, though. No drinking for him. He's not the kind of man to ever let his guard down.

I'm escorted upstairs and deposited back into my tower, my guards eager to return downstairs to their own meals. A bowl of water waits for me. Cold, of course. I don't merit hot water. The door isn't even latched before I'm tearing off my filthy clothes and splashing water across my body. My skin feels raw from the goblins' poisonous touch, and just being around Fomorians makes me crave cleanliness. I scrub until my skin stings and wash my hair, then wrap myself up in the clean clothes I do have. They are Fomorian clothes, so large I keep them strategically pinned, but at least I stay warm. It's only when I'm dry and snuggled in that I begin trembling.

*I don't know how much longer I can do this.* Another thought answers the first, stronger and bolder. *As long as you have to.*

I rise in response, jumping up and down to loosen my cold, clenched muscles. Eyes closed, I take ten deep breaths, hands raised up to the sky. Channeling Danen, I bend my knees and move through my defensive postures.

Half an hour later, I'm warmed up and ready. I move more quickly now, calling up lessons from the depths of my memories, dredging up every ounce of wisdom Danen tried to impart. I kick and punch, lashing out with all my strength, which in my current condition isn't much. I tire easily, but I push through anyway. He would expect me to. Dodge and thrust. Jump and duck. I've spent every night training my body to move like

Danen's. Someday I'll need it. I just hope it's enough.

*I'm not giving up, Danen. I promise.*

As always, just the thought of him stirs memories I wish I could banish. The crack of his neck as Halasuwa broke his body. His limp form lying on the ground. The Wild Hunt descending from the sky and stealing him away from the battlefield. He's out there. Somewhere. I have to believe he's out there.

I have Fae still out there, too. I don't know how many, or what condition they're in, or even where to find them, but I choose to believe they're out there. They're too out of reach, though. Too many unknowns separate them from me. I can't make promises to them. So I keep my focus narrow and make my promises to Danen, knowing he'd be the one expecting me to get myself out of this mess and put everything right. If only I knew how to do that.

I train until the first rumbling voices reach my window from the courtyard. The lightweights, abandoning the party downstairs and making their way to the tunnels and caverns they call home. The movements of the Fomorians are the only way I can track the passage of time so far from the sun. If they're leaving dinner that means it's late, but not too late. The heavy hitters will drink until they pass out there at the tables. Others will filter through the fortress searching for empty beds, or at least empty corridors. The transition is my cue to go to bed, though. I've long gotten used to the flimsy straw mattress and the threadbare blanket, and my fatigue drags me under before my body registers the chill in the air.

The next morning my nanny arrives. 'Nanny' being a joke, of course, because female goats are called nannies. Interestingly, in all my lessons with Master Feufollet and in all my invasion discussions with, well, everyone, the subject of female Fomorians never came up, and it never occurred to me to ask. Obviously there would be females, but Fae history apparently took no notice of them. They weren't in the battle at Emain Ablach. Of this I'm sure. Not that they aren't formidable; trust me, the females are every bit as massive as the males, with their own impressive set of horns. Their snouts are shortened, like on a boxer or a pug, and their hair is less bristly.

My nanny's name is Shosce, and I only know that because one of my guards addressed her that way. She's never introduced herself to me, or spoken anything other than guttural Fomorian words I can't understand. Our people share a common language ancestor, but with the division between us our languages naturally grew apart. The warriors seem to speak more clearly, but those who stay close within Canowin Hollow speak a stronger dialect. While the core is there, I struggle to make sense of the more obscure words.

Shosce comes every few days to make sure I am being cared for and to escort me about the fortress for exercise. Her idea of exercise is vastly different from mine. My legs yearn to run free, my body screams for challenge and resistance and exertion. I settle for my walks without complaint, though. It's better than being left to rot.

Today, Shosce scowls more heavily than usual, clutching my chin in her jaw and turning my head to each side. She lingers on the cheek licked by the goblin last night but ultimately decides it doesn't need medical attention. It still stings, though, and when I try to tell her that she shakes my head and makes a throaty clucking noise. She finishes her examination, poking and prodding much like the goblins did, and apparently decides I'm healthy enough. Again, our definitions differ. I'm malnourished, having lost the muscle mass I gained training with Danen and then some. My hair is so limp and broken my maid Tupi wouldn't be able to handle it. This is just the way Halasuwa wants me, though, so this is what he gets.

Shosce leads me out of my room and two guards fall into place about ten feet behind me. I catch a glimpse of their bored expressions and have to admit I see their point. What am I going to do, overpower her? Make a run for it? Any attempt would end with me bloody and broken, or worse. Still, we put on the charade that I'm dangerous.

The hallways of the fortress itself are deserted. Even with overwhelming numbers the Fomorians still took a major hit in the battle, and many of those who survived returned to their own homes in the surrounding tunnels after the initial celebrations. Of those who reside permanently in the fortress, most likely drank heavily at dinner last night and won't stir for quite some time. The gloomy stone hallways echo beneath the hooves of my companions as we make our circuit.

Of course, Halasuwa won't allow me to be taken near any sensitive areas. The rooms we pass are spartan in decoration with an air of disuse. Leftovers from a more vibrant, bygone era. The torches burn dimly, if at all, allowing lengths of darkness to permeate the space. We finally reach the stairs on the far side and travel down, down, always down. The curse of living in the top of a tower. Now it's time for my 'fresh air'.

I do give credit to the Fomorian craftsmen who built this fortress, though whether they used their hands or their magic is lost on me. Its sheer size is impossible to view all at once. The building is nestled into the rock as if grown straight out of the ground, the cave ceiling hovering scant inches from the tallest towers. The walls look to be one solid piece of aged gray stone, divots and channels worn away by the intermittent dripping from above. My tower alone is unblemished, having been plopped right onto the top upon my arrival. Quickly, too, as if by magic.

Fomorian magic. I've yet to see any in action. I know it's objectively weaker than Fae magic, but nobody bothered to instruct me on the details. Feelings bubble up, but I quash them before they can fully manifest. No use dwelling on the things I can't change. If anyone had seen this coming I would have been instructed differently. Treated differently.

*Hanathen saw this coming.* My mother, the queen, in her limited prophetic vision warned me of the incoming Fomorians. She told me I was the only one who could save my people. Fat lot of good that did me, huh? I failed anyway.

From this position, I can see the openings of four different tunnels heading away from the fortress and venturing deeper into the rock walls surrounding us. More tunnels open on the far side, out of my view. Much as I've tried, I can't remember which tunnel brought me here from the Realm. Halasuwa wasn't shy about allowing me to see my surroundings, fully confident I was never leaving his possession. Even if I were to bolt, I would be instantly lost. Everything looks the same; I can't see the subtle differences that allow the Fomorians to navigate so easily.

A commotion down one of the branching tunnels draws Shosce's attention. She stares hard in that direction before shaking her head and turning a different way.

"Troublemakers," one of the guards mutters behind me.

"They should know better," the other answers, obviously knowing what's going on.

I strain my eyes, but of course I can't see in the

dark anymore. I open my mouth to ask before remembering they wouldn't tell me anyway. It's a quiet life I lead now.

What happens next is anything but quiet. Two forms detach from the darkness inside the farthest tunnel to the left and run straight at me. The sight is so bizarre it takes a moment for me to register them as rams. As they come into the light, I recognize them as the ones shooting me dirty looks from Caspian's table last night. They bellow as they charge my guard head-on.

## Chapter Three

Shosce roars back in defiance and lowers her horns to meet the charge. The guard on my right steps up beside her, ready to defend me against whatever nefarious plans my attackers have. The guard on the left moves forward, too.

Then he snatches me around the waist and bolts in the opposite direction. Shosce calls out in alarm but my guard/kidnapper pays her no heed.

I scream. There's not much else I can do.

The guard slings me over his shoulder and barrels into the tunnel on the far right.

Before the darkness closes in around us, I see Shosce and the abandoned guard clash with the decoys, unable to change direction quickly enough to follow me instead. Then we turn a corner and the light vanishes entirely. I beat feebly against my kidnapper's back, but I might as well be pounding on a mountain. The hard muscle doesn't yield and the kidnapper doesn't slow, following a path only he can see.

"Where are you taking me?" I ask with all the indignity I can muster. Which isn't much, seeing how every other step jams his shoulder into my stomach and knocks the breath out of me in a huff.

"You don't belong here," he growls, having gotten the gist of the question anyway.

*That can't be good.* I highly doubt he plans to release me back into the wild. I rack my brain for a way out of this but am interrupted by a screeching sound. Something collides with my kidnapper in the darkness, knocking him sideways into the wall of the tunnel.

My neck snaps to the side as he stumbles and the

screech sounds again. This time, I wrap my arms around my head in anticipation. The second hit knocks him over backward and his hold on me loosens. I curl into a ball as we fall together, slamming into the gritty rock of the floor and sliding several feet before stopping.

I'm slow to respond to my sudden freedom. Everything hurts. I uncurl gingerly, wincing as bits of gravel cut into the bare skin of my hands and face. My kidnapper has no such limitations. I hear his bulk scurrying in the darkness and shove myself to my feet.

"Over here!" The voices aren't calling to me. Pounding feet announce the arrival of reinforcements, and if any of them find me I'm a goner.

One more screech and a burst of fiery light shows a bundle of brown feathers colliding with my kidnapper's face. I don't have time to ponder such a sight; the same light shows me a side tunnel I didn't know was there, leading downward at a sharp angle and away from the rapidly approaching Fomorians.

I lurch toward the tunnel, leaving my kidnapper and his bizarre assailant behind. My weak ankle sends pains up my leg at the pace, but I grit my teeth and push on. As the light behind me goes out, I press my left hand to the wall and leave it there, running as quickly as I can in my new direction.

*This could be it. Can I actually find my way out of here?*

When an iron hand closes around my arm, I snap backward and yelp. Another light flares up, this one attached to Shosce's other hand. "Going somewhere?" she asks. They're the first clear words I've heard from her, her usual dialect dropped from her voice.

I start shaking. "He—he—he took me. He said—he said—"

"Oh, enough." Without loosening her hold, she hauls me back the way I came. I know when we pass the place my kidnapper was attacked by the blood and feathers littering the floor.

"What was he going to do?" I can't help asking.

"Defy the General." The set of her jaw tells me I won't get anything else from her. She marches me all the way back to the tunnel opening before releasing my arm. I never thought I'd be glad to see the stark, imposing fortress. The courtyard is uncharacteristically full and I automatically shrink against Shosce in the face of so many Fomorians.

She grunts but doesn't push me away. They're not here for me, though.

Three Fomorians kneel on the ground. One of them has deep scratches across his face, marring his features beyond recognition.

Halasuwa stands before the trio, axe in hand. Upon seeing me, he lifts his chin at Shosce, who lifts her chin back. I know what this is. I turn my head as Halasuwa raises his axe, but I can't miss the thunk as the first of the traitors dies.

In a rare gesture of mercy, Shosce doesn't make me watch, steering me instead around to a side door.

"Hold." The voice has my head snapping up, a thousand memories of sunshine rushing through my mind. My spirit lifts like a leaf on the breeze, and I curse myself for having such a strong reaction.

Caspian was my first confidante, my first friend in the alien Fae Realm. The atrocities he committed are unforgivable, and though my mind condemns him my soul still acknowledges the connection between us. I hate it.

"You have no place here." Shosce rises to her full height and puts on her best scowl.

"Do you think denying me is a good idea?"

"Say the words, then. General Halasuwa denied you

access to the Queen. Tell me your status has changed." The authority in Shosce's voice has me scrambling. I assumed my nanny was some helpless peasant roped into a thankless task. *Is it possible she's somebody important? How did I miss that?*

"The queen received ill attention from the General's guests last night, and has had quite the misadventure at a traitor's hands. She may have suffered in ways only detectable to another Fae."

"See? You can't do it. Fae can't lie." Shosce grunts to make her point. It's a lesson I learned all too late. Fae tell a lot of untruths for being unable to lie, and Caspian is a master. "You need to leave."

"Lady Shosce, I implore you. I have had no contact with the Queen since the conquest, as instructed. I acknowledge that my actions were questionable, and you have every right to question my—"

"You betrayed our people as only a Fae can—with subtlety, trickery, and deceit. I do not know why the General suffers you to live, let alone to have free reign in our very home, unless you have further beguiled him into once again trusting you. Your words may sway him, Fae, but they will not sway me. I have my orders, and I will not allow you to fraternize with our enemy."

"Caspian is no loyal subject of mine." All eyes turn to me as my voice breaks the tension.

Caspian's eyes meet mine, and I wipe all expression from my face. I keep my words low and quiet, making sure Shosce knows I'm not asserting any kind of authority. "He was always Halasuwa's, and never mine. Even when it seemed like he might be. You can have him." I turn bodily away to emphasize the point. No one tries to stop me as I cross the remaining distance to the fortress. I pull open the door and wait. Eventually Shosce catches up and takes me back upstairs in silence.

Alone, a handful of tears trail down my cheeks. I believe every word I said. I still don't understand everything that happened in the battle. It sure felt like Caspian was saving my life at the time, but maybe that was a carefully planned manipulation, too? Regardless of how everything ended, one truth is clear. Caspian is a liar, and I can't trust him.

I feel the owl before I see it. As if summoned by my melancholy, it glides to a graceful perch on the edge of my windowsill and blinks its large eyes at me. For the first time, I'm not happy to see it. "What are you doing here?" I ask, throwing my hands up. "You're not an accident. Owls don't live underground. You're here for me, I know it, but you never say anything."

The great horned owl blinks again and hoots softly.

"That's not what I meant, and you know it. Are you a messenger? Did Hanathen send you? Someone else? Are you a sign? Please, just tell me. Tell me."

My voice is starting to raise and I advance on the bird. As I get closer, I notice the bare spots along its back where the feathers have been ripped away and the tint of blood on the tips of its talons. "You? You attacked him? Why? Did you want me to escape? Is that it? If so, it wasn't a very well-thought-out plan."

I take another step and the owl backs up and flaps its wings, ready to fly if I become a threat. "Is this really all that's left? Am I going to rot away in this tower forever? I can't do that, don't you see?" My voice chokes up, the words sticking in my throat. "This is all my fault. I failed. I failed Hanathen, I failed the Fae. I have to fix it. I need to get out of here so I can put it right, but I don't know how."

I lunge for the owl and it topples off the sill, taking flight as I reach for it. In only a few flaps, it's already lost from view in the dark emptiness. I drop against the sill, whimpering, defeated. "What do you want from me?"

## Chapter Four

*Two exercise days in a row?* I don't question Shosce's unexpected appearance, but I do follow her with apprehension across the hall and into the stairwell. *Did someone hear me talking to the owl last night? Or do they think I was involved in my own kidnapping?* My concerns are validated when we don't go down the stairs. We go up.

I've never been up. Up consists of only four stairs, basically a bridge to the other side of the tower where a hatch opens out onto the roof of the fortress. Far from flat, this section is sharply pitched as it curves around the tower and extends to the rest of the structure. Shosce navigates the incline easily, her goat hooves making short work of the slippery stone. I scrabble after her, feet wide, hands out to catch myself if I fall. I slide my feet, too slowly for her taste, and she huffs impatiently every time I pause.

I finally make it to a broader expanse of roof and discover my guards didn't follow us out here. A feeling of unease tingles over my back as I turn back to Shosce. Her face gives nothing away, but she obviously knows what I'm thinking. "There's nowhere for you to go," she says bluntly.

While true, that same sentiment could be applied to any time I'm out of my room. There's nowhere for me to go. *Unless there is...* Are there potential escape routes in my mundane activities that I simply haven't noticed? The thought makes my pulse quicken. Maybe escape is more possible than I've previously believed.

Shosce hasn't waited for me to muse these things out. I have to walk too fast to catch up with her or risk losing her in the dim light. It's because of this dim light I don't notice we're not alone until a massive figure suddenly looms in front of us. He's the largest Fomorian I've ever seen, and I've seen my share. The distinctive curl of his horns and the slant to his shoulders courtesy of the limp I gave him are intimately familiar to me.

"Thank you, Sister. You are dismissed."

My skin crawls at Halasuwa's voice. No good can come of this clandestine meeting, away from prying eyes. He could probably chuck me over the side of the fortress without even exerting himself. For that matter, he wouldn't have to drag me all the way up here just to kill me. My death would be celebrated in the halls below.

"Little queen."

I don't answer. He didn't ask me a question, and there is no one here to perform for. Cold chills creep up my body from the stone beneath my feet, but I don't dare move.

"I am old, little queen. I warred against your people centuries before you were even born. I've seen my own race fall and built it again from the ashes. The days we spent suffering beneath this mountain felt interminable. You know all this. You feel all this. Your presence here represents the pinnacle of Fomorian might. Our ancient enemy has finally fallen, and my people are free to go about the world once more."

I can't help myself. Perhaps the seclusion makes me bolder. "Why are you telling me this?" Nothing about this conversation reflects the Halasuwa I know. He does not wax poetic. He does not show vulnerability. He does not speak to me without scorn and derision in his voice.

"When we thirsted for vengeance, we were united. For centuries, our one goal was the absolute destruction of the Fae. Now that you are destroyed, my people have begun to argue about what comes next."

*Ahh.* My kidnapping yesterday is beginning to make

more sense. "They're dividing into factions. And some of them don't want to follow you anymore." I can't quite keep the satisfaction out of my voice. Seeing the Fomorians tear themselves apart would be a beautiful kind of justice. Although, I'd rather be kept out of the middle of it.

Halasuwa snarls but doesn't contradict me. "I did not see how strong this spirit of rebellion was until yesterday. Executing my own warriors is not a task I enjoy. I will not be able to lead my people into the future by clinging to the past. And you are the ultimate reminder of the past. I thought your presence here would embolden my people, but I refuse to let you become the impetus for our division." He levels his gaze at me and makes sure I meet his eyes before delivering the final blow. "Baark, the goblin ambassador, offered me a significant bounty for you. I told him I would consider it."

My breath leaves me in a rush and my knees give out. Of all the scenarios I've envisioned, this one never even occurred to me. "Why are you telling me this?" I ask again, my voice now a whisper. I'm aware I'm repeating myself, but the answer to this question is vitally important. "I've done everything you've commanded. What more do you want from me?"

He sighs, deep and heavy, a sound encompassing the weight of centuries of leadership. "I wanted to say these things out loud to someone who doesn't matter. Who is in no position to use them against me."

"What if I tell someone?" My voice is back, now that I've gotten control over myself and I don't seem to be in imminent danger of being sold. "Surely your people would view such an admission as weakness? Such information could be valuable to me."

He scoffs. "Who would believe you?"

That sounds more like the Halasuwa I know.

"But just so you understand. Open your mouth and I will sell you to the goblins."

"You might do that anyway."

"I might."

A silent moment stretches, then Halasuwa walks away. *Guess we're done.* He didn't give me any instructions, but I assume Shosce will return to collect me. *It's not like I can go anywhere.*

I'm a little surprised Halasuwa fits up here on the roof. The cave ceiling is close, touching the roof in some places. I wouldn't think his bulk would fit. As I ponder this, I move to where Halasuwa was standing, reaching up high to see if I can touch the ceiling, and I see it.

A pinprick of light. Pure, genuine light shining down from the ceiling above. It's just out of reach, but when I hold out my hand a faint glow lights up the back of it.

"The moon is full tonight."

To my credit I don't scream. I've come to expect Caspian to suddenly appear out of nowhere. Not even he can distract me from the glorious miracle that is this dot of light. "This is moonlight?"

"Can't you feel it?"

*I can.* How it reaches this far down I don't know, but a tendril of warmth spreads over the back of my hand. I suck in a breath as tears of happiness spill down my cheeks. *I'm touching moonlight.*

My moment of rapture is short-lived as Caspian steps into view. I don't retreat, and he stops a short distance away and stays uncharacteristically quiet.

I don't speak either, and it takes a few moments to see what he's trying to get me to notice. "Halasuwa was standing here. In the moonlight."

"Yes."

*Moonlight shows things for what they are.* It's a truth

long accepted by the Fae, and often used to our advantage. "He didn't mean to tell me those things, did he?"

"I suspect not, though I am no longer in his counsels."

"Why are you here, Caspian? What more can you do to me?"

He flinches. "I deserve that. I came not with flowery words, but a gift." He holds out his hand, palm up. I have to step closer to see what's inside. It's a sliver of rock, jagged like it was broken off a larger piece, with a thin cord dangling from one end.

"What is it?" I ask, not touching it. Who knows what kind of trick this might be.

"Not enough," he answers cryptically. He lifts the rock high and moves way too close into my personal space. I backpedal, but he doesn't try anything, just touches the rock to the pinpoint of moonlight. It pulses, sending a blinding flash out into the darkness and instantly blinding me. When I recover, I can see the rock is now glowing brightly in Caspian's palm.

"What did you do?" *You can't trust him. You can't trust him!* Yet I find myself reaching for the glowing rock anyway.

"I caught the moonlight in the clear quartz." He says it like it's a simple thing, like moonlight in the darkness isn't the most incredible gift I've ever received.

"You risked everything, for both of us, to catch moonlight for me?"

"Yes."

A host of possibilities slams into my mind. *Moonlight shows things for what they are. It will show me a way out of here.*

"Yes, My Lady." Of course he knows what I'm thinking. He always has. Even now I can't hide my thoughts properly.

"Shosce."

"What?"

But he's already gone, melting away into the darkness as if he was never there at all. At the same time, I hear hoof beats behind me as Shosce approaches. I school my features quickly and turn away so she won't read something on my face she shouldn't. "So he didn't kill you after all." There's no emotion in her voice to tell me how she feels about that.

"He threatened to sell me to the goblins."

"Hmm."

"You're his sister?" Somehow that tidbit survived after all of the revelations following it.

She doesn't answer, just leads the way back across the roof. It doesn't matter. My days here are officially numbered. Speaking of which...

My hand goes to the bump in my shirt where the moonlight quartz rests. Shosce said nothing about the flash of light, though she had to have been close enough to see it. How did it pass her notice? And how did Caspian capture the moonlight in the first place?

*Fomorian magic.* I've finally seen it at work, and it was nothing like I would have expected. That could be due to the user. I can't see a full-blooded Fomorian having any desire to capture moonlight.

It doesn't matter. None of it matters. I'm finally leaving. And Caspian made it happen. *My Lady? Is he* my *Caspian after all?*

## Chapter Five

I make my plans. I'll escape on the night of the new moon, when the skies will be dark and there will be nothing to give me away. The moonlight in my quartz is all I need to find a route out of here. That gives me fifteen days. I trust the moonlight will show me the way, but how do I search without alerting the Fomorians? I puzzle on it until I'm too tired to think straight, then with regret I bury the moonlight inside my pillow and fall asleep.

The next morning, I burn my candle bright, to hopefully hide the moonlight from prying eyes. When I remove the quartz, I find it just as beautiful as I did last night.

*Don't get lost in it, Eve. You have work to do.*

But how?

I stand in the middle of the room and hold the quartz in my palm, much like Caspian did. The moonlight disperses in a soft glow, lighting up the far edges of the room before disappearing into the cold, gray stone. Or ... not.

*It's an illusion. My room is an illusion.*

Well, yes and no. It physically exists, but it isn't the inescapable prison I've believed it is. The stone-slab walls are nothing more than timber framing, not even mudded to seal the cracks. My ceiling is nonexistent, open to the cave ceiling overhead. My impenetrable door? Merely a heavy curtain.

*Halasuwa told me he built this tower for me to spend my days. I never questioned how they accomplished such a thing so quickly. They're trusting the strength of Fomorian magic to keep me in here. I could walk out anytime.*

I step forward to do just that, but quickly stop myself. I can't. The second I do they'll know I know, and I'll lose my chance. Does Caspian know? He has to.

It burns me to sit in my room all day. Today is not an exercise day, which means no sign of Shosce. Just three scraps of food delivered at regular intervals without any personal interaction at all. As much as I try to see past it, without the moonlight, the illusion of my room persists. The heavy door stands firm, the walls remain unyielding gray stone, and I remain trapped. Unlike most days, though, I sit against the wall by the door instead of by the window. Even though it looks and feels like a door, I know it is only a curtain, so I strain my ears to see how much I can hear of the goings-on on the other side.

The answer? Not much. I hear my meal delivery about two steps before the door opens, and I hear them huff in annoyance once their job is complete. What's better, though, is I can hear my two guards talking to each other from each side of the hall. Not enough to make out their words, but enough to know they're there and roughly where they're standing.

Eventually the fortress grows quiet, and the heaviness I associate with bedtime descends on the grounds. My restless body can't take it anymore and I dig out my quartz, releasing the comforting glow of moonlight into my room. My eyes settle on the curtain and a dangerous level of curiosity rises inside. For too long I've been stripped of any kind of autonomy. It would be foolish to escape tonight … but I can at least have a look around.

Adrenaline courses through my veins as I lay flat and snag the bottom corner of the curtain. Peeling it back, I can see my guards alert and attentive, standing just outside. That won't do. I'll never make it past them. My eyes drift upwards instead, lingering on the edge of the wall where the ceiling isn't and the open space beyond.

*If I could just make it up there.*

With little furniture my options are limited, but the window may be my best bet. A quick glance out shows me a deserted courtyard and a very long way to fall. I grit my teeth and grip the sill anyway. The unsealed cracks in the wall provide my handholds, and even though my arms shake violently I manage to reach the top. Only to find myself straddling the wall on the opposite side of the tower from the main roof.

*I didn't think any of this through.* I can't linger here, though. Someone will eventually come outside, and the moonlight will draw their eyes to me like a beacon. I stuff the quartz inside the neckline of my shirt and begin the process of scooting around the edge of the tower until I can safely clamber onto the roof. Once I do, I promptly collapse, heaving in breaths and willing my traitorous body to be able to get up again.

Splinters prickle my palms and fingers, but most are too tiny to dig out with my fingernails. I wince against the pain and force myself back to my feet. The door I came through yesterday with Shosce is close, and within minutes I'm back inside the fortress once more. I pass my own door quickly, descending one more level before chancing re-entry.

*This is stupid. This is stupid. This is stupid.*

Yet I feel alive for the first time in a very long time. If I'm caught I'll be sold or killed for sure, but the rush of taking charge of my own life drowns out the consequences. I keep the moonlight hidden as I prowl through the empty upper halls of the fortress, peeking into dust-filled rooms and exploring forgotten corners. Even with the increase in their numbers, the Fomorian population is nowhere near as big as it once was. The main living quarters are located at an underground level, so these upper floors haven't seen traffic in years, if not centuries.

My legs ache but still I press on, my mind churning out possible escape scenarios. I locate five different staircases, some more obviously used than others. I had originally written off the tunnels, but now with the moonlight in my hand anything feels possible. Still, they're complex and a total mystery, not to mention housing the bulk of the Fomorians living in Canowin Hollow. Any escape plan involving the tunnels requires me to either sneak past all of them or be able to outrun them.

*Is there another way out of Canowin Hollow that doesn't use the tunnels?*

I don't see how I could find the answer to that question without arousing suspicion.

I wander as long as I dare, avoiding any space that looks recently occupied, before deciding I need to head back. Intentionally locking myself back into my tower makes my heart hurt, but I soothe myself with the knowledge that this time it's only temporary. I'm getting out of here. Just knowing that I can scale my room and access the roof makes my tower feel slightly less confining.

Two hallways from my staircase I encounter my first Fomorians. They weren't here when I passed this way the first time, and I duck through the first doorway I come to when I hear their voices. The voices don't move, though, and I track them to an abandoned library where the weight of the books has crushed the rotted wood of the shelving until everything lies in haphazard piles across the floor.

"If we're lucky, Baark will take care of the problem for us."

"Keep your voice down! And don't let Kharn hear

you say that. It isn't enough for the Fae to simply be gone. She must be dead if we are to rise."

"If Baark has his way, she will be as good as dead."

"Not good enough. If the goblin steals her without the General's blessing, he will hunt him down and steal her back, and then we're right back where we started. As long as she lives, she will draw the General's focus."

There's a long pause. I hold my breath, waiting to see which fate the whisperers will land on.

"You're right. Tell Kharn I'm in. When he's ready to move, I'll back him."

I back slowly away. Nothing good can come from hearing any more of this conversation, and I have to get back to my tower. They're blocking my way, though, and I don't dare try to creep past their door. I backtrack to another staircase and follow it up to the roof. It takes me a moment to get my bearings, and even longer to scurry across the dangerous surface, but I finally make it back to the familiarity of my tower. When I come to the edge of my room, I don't hesitate, lowering myself as far as my arms will reach and dropping the remaining distance to the floor. I hit like a lead weight and my knees buckle, sending me sprawling.

I stay where I landed, panting on the stone floor. The adrenaline abruptly dies and my body becomes too heavy to move. While I drift off to sleep, I ponder what the faceless Fomorians had to say about my future. The name Kharn sounds vaguely familiar. He's some leader in Halasuwa's army. Baark, though, is much more recent. He's the goblin ambassador, the one who was so taken with me at dinner. The one Halasuwa is considering selling me to. Apparently, he's still interested. And if they're concerned about him "stealing me away"? That just means I can't fail.

## Chapter Six

The next two weeks pass interminably slowly. I barely sleep, acutely aware of the vulnerability of the barrier between me and my enemies. Every time Shosce collects me, I panic, certain she'll discover the quartz I desperately keep hidden. Her discovery of my splinters was bad enough. She scowled and huffed and plucked at my hands, digging out every sliver before demanding to know how they got there. I skirted the truth, asking her how I could have gotten wooden splinters from stone walls. She had to accept my words, since I am meant to believe my walls are genuinely stone.

I don't scale the tower again. My luck held once. I can't risk getting caught. Not when I'm so close. I spend the rest of my days avoiding Shosce's face for fear she'll see something on mine. The slightest glimmer of hope could have her tossing my room or carting me off to the goblins. Thankfully, Halasuwa doesn't summon me, either, and the night of the new moon arrives at last.

I have only a vague plan for where I'm going. Through a few subtle questions, I learned that the tunnels are the only way into and out of Canowin Hollow. As terrifying as venturing into them is, I have to trust that the moonlight will come through for me. It will show me the way.

Before I start up the wall, I check the status of my two guards. They're right where they're supposed to be, but before I withdraw, the guard on the right tilts to the side. A second later, he's collapsing into his fellow on the left, who goes down under the weight. Upon hitting the floor, neither of them move.

I wait for several heartbeats, but they don't make

a sound. "Caspian? Did you do this?" I whisper into the hall. No answer comes. I steal out into the darkness and head for the stairs. They'll expect me to go up. Any reasonable Fae would go up, toward the surface, toward the light, toward freedom. So I need to go down, as painful a notion as that is. I finally bring out the quartz, looping the cord around my neck so I don't lose it. Moonlight shines forth, showing me where to place my feet on the treacherous steps.

I descend two levels before exiting the staircase. A furtive trip through the hallways brings me to another one, narrower and sunk further into disrepair. So far, everything is quiet. I waited as late into the night as I dared, hoping to put some distance behind me while the bulk of the Fomorians sleep. I creep down the stairs, using as little light as possible, ears straining for the slightest sound.

Still, when the alarm sounds it takes me by surprise. *How could they know already?* Shouts ring out and the clomp of hooves echoes both above and below me. A door opens from a lower level and I scurry backward, fleeing into the first hallway and scrambling for cover. When the voices come, though, they aren't the deep growls of Fomorian warriors.

"Little queen, little queen, come out, come out. I know you're here. I can smell you." The hiss of Baark's voice makes my skin crawl. My cheek burns with phantom pain as it remembers the feel of his tongue. "You are not where you are supposed to be, for that is the first place I looked. Does the General know you are prowling his halls when you should be sleeping? Hmm?"

The only weapon I have is a wooden rod I pried loose from the underside of my bed frame. Not much use against a Fomorian, but better than my bare hands. Baark is smaller than me, but fighting him would be like trying to fight a snake. He's strong, and wily, and fast. Fleeing is the better option.

More doors slam and Fomorian voices finally reach me. "Search every room! Find the queen! And any wretched goblin you find ... kill it!"

Baark chuckles. "Do you think they will save you? Oh no. They will not find you in time." He leaps through my doorway, eyes shining in the dark like the night creature he is. "Found you," he whispers.

I bolt, diving out from behind the curtains and running as fast as I can for the door.

Baark is faster. His body collides with mine and the two of us roll in a tangle before slamming into the wall. His nails dig trenches into my arms as he tries to subdue me. I kick and flail wildly, anything to keep him from grabbing hold. As he lands a blow to my chest a strangled yelp bursts out, and the hallway fills with pounding hooves.

"In here!" Two Fomorians rush in, and my body betrays me by being glad to see them.

Baark loosens his hold and turns to face the greater threat. He flings a dagger in their direction before charging them full-on.

The Fomorians charge him in kind, leaving a sliver of open space behind them. I scramble toward freedom, sliding through the doorway as the opponents collide. The hallway isn't any safer. The ruckus we've been kicking up has announced my presence to the entire fortress. Fomorians approach from one end of the hallway. Goblins rush in from the other. There are only three doors I can reach before I'm overrun.

"Come on, come on," I murmur, yanking my quartz out from under my shirt. Light blazes forth, blinding my enemies and stopping them in their tracks with painful screams. "Which way?"

The moonlight narrows into a single beam, lighting on a door across the hall. I run for it, diving inside before my pursuers can recover. Behind me, I hear their roars of anger and frustration, and the two forces clash together to keep the other from reaching me first.

My time is now measured in breaths. *Okay, what's in here? How is this room going to help?* I raise the quartz, but all it does is highlight the wooden paneling on the back wall. Upon closer inspection the paneling puckers and bulges in places. I run my fingers over it, pushing lightly, and a piece crumbles under the pressure. Emboldened, I dig my hands in, pulling chunks out and raining debris onto the floor. Soon I have a hole large enough for me to crawl inside. I squeeze myself in without hesitation.

Before I fully clear the hole, an iron hand seizes my ankle. "Hiding in the wall, my little present? That's not very helpful."

I kick out at Baark, but the space is too cramped for me to maneuver. He hauls backward on my leg, stronger than I am. I feel myself sliding backward and reach for something, anything, to grab hold of. There's nothing.

With another firm pull, he yanks me the rest of the way out of the wall and pounces on me again. I swing with the only thing I have available—my wooden rod. The end is jagged where I broke it off, and Baark's momentum carries him right into the broken tip. I hear the squelch as his flesh parts, but I don't stick around to see the damage. The second his grip releases, I scurry back through the hole, plunging headfirst down the filthy, twisting passage inside.

Baark cries and curses behind me, a sound that turns to strangled screams as the Fomorians find him. I move faster. Without warning, the passage drops several feet, dumping me down to what I believe is the next lower level.

*Who used this passageway, and for what purpose? No Fomorian would ever fit in here.*

The tunnel makes several more drops, finally landing me in a cramped space without an exit. I've reached the end, but with no idea where I am or how I get out of here. Commotion from the outside has me freezing in place. Heavy footfalls tell me many Fomorians are out there, but they don't seem to know I'm in here. They call out to one another in muffled voices, but I can't make out the words through the wall.

I try to squirm around and see where I need to go next, but there's just no room. Even my small frame barely fits, and every movement requires pushing on the stone walls around me. I consider going back up, but instantly dismiss the idea. The passage is nearly vertical, and even if I could climb back up nothing good awaits me there.

Then I squirm a bit too hard and the stone I'm leaning against gives way. The whole wall shifts and I tumble backward, end over end in a shower of dust. I scramble to my feet and find myself in a dark storeroom. Shelves lined with foodstuffs fill each wall and an open door reveals roaring fires and lines of tables. The kitchen is filled with more light than I've seen in one place in months. This late at night activity should be low, but tonight the fortress is swarming with warriors and goblins alike. Who knows what I'll find in the kitchen?

I creep to the doorway and peak out, relieved to see only one form moving about the otherwise deserted space. It's too small to be a Fomorian, but I don't recognize the race of the creature. Not a goblin, though.

As I watch, it dumps a bucket of water on the floor and goes to work with a mop. Food scraps, offal, and miscellaneous fluids all get herded toward a dip in the middle of the floor where they vanish from sight with an accompanying plopping sound. Some kind of disposal?

I scurry backward as a troop of guards comes bursting through the door. I recognize the one in the lead from the hallway upstairs. Blood drips off their weapons, leaving sizzling spots on the stone floor. "She has to be here! All the old passages end up here!"

The guards spread out, ignoring the worker while digging their hands into flour barrels and knocking over woodpiles. I watch their shadows move closer to my hiding place, knowing it's only a matter of minutes until I'm found.

"What about the channel?"

"She wouldn't dare. Not with the Nix."

"She may not know of the Nix."

Two guards separate from the others and approach the dip in the middle of the floor. Kneeling down, they grasp a pair of handles set into the floor and heave. With effort, they haul a grate into the air and let it clunk down onto the stone floor.

Over their words, I hear the faint sound of rushing water.

"See? She's not in there. Wouldn't be able to lift it anyway."

"What's wrong with the General? Can't he track her?"

"Watch what you say about the General. He's already spitting mad about whatever the goblin did to interfere with his magic. He catches you talking like that…"

"Yeah, yeah. Let's get this thing put back before someone falls in and gets swept away."

The only idea I have is a crazy one. I'll never

make it to the tunnels now. Guards are tearing apart the kitchen, and even if I could get back into that passage, the hole in the wall can't be hidden. There's no escape through the kitchen. But there's currently a route open underneath it.

I eye the grate as the guards hoist it again. Even they strain under its weight. But the water in there goes somewhere, hopefully far from here. I make my decision and move before I can second-guess it.

I race into the open kitchen, running as fast as I can for the hole in the floor. Shouts go up as I'm seen, but no one moves fast enough to stop me. Even on my tense, achy legs and my wobbly ankle I gain the hole in seconds. With the wet, slimy floor, I lose my footing, my momentum carrying me into a slide and dropping me into the hole.

# JESSICA GOEKEN

## Chapter Seven

I suck in a half breath before I hit the water, the current instantly sweeping me away from the Fomorians yelling above me. I go under and lose all my senses as the freezing water tumbles me in all directions. I curl into the fetal position, locking my elbows around my knees and tucking my head as tightly as I can.

My half breath doesn't last long. My lungs protest, telling me I need more air. My body yearns to swim, to fight, to find the surface. I don't even know if there is a surface. Who knows how far this river runs underground before emerging? I hurtle along, flung this way and that, bashing repeatedly into something rough and unyielding.

I can't breathe. Against my will, my mouth opens, water flooding in, gagging me, forcing itself down. I hit something again, knocking my arms loose and wrenching my head to the side.

*I'm going to die.*

Then everything stops. The angry rush of water dwindles to a gentle wave and I find myself bobbing like a top. My body reacts, legs kicking out, propelling me ... somewhere. I break the surface and spew water, coughing and gagging while trying to keep myself afloat. The world is dark. Cold. Exhaustion pulls at my limbs, but I don't stop moving them. I can't. I have to get away.

I'm still underground, probably in a cave of some sort. I'm just thankful there's open air. There must be an exit somewhere. I just have to find it. The idea of going under again makes me shiver, but if that's what I have to do, so be it. I'd much rather find a ledge or a beach or something...

Something splashes to my left. I spin in that

direction, knowing full well I won't see anything.

*They wouldn't have followed me, right? No way they jumped in behind me.*

But it's possible. If not a Fomorian, then certainly a goblin. If Baark is down here in the darkness I'm a goner. I breathe as quietly as I can, straining my ears for any sound. Another splash comes, this one closer. Then something whooshes past my legs, knocking me sideways. I hear a giggle, low and malicious. Something brushes against me, then a hand grabs my foot and yanks me under.

As soon as my head is submerged, I hear music, a rhythmic thrumming that seems to echo all around me. It assaults my ears, burrowing its way into my head. I kick my feet, connecting with something and shaking myself free. I plumb the depths of my energy and swim with all I have, striking out in a random direction. My head is pounding, the music still bouncing around inside. Then I hear it with my ears, too, dancing above the water, like it's pursuing me. On my next stroke, I touch scales, my hand running the length of some enormous fish. It flaps and splashes, sending a wave of water over my head.

Then a voice joins the music, throaty words I don't understand that make my heart race in panic. My response is an ancient one, bubbling up out of my ancestral Fae memories. The Fomorian guards said something about a Nix. Putting a name to the threat doesn't make me feel better. I don't know what a Nix is, but I'm sure I'm about to find out.

I stall in the water, my body suddenly leaden, arms and legs refusing to do what I want them to do as the singer comes closer. I feel their presence drawing nearer to me, a disturbance in the very atmosphere. More hands clutch at me, but I'm powerless to fend them off. Needle-sharp teeth graze my skin, nibbling at places where my clothing has been torn away. Then three pairs of teeth sink into my legs simultaneously. I gasp from the pain, but the song's paralysis has fully taken hold. The singer is right in front of me now. I feel their breath on my face, their fingers caressing my cheek.

Then they hiss. The water suddenly froths and boils, and my attackers vanish. A glow appears beneath my feet, waves surging up around me. Another set of arms surrounds me, strong and protective, and I'm lifted straight out of the water. Power weighs down the air. Warmth flows into me, my skin tingling at the touch. My savior bears me forward until pebbles crunch under their feet. I'm lowered to the ground and I finally get a look at my rescuer. He towers above me, tangled black hair swept back from his face, flames where his eyes should be. His entire body is lit from within by a dull orange glow, the only light pushing back against the overwhelming darkness.

"Eredin Glas." His name is a whisper on my lips, as if speaking it aloud will cause him to vanish like the apparition he must be.

His face lowers to mine, his mouth grimly set. His hands grab my face, those terrifyingly beautiful eyes boring into mine, and I hear the echo of words he doesn't say. I don't understand them, but the paralyzing song abruptly cuts off. My body becomes my own again as the Nix's spell fades away.

A shriek pierces the air and he whirls to face the water. Growling, he regains his feet and retrieves a scythe from across his back.

Still beyond tired, I prop myself up on my elbows to watch him wade out thigh-deep into the water.

"Come on!" he roars into the darkness, and several shapes rush him at once. They speed through the water, but the King of the Wild Hunt is more than a match for them. He moves almost too fast for my eyes to follow, but I do see the arcs of blood in the air and hear the screams of the Nix. I see their forms only briefly as they attack both above and below the water, long, powerful fish tails propelling female human torsos. Their hair is long and straggly, their fingers tipped with inch-long talons.

One Nix leaps out of the water behind Eredin Glas and digs her talons into his back.

He roars in pain, seizes her around the neck, and launches her into the air. She lands hard about twenty feet from me and lays on the beach gasping, thrashing her tail. She flips herself over, eyes locking onto mine, before realizing she doesn't need water to kill me. Her mouth opens wide in an evil grin, showcasing rows of shark's teeth. With a shriek, she crawls toward me, powerful arms dragging herself across the rocks.

I finally move. Adrenaline surges into my muscles and I shove myself upright, digging through the rocks surrounding me for some kind of weapon. I find one with a sharp edge just as she hits me. She claws at my face as my arm comes down, swinging with all the strength I have. The first blow doesn't faze her, so I hit her again. And again, while using my other arm to hold her at bay. She's strong but off balance on the beach and doesn't have the leverage to pull me down to her level.

One of my blows finally hits home, driving the sharp edge of the rock into the corner of her eye. She screams and recoils, and I hit her again. Blood flies, and I hit her again. When she finally stops moving, I collapse, wheezing, on top of her.

All is silent around me. I didn't even see Eredin Glas come back out of the water, but suddenly that gentle orange glow fills the space around me. "That's more like the Queen I was expecting."

His voice sends a thrill through me and I'm thankful I'm looking away from him. My mind sweeps back to the one time we met face-to-face and the absolute desire I felt for him. I was in a position of power then, confident in myself and with allies at my back. I have no power now.

"Why are you here?" I drag myself off the Nix, well aware of the picture I present. Starved, drowned, and now covered in Nix blood. Still, I stand and turn to him, raising my gaze to his without flinching.

The flames in his eyes fade, revealing soft brown backlit by a flickering fire. "You're injured."

"So are you."

Lacerations cover his arms, but even as I say it, they knit themselves closed.

"Neat trick."

"Sit."

I sit. What else am I going to do, argue with him? Insist I'm fine? Leave?

Blood flows freely down my legs, courtesy of the Nix bites. Other patches of skin are shredded from my trip downriver, and everything hurts. The pounding in my head and churning in my stomach tell me I have a concussion.

"You would have let them eat you."

"I didn't have a choice."

"It is true, then? Fae magic is broken?"

I don't answer. Not only don't I want to, but the answer is more complicated than a simple yes or no. Fae magic *is* broken. But some remnant of it remains, and I don't yet know what to do with that information.

He doesn't press the issue. Instead, he lays hands on me, gently, and that not-voice flows through my body again. Energy swirls around me, through me, and I gasp as my wounds close the same as his did. When he pulls back, he meets my gaze, searching for … something.

"Thank you."

"My pleasure."

Awkward silence stretches between us, so I shift my attention back to the Nix. Her head is a battered mess, but the rest of her is simply gray. Gray skin, gray hair, gray scales, perfectly adapted to be invisible in an underground lake. A lake I nearly didn't come out of. I repeat the words, softer this time. "Thank you."

I look back at Eredin Glas, my question suddenly needing an answer. "Why are you here?"

He stands again, holding out a hand for me to take. "I thought that was obvious. I'm here to rescue you."

## Chapter Eight

I don't take his hand. I do stand, though, putting us closer to equal footing, and take a step back for good measure. "Why?"

He laughs, a sound so big it echoes off the not-visible cavern walls. It's a vocal reminder of who exactly I'm dealing with and the things he is capable of. "Do you not need rescuing?"

I do need rescuing. That's the problem.

He extends his hand again. "Come with me, Eve. Leave this darkness behind."

I so want to leave the darkness behind. He sees the yearning in my eyes and knows my posturing for what it is, but I do it anyway. "Out of the goodness of your heart? What do you want from me, Eredin Glas?"

His eyes flash, the storm inside not willing to stay hidden much longer. The familiarity drops from his voice, and we are once again royals standing on opposing sides. "In our last stalemate, we parted peaceably, but we are no longer evenly matched. Will you accept my rescue, Eve La Stella, or would you choose captivity again?"

I did choose captivity. I chose to be taken by the Fomorians rather than be killed at Emain Ablach. If I make him leave me here, I will undoubtedly fall into Fomorian hands again, but I don't think that's what he means. "If I don't go with you willingly, you will take me?"

"I will not leave here without you, Eve. It is up to you to decide how you come with me."

My temper flares, white hot after being suppressed for so long. "Why now? Why not months ago? Your power is more than a match for Halasuwa.

Why leave me to rot in a Fomorian prison if you could have walked in whenever you wanted?"

His voice is deadly calm when he answers. "I am here to rescue a queen. I had to wait for you to become one again."

That shuts me up. I could give him the reasons I waited to escape, but they would sound like excuses. Even to me, they sound like excuses. Maybe I could have acted before now. Without Caspian, without moonlight. Maybe I could have made it. I'll never know, and the time has passed to find out. The important thing is what happens now. And what's important is returning to my people. The first step is, of course, getting out of this cave.

While I contemplate these thoughts a rush of wind blows past my hair. Wings rustle and I drop back into a defensive stance, but then a brown blur settles itself on Eredin Glas's shoulder and blinks large, round eyes at me. I stare at the owl, looking between it and the self-satisfied smirk on Eredin Glas's face. "It was you?"

He doesn't answer, letting me work through the ramifications for myself. The great horned owl used to be a sign, connecting me to my dead mother. When it appeared to me in Canowin Hollow, the most un-Fae place imaginable, it was easy to believe she was still looking out for me. But the owl was just a trick.

I let my anger drain away. "I accept your rescue, Eredin Glas." I'm careful not to say anything else. Anything that will bind me to whatever price he will expect me to pay. Because he does want something. Last time he tracked me down, he wanted me to join the Hunt. Is it possible that's still what he wants, powerless as I am?

He smiles again, a charming smile that would turn any head, mortal or otherwise. "I am pleased. Take my hand, and we will leave this foul place together."

I take his hand, and he startles me by swooping an arm under my knees. In one swift motion, I'm cradled in his arms, just like when he carried me to shore. The heat of his body presses against me, reminding me just how cold I am, and against my better judgment I snuggle in closer.

He wades back into the water.

"Where are we going?" I can't keep the tremble out of my voice as the cold water splashes against my backside.

"The same way I came. Take a deep breath."

I grab a lungful of air as we drop underwater. Eredin Glas still glows, and I'm able to see through the water around us. We sink like a stone, straight to the bottom, where another glowing orb meets us. This one is a gentle violet, and it pulses against the water surrounding it. I clutch Eredin Glas's neck as we drift closer and my lungs start to burn. We fall into the orb, and purple light flashes so brightly I'm blinded.

When it fades, we're still in the water, but the color has changed to a crystal blue-green and my eyes sting. I gasp with the shift and inhale a large mouthful of saltwater. Coughing and gagging, I spasm in Eredin Glas's arms, but he holds me tighter and shoots toward the surface. A second later, we break through and I'm able to clear my lungs properly. I suck in air, still coughing, as Eredin Glas swims one-handed toward the shore.

When we reach the beach, I'm finally able to pay attention to my surroundings. The sand is fine and white, and soft as powder. The sky stretches above us, vast and lit with millions of blinking stars. I lay on the beach and stare at the sky, not even fighting as tears course down my cheeks.

*I feared I would never see it again.*

Night still prevails, and no moon shines down on me, but the darkness is so pure and so clean as to be the complete opposite of the Fomorian darkness. The air is gentle and warm on my skin, with a sweet smell I can't place. I want to sink into this moment, into this air and this sand and this sky, but Eredin Glas hovers over me, dripping water into my personal space.

I rise to my feet, aware of the sand clinging to every wet inch of me. I need to push my feelings aside and make some kind of overture here. "Thank you, Eredin Glas. My freedom is a precious gift, and you have restored it to me."

The 'freedom' here is an assumption on my part, one I'm sure he doesn't miss. Freedom from the Fomorians, yes, but by his own words I may not belong entirely to myself just yet.

"The darkness did not become you, Your Majesty."

His reply still doesn't tell me where I stand, but a sound from behind me keeps me from pressing the issue. The stomp of a hoof, followed by the squeak of a shifting harness. I turn slowly, loathe to tear my gaze from the sea and confront whatever lurks behind me. Especially with the state I'm in. I assume it's not a threat, otherwise we would not be casually standing on this beach, which means there's only one logical thing it could be.

Behind us, far up in the tree line, stands the Wild Hunt. A motley collection, they shift impatiently on their feet and stare openly at the two of us. There are a few dozen, tops. Not as many as I expected. Their dark clothing blends them into the shadows of the trees, and I can only tell them apart when they move. My eyes don't linger on them long. Instead, I'm drawn to the wildness stretching out behind them. Colossal trees tower above them, tall enough to block my view of the stars. Even in the darkness I can see the richness of their colors, the vibrant greens second only to my own Realm. The trees stretch endlessly in both directions, following the beach, until they disappear beyond my sight.

"It's beautiful," I breathe.

"Thank you, Your Majesty."

"Where are we?"

Pride glows in Eredin Glas's voice. "This is my home. Welcome to Hellequin Wood."

A trio of hunters breaks rank and approaches on foot.

Eredin Glas steps forward to meet them, and after a moment of indecision I follow. He outpaces me easily, and his body blocks them as they speak.

"Welcome home, my liege. I trust all is well?" The voice is deep, with a richness that only comes with age.

"Hail, Jarild. All is well." They clasp hands, and the action seems to signal some kind of change among the hunters. They murmur and move about, some disappearing into the trees, others wandering down the beach.

I finally reach Eredin Glas's side and get a glimpse of Jarild. In the open air the starlight is bright enough to see his face, and I do a double-take. "You're human," I say without thinking.

"I am, Your Majesty."

"Jarild, may I present Her Majesty, Eve La Stella, Queen of the Fae."

Eredin Glas's words slam into me, reminding me of my place. I draw myself up and straighten my shoulders. "Apologies for my brashness, Jarild. I had little use for manners among the Fomorians, and it would seem I have forgotten how to use them."

"No apologies necessary, Your Majesty. You will find little ceremony among the Hunt, and few words that will give offense."

"Thank you," I reply automatically, turning over his words. *How long does he expect me to be staying?*

Eredin Glas takes the conversation back. "This has been a long and difficult night. Eve, allow me to escort you to my home, where you may rest."

*The King of the Wild Hunt has a home?* My tired mind fixates so strongly on the notion that I stop paying attention to my feet. I stumble and fall forward, only to find myself caught by the last of the trio of hunters. I never spared the other two a glance, but now strong white arms catch me around the middle and set me back up on my feet. I look up to find a pair of familiar black eyes boring into mine.

My heart stops and my voice catches in my throat. I clutch at his arms, my legs suddenly too weak to stand. I reach for his face, but stop when I see no recognition in his expression. "Danen?"

## Chapter Nine

"Danen?"

"Yes, Your Majesty?" His voice is the same, but something is missing. He addresses me now as the visiting royalty I am, not as the Queen he pledged his loyalty to, and certainly not as the friend and confidante I grew to be.

I stumble away from him, a vice-like pressure around my chest. I can't handle this right now. I'm too tired, too broken, too hurt. *I watched him die. And I watched Eredin Glas take him.* But this creature standing before me isn't Danen. It can't be.

Once again Eredin Glas appears, taking my arm and steering me into the trees. I have little dignity left to lose, so I don't bother holding back the sobs that break uncontrollably from my throat. I was doing a decent job holding it together, all things considered, but Danen was just too much. I can't hold it in anymore. I can't even see past the tears clogging my eyes, and at some point, I realize I'm being carried again.

I should be indignant. He keeps picking me up like I gave him permission. His level of familiarity with me would be concerning if I were thinking straight, but I'm not. Not at all.

Eredin Glas carries me off into the darkness, and I can't summon the emotional strength to care. He puts me somewhere soft and warm, but I don't even bother to look. I let myself fade into oblivion and can only hope that sleep will make everything clearer.

****

A gentle breeze tickling my skin is the first thing I notice when I wake up. It's so out of the ordinary that I start violently, thrashing in the blankets until I lurch out of bed and crash onto the hard floor. I can't see, and I paw at my face in a panic until I remember that I cried myself to sleep. My eyes are gunked shut, and after picking at them for a minute I'm able to painfully crack the lids open. Blessed sunlight greets me, washing away the last of my fears about some Fomorian trickery. I'm in the home of the Wild Hunt. With Eredin Glas.

Sunlight. It almost hurts, but my aching eyes drink it in anyway. The warmth of it on my skin is euphoric. As my vision adjusts, the details surrounding me come into focus. My bed is a large cushion taking up most of a bamboo platform. Gauzy curtains flutter in the same breeze that's wafting the salty sea air at me. Down a short ladder is grass, wonderful, luscious grass that bounces under my feet. I sink to my knees, burying my hands in it, tears once again streaking my cheeks. The sky above is cloudless blue, the sun blazing with afternoon intensity. Gargantuan trees spread out below what must be a plateau, with the glint of the sea in the distance.

"Good day, Your Majesty. I trust you slept well."

His voice intrudes on my very private moment and I don't immediately respond. I catch my breath and wipe at my face, trying to keep my voice from trembling when I answer. "I did sleep well, thank you."

When I turn my head, Eredin Glas stands behind me. I gain my feet and fully face him, aware that we are the only people in the immediate vicinity. Other platforms similar to mine dot the plateau, irregularly placed around a large cooking fire set deep into the earth. A tripod straddles the fire with a bubbling pot hanging beneath.

The King himself is stunning in the sunlight. He's still larger than life, alluring in the way only someone confident in their own power can be, but softened by the lack of crackling magic and weaponry. He wears a simple linen shirt and pants, his bare feet smudged from walking through the dirt. There's an air of approachability about him, like he really is the simple hunter he appears to be.

A pair of hounds lay by the fire, splotched and long-legged. One gnaws a bone while the other nibbles at something stuck in the fur of his hindquarters. The scene is so serene as to be staged, presenting the King in a trustworthy, almost vulnerable, light.

I, on the other hand, look horrendous. I don't need a mirror to tell me that. I haven't bathed properly in months, and the last twenty-four hours have been especially foul. Now that the immediate danger is passed, I need to at least attempt to represent my station.

"Are you hungry?" Eredin Glas ignores my appearance, my rapturous episode in the grass, and my coming-undone last night. The question seems innocent enough, but I return his open smile with a guarded expression.

"I am hungry, yes." I don't move. He didn't offer me anything, and I'm not going to make assumptions about his intentions.

"Then sit, please." Without waiting for a response, he turns his back on me, retrieves a bowl, and ladles out a spoonful of whatever is stewing in the pot.

The smell hits me and I'm instantly ravenous. My legs act of their own accord, carrying me forward until they reach an overturned log sawn in half to create benches. I sink onto the bench as Eredin Glas thrusts a bowl of stew into my hands. He didn't give me a spoon, so I tilt it up and drink directly from the smooth, wooden surface, sucking in chunks of meat and vegetables. It's the most delicious thing I've ever tasted, and I've eaten the best Fae cooking the Realm has to offer. *Had.*

Eredin Glas is quiet while I eat, and I'm done in only a few minutes. My stomach cramps at the sudden fullness, but I ignore it. I wipe my mouth with the back of my hand, noting his eyes on me. It's not like I can get more gross, but the scrutiny still makes me self-conscious. I cast about for a topic, and my eyes catch on the open-bedded platforms again. "This is an unusual dwelling for a king."

The observation makes him grin. "I am a hunter first. I despise confinement. The open air suits me. As I believe it suits you."

*It does suit me. My soul feels at peace here.* I don't want him to know that. I don't want him to know anything I don't verbally tell him. To hide my thoughts, I ask the first question that comes to mind. "Did you design these platforms yourself, then?"

He chuckles. "I wish I could say that I did. Alas, I lack such creativity. I borrowed the design from the palafitos I saw in Chile. Mine are not painted quite so brightly, however." He doesn't continue the conversation, content to wait for me to broach the next topic.

*What does he want from me?* He'll tell me eventually, I'm sure, but sitting around waiting is an abdication of authority I'm not willing to grant him. Time to force his hand. Setting down my bowl, I stand, fighting against the lingering aches and fatigue. "I thank you for your hospitality, Eredin Glas, and for your protection through the night. However, it is time for me to return to my people."

His expression darkens. I haven't known him long, but he's even worse about showing his thoughts than I am. He knows I can't leave on my own, and he's annoyed I'm even playing this game. Worse, I'm rusty, the politics of the Fae court taking a backseat to the submission required by the Fomorians.

Eredin Glas stands to match me and steps into my personal space. He's easily head and shoulders taller than

I am, and obviously used to using his size to intimidate, but others have tried this trick before. I don't back down.

"I am not going to play games with you, Eve. I will speak plainly with you when I am ready to do so. Until that time, your attempts at establishing dominance in this relationship will only make you look childish and foolhardy. Now, I have provided for your every need while you are my guest. You need not fear my hunters and you may explore the Wood at your leisure. I have assigned a hunter to your beck and call, and will be available should you require me. Your time is your own, and should you wish to bathe you have only to ask."

The subtle dig doesn't land. I know I'm gross, and a bath sounds incredible. I don't say that, though. I don't say anything. Obviously done with me, Eredin Glas brushes past and makes his way down a winding game trail. In less than a minute, he is lost among the trees and disappears from view.

"Your Majesty? My liege has requested that I attend you. Is there any way I may assist you?"

My blood runs cold. I turn to find Danen not five feet from me, having materialized out of thin air. "You don't know me at all?" The words are out before I think them. My pulse pounds so loudly in my chest it's a wonder he can't hear it.

"You are Eve La Stella, Queen of the exiled Fae."

"That's what I was afraid of." The words are a whisper, more to myself than to him. A molten feeling in my gut having less to do with Danen and more to do with Eredin Glas begins to churn. *Not playing games, huh? Then what do you call this?* He knows who Danen is. He saw him at my side in the human world. He watched the battle with the Fomorians from the sky over Emain Ablach. He saw Danen give his life to protect mine. He didn't choose some random hunter to guard me. And a guard Danen is, regardless of the flowery terms his King used.

Eredin Glas can claim all he wants that he's not playing games, but every move he's made has been carefully calculated. He isn't Fae. He can lie.

## Chapter Ten

"How may I assist you, Your Majesty?"

Danen's voice, without emotion or inflection, breaks my heart. 'Your Majesty' sounds so foreign on his lips. What I wouldn't give for a 'My Queen', or even just my name. Some indication that our relationship is intact. How did this happen? Are all the hunters like this? Devoid of their lives before they joined the Hunt? Or is there something else at work?

I *will* figure this out. I will get *my* Danen back. I bite back another round of tears and think logically. Eredin Glas is dangling Danen in front of me for a reason. He knows that I care about him. The King obviously isn't concerned about the two of us absconding, so breaking whatever hold he has on Danen isn't going to be easy. I need to be at the top of my game to come out ahead in whatever game Eredin Glas is playing. And to do that, I need to be strong. Healthy. Clean.

"I could use a bath." The words feel strange on my tongue, said so casually to Danen. There was something between us. Before. I never could have asked him to help me with such a task then, in case he interpreted the request more intimately than I intended. No intimacy exists between us now.

"Right this way, Your Majesty." Danen leads me in the opposite direction of Eredin Glas, stopping only to retrieve a basket from beside the ladder of my palafito. *Do things just appear out of thin air here? I swear that wasn't there when I came down.*

The path we take wanders leisurely among the trees then drops off the edge of the plateau, curving to follow the natural slope of the terrain. The roar of water reaches my ears about halfway down, and not long after

Danen slips into a narrow crevasse in the craggy rock face. The water grows louder, and soon the crevasse opens up to a waterfall that reaches up to the sky. I squint at the top, trying to figure out where it comes from, but mist obscures the source. Sunshine turns the spray into rainbow lights playing on the rocks, so it must open to the top of the plateau somewhere.

"Your privacy is assured, Your Majesty. I will wait at the entrance until you are finished." Danen deposits the basket on an outcropping of rock and retreats, disappearing back through the winding crevasse. The basket is filled with hygiene products and piles of linen, so I dig out what I hope is soap and start the process of peeling off the scraps of clothing I'm still wearing.

My escape from the Fomorians was not kind to my clothing. Shosce provided me with pants and shirts to wear, all designed for Fomorian bodies, so they swamped me on the best of days. After my trip downriver and being attacked by the Nix, they're little more than patches covering the important parts. I drop the scraps in a pile. I'll go naked before putting them on again.

When the pile bursts into flames, I yelp and jump back. The fire is controlled, though, and extinguishes itself a moment later when the scraps have been reduced to a fine ash. The breeze picks the ash up and scatters it, and it's like the Fomorian clothes never existed at all.

The waterfall is cold, but not unpleasantly so. The soap smells like coconut and aloe vera, and leaves my skin silky smooth. I scrub until my arms start shaking. Eredin Glas healed my injuries, every scar and blemish I possessed, but did nothing for my malnourishment and weakness. Even knowing how brutal my captivity was on my body it's still difficult to look at the way my ribs protrude from my torso and how the skin on my arms and legs stretches right over the bone. I can feel the difference in the hollowness of my cheeks, the brittleness of my hair, the way just washing myself leaves me winded and aching. I'm not who I once was, in more ways than one.

I dunk my head back under the water and squeeze my eyes shut, almost wishing for the oblivion of Canowin Hollow. This world is too bright, too beautiful. I don't have a place in it anymore.

I sink to my knees, letting the push of the water against my body beat me down. The tears come again, different than the tears I shed last night. Last night's tears were overwhelming and desperate. I shed them because my body had nothing left. Today I have something, and it is for this that I cry now. I have the knowledge that I am broken, that my world is broken, but is not yet ended. My life should have been over. Canowin Hollow was my grave. Yet here I am, back in the light, and it is too much. I kneel in the cold waterfall until my legs are numb and the chill has sunk down to the bone. Then I stand. I wipe the tears from my face despite the rushing water. *I'm not dead yet. Danen isn't dead. There are more Fae out there, and they aren't dead yet, either.*

Stepping from the water, I examine my body once more. It's weak, yes, but it can grow strong again. Here in Hellequin Wood I can grow strong again. I can rest, I can eat, I can train. I will be the queen my people need, and I will return for them.

Outside of the waterfall the warm air quickly dries my skin. The pile of linen in the basket is what looks to be a lightweight sundress covered in dainty purple flowers, with straps for my shoulders and flowy around my legs. I've never been a fan of dresses, but I slip it on anyway. With my wasted muscle the dress is baggy in places it shouldn't be, but it fits well enough. There are no shoes. Eredin Glas goes barefoot, so I shouldn't be surprised.

My hair takes a long time to comb out. The soap got it clean but was ill-equipped to tackle the perpetual knots and breakage. When I finally tame it, I braid it back away from my face and tie the end off. Then I repack the basket and go looking for Danen.

When I reach the opening, I'm surprised to find that evening has fallen. I dawdled, yes, but the light in the crevasse never changed. A look over my shoulder validates my confusion—sunlight still fills the crevasse. "Danen?"

"I am here, Your Majesty." He appears out of the dimness, rising from his perch on top of a large boulder. "Is all well?"

I can't answer that question honestly, so I opt not to answer it at all. Instead, I wave my hand out over the ledge and toward the ocean of trees reaching past my sight line. "This is Hellequin Wood?"

He takes the question for the invitation it is. "Hellequin Wood has been home to the Wild Hunt since Eredin Glas became our King. We may travel across worlds, but this is the safe haven to which we will always return. Eredin Glas formed the Wood and the creatures in it. The land is as much a part of him as his body or his magic. The two cannot be separated."

*He said "we".*

Danen believes he belongs to the Wild Hunt. In the strictest sense, he does, but he also feels it in his heart. His home is here. His family is here.

*But now I'm here, too, so where does that leave us?*

"Would you like me to take you somewhere, Your Majesty?" Danen's question makes me realize I've been standing here, staring out at the trees, for way too long. By his tone he's already asked me that question, or some version of it, more than once.

I study his face. He looks like my Danen. I know every inch of those sharp cheekbones, those shadowed eyes, that coal black hair. That snow white skin, those corded muscles, that proud, feline grace. I *know* him. But he doesn't know me.

I swallow the lump in my throat. "I would like to return to the top, please."

"Of course."

# JESSICA GOEKEN

## Chapter Eleven

Danen leads me back the way we came, following the ledge that circles the outside of the plateau. It's quite a bit darker than the descent, though, so I walk closely behind him so as not to lose my footing.

"May I ask you a question?"

"Yes, Your Majesty."

I take a deep breath. *Here we go.* If only I could see his face. "Who were you before you joined the Hunt?"

His step falters, and my heart leaps. "I have only ever belonged to the Hunt."

My heart crashes and burns. He couldn't say it if he didn't believe it. But if he died, is he still Fae? And if he's not Fae, he can lie. It's all so confusing. He hesitated, though. He doubts.

"Do your memories tell you that? Or only the word of your King?"

"Why do you ask this, Your Majesty? Do you seek my answers only, or the history of every hunter in the Wood?" Danen's voice remains aloof and detached. He truly has no idea that he used to be anyone other than who he is now.

*One more push.* "What if I told you that what you believe isn't true? That you were someone else once. Someone important."

He shakes his head and walks faster. "I was told the Fae could not lie, Your Majesty. If you believe your words, then you must be mistaken. I am a hunter. Only a hunter." He draws farther ahead, topping the plateau before I can catch up.

Eredin Glas waits at the fire. He looks much the same as when he left, save for the loose hair around his shoulders. The dark locks soften the edges of his face. A four-legged creature spins slowly on a spit, crackling and dripping grease. A large bowl set in the middle of one of the benches holds small, round loaves of bread. "Thank you for watching over our guest, Danen. She is safe with me for the night. You are dismissed."

"Yes, my liege." Danen bows and leaves, not even looking at me. I look at him, though, and I know he feels my eyes. When I can no longer see him in the darkness, I turn back to Eredin Glas with a glare. "What did you do to him?"

"Good evening to you, too. You look lovely. Lilac suits you."

"I need answers, Eredin Glas, and it is time you give them to me. I will not simply lounge here in ignorance until you decide that I am worth indulging."

"Found your bite, did you? You may ask me anything you wish."

His cordiality throws me off. I was expecting a fight. Why isn't he fighting?

Alert for any tricks, I wade in cautiously. "When warriors join your Hunt, are they still alive? Or do you take them after they are dead?"

Eredin Glas settles onto the ground, leaning back against the bench and folding his fingers. "Do you remember your own condition for allowing me to hunt in your Realm?" he counters, his tone still easy, his posture relaxed.

I remember. "I told you that you could only take Fae who were willing, and use no coercion."

"Precisely." He snags a roll from the basket and tears off a piece. "Now, how can I coerce someone who is dead?"

Assumptions and double-talk are the Fae way, but I won't allow the King to draw me in. "That's not an answer."

He sighs, deflating a little. Like I'm ruining his fun. "I cannot conscript the dead. Once they pass through the veil they are lost to me."

*Danen's alive! Which also means he's still Fae. And maybe I can still get him back.*

The King's eyes meet mine, and I see the flames flickering behind the chocolate orbs. His temper is still in there, just banked. For now. "Now it's time for you to stop being coy. Ask me what you want to ask me. We agreed once to speak plainly together, did we not?"

A situational agreement that holds no bearing on our current circumstance. I don't mention that, though. I take a deep breath. "Why doesn't Danen remember me? Are all of your hunters ignorant of their pasts, or did you do something to him?"

"If my hunters did not know who they were, they would not be as valuable to me as they are. I choose them for their valor, their bravery, their loyalty. Those traits do not resonate in an empty shell. Danen does not remember you because I stole his memories from him."

"What?"

He pats the ground next to him. "Come, sit down and eat. You must be hungry, and we have much to discuss."

"I will not until you have explained yourself!" The words fly out of my mouth before I consider them. My eyes widen in horror as my jaw snaps shut, but it's too late. The oath has been made. I have no choice but to keep it. I have just vowed to neither sit down nor eat until Eredin Glas explains his actions to me. My fate is entirely in his hands. If he so chooses, he can let me stand here until the end of time, or at least until I starve to death.

His brows raise, the severity of the situation not lost on him. "Interesting," is all he says.

I let several minutes pass before I give in, the only

sound between us the crackling of the fire and the distant chirping of crickets. "What's interesting?"

Eredin Glas rises to his feet, circling me as he looks me up and down. "Your oath is bound by Fae magic, as is your inability to lie. If Fae magic is broken, how then do these rules still stand?"

Do they? Not lying has always been bound to my nature. I haven't even tried to lie, knowing that I can't.

Eredin Glas is thinking the same thing. With a flourish, he slices a sliver off of the roasting beast. A second later, he puts it in my hand. The smell reaches my nose and my stomach goes crazy, rumbling and gurgling so loud we both hear it.

I meet his eyes, then slowly lift the piece of meat. Closer. Closer. I open my mouth, and my hand stalls. The meat nearly touches my teeth, but I can't move it any closer. My arm cramps and tears spring to my eyes, but still, I can't eat it. The oath holds. I drop my hand in defeat.

"Interesting," he repeats, then steps back and stares at me.

I know what he wants. An answer to a question I was hoping I could ignore a little longer. An answer that is none of his business, except that my business is now his business. "Fae magic *is* broken. But a remnant remains. I don't know how much, and I certainly don't understand how."

"Can you perform magic?"

"No." The admission crushes me, and a hint of triumph tinges his expression.

"Danen's loyalty to you is unquestionable. When I looked into his eyes as he lay dying on that battlefield, I could see the truth. I wanted him, yes, but he didn't feel the call of the hounds. He only wanted to stay alive. Staying alive meant saving you. I loved him for that.

However, that same loyalty would have had him whisking you out of Hellequin Wood the moment you set foot on this island. And that I simply cannot have."

My knees sag as my oath is lifted. I stumble forward to the bench and sink onto it gratefully. I stuff the piece of meat in my mouth and groan. When I recover, though, I glare at Eredin Glas. "You stole his memories to deprive me of allies? To keep me here against my will?"

"His memories are still his own, just buried where he cannot reach them. At the appointed time, I will release them, and he will be himself again."

Dread pools in my gut. "And what is the appointed time?"

"When you vow to become my queen."

# JESSICA GOEKEN

## Chapter Twelve

I leap back up again. "I will never—"

"Ah ah. Watch your words, Eve. Some things can't be taken back." The King is emerging again, in Eredin Glas's words and bearing. He can only suppress his nature for so long. He stands to match me, lording his size over mine.

I cut off abruptly, aware of what I almost did. Again. *Why am I so discombobulated around him?* I need to get a handle on myself, and fast. With a deep breath, I shove my temper down and choose my next words carefully. "You said you weren't playing games with me, yet Danen's entire presence is a game. But my duty is to more than just him. By all rights, he should be dead. Why would I bind myself to you for a single Fae and abandon the rest of my people to exile?"

"If you would do that, then you wouldn't be the queen I desire. No, Danen is not here to force your hand. On the contrary, I look forward to unleashing his power as he fully embraces the Hunt. Your Danen is a formidable warrior, and his skills are unmatched even among many of my hunters."

"Then I ask again, why would I bind myself to you and abandon my people?"

"To save them."

Not the answer I was expecting. The King has a way of taking me completely by surprise.

He continues. "The majority of your people are dead. That fact cannot be erased. The remaining Fae believe *you* to be dead. Even those who survived the battle at Emain Ablach do not know what became of you, and you have yet to reappear after nearly a year of absence. They live broken lives in the human world. They devolved into warring factions and are hunted by Fomorian patrols."

With every word he speaks my spirits sink lower. *This isn't right. The synod was supposed to be taking care of them. They're supposed to be safe.* "I need to go to them. I need to see them." All strength has fled my voice, taking with it any chance I had of gaining the upper hand in this conversation.

He moves in front of me, ignoring my murmured words, hand gently lifting my chin. His voice drops, growing tender and intimate. "The Fae need not remain lost. Regaining their magic will once again give them control of their own destinies. They will flourish, and in time they will be strong and proud again. Swear yourself to me, and I will restore Fae magic."

My breath leaves me in a rush. My legs wobble but thankfully keep me upright. "Can you do that?" I ask in a whisper, unable to hide a glimmer of hope.

"I can."

I search his face. If he can do what he says he can…

"You know what happened, then. You know why Fae magic failed." *If he can make this make sense, if he can put everything to rights, then I need to know.*

His eyes search mine, looking for my angle. "I do."

My voice grows earnest. I can't tear my eyes away from his. "Then tell me. Tell me what it is I did wrong, what mistake I made, what danger I did not foresee." My voice cracks, betraying the hurt and uncertainty I've been trying to hide from him. Tears prickle behind my eyes once more. "*I* did this. I doomed them, I doomed us all, but I don't understand what I did wrong, so if you truly know, please, tell me."

Eredin Glas takes my hands in his and draws them in toward his chest. "Oh, Eve. I want to give you everything you're looking for. I want to give you the answers that will bring you peace. But I cannot give you one answer without also giving away the other. To tell you why Fae magic is broken would be akin to telling you how it can be restored, and that would be a torturous thing for you to know."

I stiffen in his embrace. "Torturous why?"

"Because you cannot restore Fae magic of your own accord. To have that knowledge and be powerless to act on it? I will not burden you so."

I've been here less than a day and he's already lied to me at least once. Not to mention the deception with the owl. How can I trust him now? I shove his hands away and take a step back. "This is why you rescued me. To dangle this knowledge in front of me and trick me into being your queen."

"Trick?" His eyes flash, flames flaring up to obliterate the soft brown. In an instant, he's alien once again, power radiating off him in waves. The reminder is good. I can't let myself forget who he is.

"Yes, trick. You play the part of a savior, but you continue to reveal ulterior motives. Fine, let's play your game. You wish to make a Fae deal. You refuse to give me any information that might help me unless I agree to your conditions. Swear myself to you. What exactly does that entail? What do you want me for?"

The King grinds his teeth, scowling at me in a way that totally belies the coziness he was portraying just a few minutes ago. This conversation is not going the way he planned. I see the moment he decides to tell me the truth. The flames bank in his eyes and his shoulders lose some of their tension. "I want your magic. That's no secret. You hold greater power than anyone in your bloodline since Titania. I felt you across the worlds and sought to add you to my Hunt, but that position was too small for you.

"If you swear yourself to me, I will possess your magic without having to tear it from you. It will be at my beck and call, and I will not have to extinguish you from this world. You will rule at my side as my queen, and together we will ride the skies and bring terror on all who fall before us."

It's a pretty speech. And a terrifying one. One I believe. Eredin Glas tried to claim me once. Hunted me across the human world. He failed. I would be a fool to believe he wouldn't try again.

I also can't make a rash decision. My people need me to be their queen, now more than ever. With forced formality to cover my raging emotions, I answer. "Thank you for your honesty. I will consider your proposal, Eredin Glas."

His eyes shutter. The sliver of vulnerability he showed me snaps shut and his spine stiffens once again. "This is what I want, Eve, and I want to give you the time to consider your decision. I will not wait forever, though, and I make a habit of getting what I want."

It's not a threat, exactly, but neither are they friendly words to part on. At least I know where I stand as he strides off into the darkness, leaving me behind at the fire with the roasted creature and the basket of bread.

I sink back down onto the bench, my exhaustion stealing my remaining strength in a rush. My first impulse is, of course I can't abdicate my crown. How could he even ask that of me? Yet I told him I would consider it, and I am bound by those words.

From the back of my mind, questions arise. *If I do agree, will he really keep his word? Is he really capable of restoring Fae magic, or is that just a ploy to force my compliance?* And, most importantly, *If he can do it, why can't I?* He said I can't, but that doesn't necessarily make it true.

He said one other thing, too. Well, he didn't contradict me when I said it, which isn't quite the same thing. *It was my fault*. It's the one truth I can't escape no matter how far away my enemies carry me. Something I did broke Fae magic, and until I understand what that was, I will never be able to put it right. All of the dead Fae can be laid at my feet, for the decisions I did and didn't make. How do I ever return to them bearing such a weight?

My vision swims, hunger and fatigue a lethal combination. The plateau around me is quiet with nighttime activity, which means it isn't quiet at all. Not in the little ways that matter. In the absence of our voices, I can hear the birds and rodents rustling in the tree branches overhead and the leaves on the ground, settling in for sleep. The gentle reminder begs me to go to bed, too, pulling at my eyelids, but I can't rest yet. I take the spit off the fire, singeing my fingers but landing the creature safely across the edges of the bread bowl. For the moment, I have to focus on my most pressing objective: get strong again.

I tackle the bread while the meat cools, stuffing it in my face in a decidedly non-queenly manner. It's delicious, leaving me wondering if Eredin Glas is the cook.

The meat is still too hot when I finally start in on it, but I don't care. Without plates or silverware, I'm reduced to peeling pieces off with my fingers. It isn't a small animal, but I stuff every bite inside anyway. I need to rebuild myself, and fast.

When I finally seek my bed, the moon is high overhead, the tiniest sliver of light peeking down from the sky. "Thank you for getting me out of there," I whisper up at it as I snuggle down into my blankets. My bed may only be a cushion on the floor, but it's soft and cozy, and despite the turmoil in my brain I fall asleep instantly.

## Chapter Thirteen

I wake up at peace, my body buried in blankets and pleasantly heavy. I consider snuggling back in, but the gentle sun coaxes me awake enough for my stomach to protest at being empty yet again. For the time I've spent hungry it's gotten quite uppity now that food is once again in abundance. The hunger drives me from bed and back to the fire, where I find myself alone with a basket of fruits and cheeses. Simple fare, but filling. I eat as much as I can, willing my body to rebuild the strength I've lost.

When I finish, Danen appears, and I get the impression he's been watching me for a while. No sign of last night's conversation shows on his face. I'm ready, though. I know what I want to do today.

"I would like to explore the Wood and meet the rest of the hunters," I tell him, keeping my voice neutral. I don't want to make him too uncomfortable to act as my guard.

"As you will, Your Majesty."

Prepared as I am, the shift in our relationship is jarring. Caspian used to be the one trailing me like a puppy. Danen's presence was stronger. Impossible to ignore. Even now, he's not easily forgotten as I wander at my leisure. I have no shoes, but the ground is soft beneath my feet and the grass feels heavenly against my skin.

We travel down the same path as last night until the ground levels out at the base of the plateau. The trees here are the tallest I've ever seen, with branches as thick as my thigh stretching from top to bottom. If I wanted to, I could scale the behemoths like a staircase and flit between them like a squirrel, never touching the ground. I stretch my arms up to the sun, drinking in its warmth, until the upper canopy hides its rays from view.

"Why does the King live alone on the plateau?" I ask Danen. "Where does the rest of the Hunt sleep?"

"We sleep wherever we wish, Your Majesty. The King allows us the freedom to live our lives largely how we wish to. Some prefer the trees, others the beach, still others prefer the rocking of a boat on the waves. My liege enjoys the view from the plateau, but he does not require solitude. His fire is often raucous with tale and song, the grass crowded with tents."

The words he's not saying are easy enough to understand. "He sent you all away for me?"

"He wishes you to be at peace, Your Majesty."

I am at peace. My thoughts are chaotic, that's true, but living under the sun once more has calmed me in ways I didn't think possible. The future looks less bleak from up there. Hellequin Wood isn't the Realm, it never could be, but if I'm being honest with myself, I could see a future in this place. It isn't home, but it speaks to my Fae nature, and my nature welcomes it.

Before I can chase that thought too far the scent of woodsmoke tickles my nose. We enter a clearing to find another fire, smaller than the King's, with a handful of simple tents encircling it. Three hunters sit at the fire. One man is animatedly telling a story in a language I don't know, to the amusement of another man and a woman. They fall silent when they see us.

"Hail." Danen greets the hunters.

"Hail," they answer, gaining their feet.

"Your Majesty, I present Farooq, Nes-Unnefer, and Lella." The hunters each nod when introduced but don't speak. "I thought it would be good for you to meet Lella, to help put you at ease."

"It's a pleasure to meet you," I say honestly. I

didn't pay much attention to individual hunters the other night on the beach, but I'm not surprised to find a woman in their midst. Eredin Glas doesn't seem the type to care where strength comes from, so long as he can claim it for his own.

"I am happy to make your acquaintance, Your Majesty."

"Eve, please."

The men move off, giving us space, though part of me wishes they would stay. I am unable to place their origins from their names and coloring, and I would welcome the chance to learn such things.

Lella is tall and strong, with chestnut skin and black hair. She's not classically beautiful, her features looking more weathered than delicate, but her eyes shine with obvious wit.

"How are you finding the Wood, Eve? Is there anything I can help you with?"

The question grates against my nerves. "Honestly, I could use a friend," I confess. "Everyone is so maddeningly helpful. I feel like Eredin Glas told you all to be polite and distant, but that isn't going to help me learn about this place, is it?"

*How much does she know about her King's plans, I wonder?*

Lella smiles, a genuine one that lights up her eyes. "Indeed. My liege wishes you to remain unbothered so you may rest, but I for one would find such an existence a bore." With a flourish, she whips a knife out of her belt and flings it at a nearby tree, where it sinks deeply into the wood. "Give me quarry to chase or a battle to be won over idleness for the rest of my days, and I will be content."

My heart warms, stirred by the kindred spirit I feel within the hunter. When she gestures to the fire I sit willingly, and she passes me a skin of something spicy to drink. "You're a queen, huh? This must be a change for you, mingling among the likes of us."

"You must not have met many Fae. We are not a fancy people. Riches mean little to us. Rather, we prefer the simple joys of growing things and wildness. Walking barefoot through the grass and speaking with people who love the land is my idea of a good day."

"Canowin Hollow must have been hell for you, then. No growing things there." Her words sound flippant but are anything but. She hasn't missed the hollowness of my own body, nor did she miss the spectacle I presented on the beach. These words stand as an invitation to talk about such things, if I wish to do so.

"No. No growing things in Canowin Hollow." I don't want to dwell on the darkness. I especially don't want to dwell on the despair and hopelessness I felt there. I let my voice trail off and my eyes wander, and she doesn't press the subject. A minute later, I change the topic. "Tell me, Lella, how long have you ridden with the Hunt? What lands do you come from?"

She clicks her tongue. "I can't say how long, for time ceases to matter once you've been removed from the world. But the last time we rode through the human world my children's children no longer walked the deserts of home."

"You're human, then?"

"None of us are any longer what we were. But I was human, once. I was Lella Ult Chikat, of the Tuareg peoples of northeastern Mali."

"And how did you draw the attention of Eredin Glas?"

Lella takes a swig of the spicy drink and blows out a breath. "What do you know of the Tuareg?"

"Little," I admit. "I've heard the name." During

my time in Africa with Caspian, we avoided people at all costs, though we caught snatches of conversation now and then. None of it pertained to us, so I made no effort to remember it.

"In the briefest of histories, the Tuareg is a clan society, and we do not all get along. My clan was peaceful, keeping herds, and this made others think us weak. We were not weak, and when they came for us, we educated them on the matter."

"He came for the battle," I muse.

"My liege enjoys a good battle, and we gave a good one that day. He plucks many of his hunters from death on the battlefield, as he took your champion. What did he see in me, to choose me over another? I do not ask."

"And now you are here."

"Yes. Now I am here, and will be until the end of days." Her words are punctuated by a horn ringing out over the Wood. Baying hounds join in, sending goosebumps over my arms, and Lella leaps to her feet. "Our quarry has been spotted," she declares, grabbing my arm and hauling me up beside her.

"What quarry?" I ask as she dives into her tent. Farooq and Nes-Unnefer reappear in the corner of my vision, pulling on boots and retrieving their weapons. The sudden bustle of activity catches me off guard until I remember that this isn't a simple woodsmen's camp, no matter how serene it appears. It's a hunters' camp.

Danen appears at my side. "Your Majesty, I must return you to the plateau."

"What quarry?" I repeat, ignoring Danen and calling after Lella.

"Magic," Lella answers as she returns, her body quivering with excitement. "For that is what the King hunts."

Her enthusiasm is contagious and anticipation rushes through my body. Danen tries to get my attention again and I make a snap decision. "I'm coming with you."

"Most excellent! You will ride at my side, and we will glory in this chase together!"

"Your Majesty, I insist—"

I step away from Danen, ignoring the whiny tone he would hate to hear coming out of his own mouth. "What do I do?"

Lella's eyes sweep over me, judging the flimsy dress I'm still wearing and finding it wanting. "You can't ride with the Hunt wearing that."

"Then let's find me something else."

## Chapter Fourteen

My new, scrounged-up clothes fit me much better than the gauzy dress ever could. I wear supple leather pants that wrap my legs, a leather vest over a billowy, long-sleeved linen shirt, and boots only slightly too big that reach halfway up my thighs. The dark brown of the leather complements my golden skin, and with my silver hair tied back in a braid I look every bit like a hunter.

Lella ties a knife onto my belt and we hurry to the beach where the rest of the Hunt has mustered.

A crazed energy consumes the beach. Horses paw at the sand, hounds strain against their tethers, hunters call back and forth to each other, and over them all presides the King. Eredin Glas sits astride his mount, a massive creature twice the size of a normal horse. His power crackles around him like static, and the flames in his eyes burn bright. He turns the weight of his gaze on me as Lella and I join the gathered hunters, and my blood pounds in my ears. It takes all my strength to meet those eyes and not tremble.

"I'm coming," I state simply.

"Good." He whistles, and a weight slams between my shoulder blades. A horse, already saddled and harnessed, is waiting for me to mount. He expected this. "His name is Gent. He's no qilin, but he won't let you fall."

A pang goes through me at his words. My qilin mount, Keshi, was left behind when Emain Ablach fell. I don't know what happened to her. With a pat on Gent's nose, I climb into the saddle, whispering sweet nothings to him about what a good boy he is.

When I'm situated, Eredin Glas lets out a bellow

that silences the beach. "Hunters! We ride far today! Our sorcerer has broken his exile!"

A raucous cheer accompanies this announcement. They obviously know who this sorcerer is and are chomping at the bit to find him.

"Three times our quarry has evaded us, but no longer. Today is the day he learns what it means to face down the Wild Hunt. Come, hunters! With me!" Eredin Glas digs his heels into his mount and the beast leaps into the air.

Gent follows on his heels, sending me flying backward at the unexpected upward motion. I recover quickly to find Eredin Glas's eyes on me again. I can't read the emotion in them, but he's smiling. A lock of his hair pulls loose from the tie at his neck and flies free behind him.

A baying chorus of hounds accompanies our ascent, and their cries pull me outside of myself. That same yearning I felt the first time I heard the hounds rushes through my body, urging me to let go and lose myself in the Hunt. More than simple freedom, my release is from bondage and oppression. At this moment, I can believe that the Hunt is where I am meant to be. I can't stop the elation that crosses my face, and when Eredin Glas sees it, he barks out a happy laugh.

The beach falls away as the horses' legs churn the air, carrying us ever higher. The sky above us splits open, blues and purples radiating out from the piercing light beyond. Our mounts carry us through as the hunters call and cheer behind us.

The portal greets us with a blast of cold air and blinding light that obliterates my senses. My head spins, and I clutch at Gent's mane to keep from tumbling off. He whinnies and adjusts his gait, and suddenly the world stops spinning around me. His legs are still moving, but my perch along his back feels motionless.

Seconds later the light fades out and we're flying through a foreign sky. Not the human world. Not the Realm. Somewhere new. *How many lands exist in this world?* I'd always felt like my world was bigger than most, knowing that the Realm was out there, that so much was open to me while the humans were so limited. I had no idea that places like Canowin Hollow or Hellequin Wood even existed. How naive I was to not realize the Realm was but one in a vast sea of lands.

And speaking of vast seas...

Water stretches beneath us as far as the eye can see. Even from this height, the wind our arrival generates whips the waves into a frenzy. The cloudless sky around us darkens as the storm accompanying the hunters forms. One look at Eredin Glas and I can see the magic pouring out of him, drawing the elements together to create such a massive weather event. It's no accident the hunters arrive in a storm. He chooses this. He wants his prey to know he's coming.

The electricity in the air fires up hunters and hounds alike. Eredin Glas tugs his horse's reins, driving him down toward the churning waters. The rest of us follow like the whipping tail of a snake. Gent's hooves stop a few feet above the water, and suddenly we're generating not just a storm but a hurricane. My body trembles in equal parts anticipation and fear. I don't believe Eredin Glas will allow his storm to hurt me, but it's a terrifying experience nonetheless.

"Eve!" The King's word barely reaches my ears over the gale.

I spur Gent onward, and we come abreast of the King's mount.

"Do you see it?" His arm points into the distance, where a dark mass has appeared on the horizon.

"What is it?" I can't make out any details through the rain and the darkness.

"The Lost Island of Atlantis."

*Atlantis? It's real?*

The hunters cry out at the sight of land, which adds fuel to the horses' frenzy. We race faster than I would've thought possible, even though I've experienced firsthand the power and speed of the Wild Hunt. This sorcerer won't stand a chance if we catch up to him.

Eredin Glas doesn't slow as we approach the island. The city of Atlantis towers above us, high stone walls atop sheer cliffs. From this vantage point I count six different waterfalls cresting the stone and crashing into the ocean far below. Our hurricane slams into those cliffs and our mounts ride the storm's momentum, leaping high enough to clear the walls with room to spare.

"Don't you think this is a little much?" I call to the King as the gale-force winds tear into structures and topple buildings. The well-ordered streets are empty, but it's impossible to miss the exquisite architecture and technological advantages of the island city. I can't tear my eyes away from the power on display. I may balk at the wanton destruction, but the euphoria from the ride isn't something I'll soon forget. I don't want to ever let it go.

"The Atlanteans knew what they were doing, shielding my quarry from me. They will not escape unscathed." There is no remnant of the gentle man who sat with me by the fire in this King riding forth to battle. He came for me like this once. Hunting my magic. A shudder passes over me, but there is no trace of fear this time. I'm here, on his side, instead of in his path.

Looking behind me, I search for Danen. I know he's back there. *There.* He's enjoying himself, just like the rest of the hunters. He doesn't feel my eyes, though. He's too lost in the hunt, too disconnected from me.

The hounds explode into howls and I know they've scented their prey. Eredin Glas leads us down to ground level and the grid-like system of streets dug like ditches into the sandy ground. Our storm tears paving stones from their moorings and obliterates the tracks of the streets altogether.

Eredin Glas careens down one street after another until abruptly his pace slows.

*He's found him.*

The King breaks from the Hunt, who continue to howl and ride with abandon, swarming over the island like locusts.

Without hesitation, I follow Eredin Glas. Gent pounds after him gleefully, eyes and nostrils wide. Outside of the winds his hooves thump dully on the sand.

Eredin Glas dismounts, sniffing the air as he approaches a low building.

Before he reaches the door, it opens and a troop of well-armored Atlanteans rushes out. They're tall and fit, with serious faces and hard eyes. Their armor appears to be made from seashells, though I doubt it's quite so brittle, the dark hues of their skin just visible at the edges. They level a quartet of harpoons at Eredin Glas.

"Stop, intruder! You are not welcome in this land."

Eredin Glas stops. He appraises the troop but does not attack. Hunters race past behind the building, having circled around and enclosed all of us in a raging ring. "You harbor one marked by the Wild Hunt, Atlantean. I would have him returned to me."

"I know of the one whom you seek. He has bartered refuge with our people. To yield him to you would be to violate the laws of hospitality."

"Hospitality? Does this law not extend both ways? You may have granted him refuge, but he has not upheld his end of the bargain. Else, how would I know he was here?"

This throws them. "Would you allow us a moment to confer?"

"Please." Eredin Glas extends his arm in a gracious gesture. For one so invested in this hunt, he is showing remarkable patience.

"Come on out, Eve."

The command takes me by surprise and I obey without thinking. I wasn't hiding, but neither did I want to flaunt my presence, either.

"What will you do if they refuse to give him to you?" I ask.

"I will take him." It isn't a threat. It's a fact. Four Atlanteans can't stand before the King of the Wild Hunt.

Their leader steps forward. "Tobias Olvehagan has violated our law of hospitality. Leave off with this storm, and you may do as you wish with him."

Eredin Glas grins. "Agreed." Instantly, the storm begins to clear. The wind falls silent, the rain stops pouring, and the clouds roll back into the sky, exposing the midday sun once more.

The Atlantean gestures and a commotion springs up at the door behind him. It opens and a frazzled-looking man is thrust outside. He is neither human nor Atlantean. His knees bend backward upon themselves and tiny spikes run down the length of his back. He scrambles to get back inside, but the door is shut firmly in his face and bolted. He spins around, wide-eyed, when Eredin Glas's shadow falls over him.

"You—you're not supposed to be here," the sorcerer stammers. He glances wildly around himself, but his defenders have abandoned him to his fate.

"I'm sure your friends told you," Eredin Glas whispers, his voice low and dangerous. "All you had to do was not do magic. That's how I feel you, you see. But you couldn't do it. You needed it too much."

"What are you going to do?" The sorcerer's voice is a whimper, but something stirs in his eyes. He isn't defeated yet. Does the King see it?

Eredin Glas reaches for the sorcerer, and that's when Olvehagan makes his move.

"Watch out!" I scream as the sorcerer wraps his hands around Eredin Glas's wrist.

He screams, a wrenching, guttural scream, and vanishes into thin air, taking Eredin Glas with him.

## Chapter Fifteen

"No!" I clutch at the empty air as hoof beats surround me.

"What happened?" Jarild demands, his festive tone turned serious at the disappearance of his King.

"He took him," I answer, gesturing at the empty air. "How did he do that?" All traces of the storm have passed, and the Hunt slowly gathers around us as their manic energy dissipates. A tingle races down my spine as Danen appears at my back, but he only checks on my welfare and turns his attention back to Jarild.

"Olvehagan is a slippery one. We've cornered him three times, and he's always managed to slip away."

"What do we do?" I ask.

Jarild gives me a puzzled expression. "We follow. What else would we do?" As he speaks, the air before him splits open, similar to the portal in the sky Eredin Glas brought us through in the first place. This one is smaller and less intense, and the hunters show no hesitation. Their mounts need no urging to gallop through the portal without even knowing what's on the other side.

"No, Your Majesty." Danen's hand closes on my upper arm as I move to follow the hunters. "My liege would never forgive me if I allowed harm to come to you in his absence."

I shake off Danen and move closer to the portal, stopping well out of range. The colors twist and swirl, making me dizzy if I concentrate on it too hard. Glimpses of the land beyond flash across my vision before being swallowed up again. A harsh, brittle landscape. The ghosts of cracked, crooked trees. A purple sky completely devoid of stars.

*What is this place?*

I backpedal as the portal flashes, then blinks out of existence. "How did they do that? How do they know where Eredin Glas is? How did they open a portal without him?"

Danen chuckles. "Have you forgotten that every hunter possesses magic, Your Majesty? The King is unquestionably the strongest of us, but we are not powerless in his absence. Even our mounts may traverse the lands freely; they are not bound by natural laws."

Danen's words tumble in my mind as we stand vigil on the Atlantean road. *Atlantean! I'm really standing in Atlantis right now!* My eyes rove over the buildings I can see, picking out pieces of Greek, Roman, Egyptian, even Mesopotamian design. Like their armor, the materials resemble the calcium carbonate of seashells, grooved and swirling with blues, greens, and pinks. Combined with the sand and the tall clumps of vegetation I almost feel as if I'm standing on the ocean floor. The dripping water and scattered flotsam from the Hunt's storm only strengthens that impression.

The departure of the Hunt signaled safety to the Atlanteans, and they emerge from their hiding places all around us. For the most part, they give Danen and me a wide berth and set about examining the damage.

My eyes follow them, noting their oddly fluid movements, almost as if they were swimming through the air. Every single one boasts close-cropped hair and heavy tattoos; from this distance I cannot tell man from woman.

"Eve La Stella, I presume?" The question comes from my left as a trio of Atlanteans approach. They stop a respectful distance away and wait for me to acknowledge them. "Time does not remember the last time we hosted a Fae on our shores."

Something tightens in my throat and I fight back a

wave of panic.

*Just because they know who you are doesn't mean anything. It might have nothing to do with Fomorians or goblins at all. Besides, nothing will happen to you with Danen standing right here. Just play it cool.*

I wave Danen down with a hand and step toward the Atlanteans. They take the gesture as acceptance and close the distance between us. "You know me, but I do not know you. Before today, I knew nothing of your existence."

The leader steps forward and crosses one arm across his chest, fist tightly closed. "We strove hard to erase the knowledge of our existence. Perhaps too hard, if even our former allies have forgotten us."

"We were allies?" I bury the suspicion in my voice and give him a polite smile instead. I would love to take his word for it, but I'd like to think I've learned that lesson already. I won't be so quick to trust again, especially someone that has no reason not to lie.

The Atlantean appears middle-aged, though his bare chest bulges with the muscles of youth. This close I can see the details of the tattoos covering his tan skin, crisscrossing ropes resembling nets twisted into dizzying patterns. And I see something tucked up under his chin, stretching to the bottoms of his earlobes. Gills?

"We were allies. Once. I am Reif, King of Atlantis, descendant of Seaton, who aided Peony, Queen of the Fae, as she repelled an incursion of sea monsters into the waters of the Realm."

*Peony?* It takes me a moment to place the name, since most of my education focused on the last five hundred years of Fae history, after the first war with the Fomorians and the uniting of the Houses. Peony was Titania's mother, making her my great-great grandmother.

"If what you say is true, then we are well met, Reif, King of Atlantis. But that does not explain how you know my name."

He inclines his head. Not quite a nod, but a simple acknowledgment. "You are suspicious. I do not blame you. News of your misfortune with the Fomorians reached us some time ago, though we are not on friendly terms with General Halasuwa."

That name jars in my ears, feeling at complete odds with the sparkling colors and the salty ocean air. I'm not certain how to respond, so I let my eyes stray back to the empty road, still waiting for a returning portal to open.

Reif follows my gaze, raising an eyebrow but not offended. "I am pleased to see you survived your ordeal under the earth, but I am curious how you came to belong to such a company." He can't hide the twinge of resentment in his final words. Understandable. The Wild Hunt just trashed his city.

I consider how much of the truth I should share with such an unknown entity and decide to stick to basic facts. "Eredin Glas rescued me from beneath Canowin Hollow. If you heard of the battle, then you know how the Fae have become scattered." I leave out the tidbit about the magic, but Reif's gaze darkens when I mention the Fae. He knows.

"The Wild Hunt gives you refuge, then?" His question is heavy with implication. I am not willing to disclose our vulnerability to someone I just met and whose allegiances I don't know, regardless of how close our ancestors once were, and he is too polite to ask me about it outright.

*He does seem to know more than he should, though.* "For now. The Fae will become strong again."

He nods once in acknowledgment. "Eredin Glas is

a powerful ally. And a mercurial one. Promises from him cannot always be trusted." Reif's sea green eyes shine, begging me to understand the words he isn't speaking. I believe I do.

Part of me yearns to speak plainly, but I hold my tongue. If I've learned anything at all it's to hold my secrets closer and be more judicious in who I trust. But, if he somehow knows how to restore Fae magic, the information would be worth finding out. "I must consider all viable offers of aid if I am to restore my people to what they once were."

He understands the request, but a shadow passes over his face. He shakes his head slowly as he answers. "Atlantis is unable to help you in this matter, but I would like for our alliance to become established once more. If you have need of future aid, call on us. We will answer."

His words aren't binding like mine would be, but I would like to believe he will keep them. Once the Fae are restored and back in our homeland we are going to need allies. Time will tell if I am able to trust Reif or not.

We both fall silent, turning our eyes in unison back to the empty road. Any other topic would feel trite in comparison. The minutes tick by, and still the Hunt does not return.

When Reif speaks next his words are directed at Danen. "Do you think they're going to come back?"

Danen answers gruffly, as if offended at the very question. "No sorcerer can match the King of the Wild Hunt."

As if Danen's words summon him, the air once again splits open. Eredin Glas himself strides through the rift, unharmed, the sorcerer unconscious and thrown across his shoulder. The Hunt spills out around him, whooping and cheering. He meets my eyes with a grin and pats the sorcerer's butt for good measure. "Worried,

Eve?"

My relief is plain on my face. "Concerned, though it appears I need not be."

"I always catch my quarry," he assures me, stepping close to loom over me. He lowers his voice and speaks into my ear. "Always."

I shiver. Whether he considers me quarry or not, the implication that he will catch me is clear. It's only been a day and I'm already tired of this dance and the conflicting things the King makes me feel.

The Atlanteans use my distraction to melt into the sudden crowd, vanishing as quickly as they appeared. They didn't escape Eredin Glas's notice, though. "Making new friends?"

I raise my chin. "Reif, King of Atlantis. A diplomatic introduction."

"Hmph." He doesn't care for my answer, but dismisses the interaction quickly enough. "Mount up! We ride for home, to feasting and celebration!"

The Hunt takes to the skies, leaving Atlantis far behind. We return to Hellequin Wood against the backdrop of a glorious sunset.

Eredin Glas drops the sorcerer into the sand before he even dismounts. "Tobias Olvehagan!" he roars, rousing the sorcerer from slumber.

Olvehagan looks up with defiance in his eyes, but cowers when he sees the full force of the Wild Hunt looking back at him. "This is it, then?"

Jarild steps forward. "Aye. Any last words?"

"Last words? I need last words to ride with the Hunt?"

Eredin Glas laughs. "I would never accept a sniveling coward like you into the Wild Hunt. I require loyalty of my hunters, and you have betrayed every trust that has ever been extended to you. A pleasant crossing to you, Tobias Olvehagan."

Without further words Jarild draws a gleaming sword from his belt. He takes Olvehagan's head with a single swing. The Hunt doesn't cheer. Their joy is in the chase, not in this macabre execution.

My eyes stay on Eredin Glas, though. He also doesn't revel in the kill, but a change does come over him. His entire being glows from within, and he sucks in a sharp breath. He moans on the exhale, and when he opens his eyes, they contain the brightest fire I've ever seen in them.

*He's absorbed the sorcerer's magic. That's what this whole thing was about.*

And it's made him stronger.

I look back at the body, only to find it gone. In its place is a pile of ash that blows away on a sudden wind.

Eredin Glas bangs his scythe against the armor on his chest. "Hunters! This night finds us victorious! Let us drink!"

# JESSICA GOEKEN

## Chapter Sixteen

A cheer goes up and activity breaks out on the beach. Eredin Glas steps closer to me, exultation evident in every move he makes. "Did you enjoy riding with the Hunt, Eve?"

I can't lie to him, and I find I don't want to. "I did enjoy it. The thrill of the Hunt is contagious. Inescapable."

He grins, the flame in his eyes glowing like a dying ember. "I knew you would. You have fire inside you, Eve, and I would unleash it on the world. Can you imagine the pair we would make, riding through the skies? All of the lands would be ours for the taking."

I can imagine it. "But this? Killing that sorcerer in cold blood just so you can steal his magic? That I cannot condone."

"You have never killed?"

I keep my mouth shut. I have killed. Human sacrifice is the only way to open the gate between the human world and the Realm. *Was.*

"The Hunt does not always end so. Even when our quarry does not possess the fortitude required of a hunter, my choice is often to strip them of their magic and leave them alive. Olvehagan has been a thorn in my side for a very long time, and he made an attempt on my life today. That is what cost him his. Think what you will of me, Eve, but remember that your hands are not clean, either."

He steps away, following his hunters toward the trees. Fires are already springing up and songs echo across the sand. After a few steps, he turns and holds out a hand. "Will you be joining us, then? To carouse with the Wild Hunt is an experience not quickly forgotten."

"I should go to bed." My heart yearns to follow Eredin Glas into the woods, to drink and feast with the hunters, to join them in their revelry and lose myself once again. But my captivity still holds sway over my body, and the day's activities have left me exhausted and sore. "And I must still tend to Gent."

"Danen will see to Gent."

As the King says the words, Danen materializes at my side, his white skin nearly glowing in the darkness, clicking at Gent and leading him up off the beach. "Go, Your Majesty. Enjoy yourself. This won't take long."

Eredin Glas still waits, hand out, eyes urging me to follow him. The sounds from the Wood increase in pace, drawing me toward the trees like so many innocents drawn toward a Fae revelry in the old stories. I find myself entranced by the music, and even though my body protests, I allow my feet to carry me forward.

*Just for a bit. I can sit and watch, and leave for bed soon.*

I precede Eredin Glas into the midst of the hunters to find the revelry in full swing. Three different bonfires blaze high enough to light the entire area. Sparkles in the branches overhead obscure even the tops of the trees and make the area feel closed in and intimate. A wooden table has appeared full of treats, delicacies, and pitchers of several differently colored drinks.

Jarild sits high on a rotting log, strumming a guitar and belting out what I assume is a song.

I wince as he hits one foul note after another, noting that no one else seems to care.

"A swallow of this and you won't care, either." Eredin Glas thrusts a wooden cup into my hand.

The smell from inside is potently sweet, the sides of the cup chilling my palms. "Where does all of this come from?" I ask, gesturing around me.

"It's magic," he whispers, downing his own drink

in a single gulp. He lets out a whoop, shakes his hair out, and throws the cup into the sky. A bolt of lightning blasts it out of the air and sends charred splinters of wood raining down in all directions.

The hunters laugh and cheer, chucking their own cups into the air.

Eredin Glas takes great pleasure in zapping them one by one, the air steadily becoming more electrified until my hair lifts and sways with the static charge. And, regardless of how many cups get thrown, the number remaining on the table doesn't change.

"You going to drink that or just hold it?" says a high-pitched voice over my shoulder.

"I haven't decided yet," I admit, tearing my gaze away from the spectacle before me.

The speaker wears hunter leathers but only stands as tall as my elbow. She smirks up at me, daring me to comment.

"I don't believe we've met. I am Eve."

"Yaikhaa."

"Hail, Yaikhaa. Have you ridden with the Hunt long?"

She doesn't look like the typical candidate for a hunter. In addition to her short stature, her frame is delicate, bordering on wraith-thin, and her blonde hair and blue eyes make her look more like a doll than a warrior. Still, the King must have chosen her for a reason.

"What is long for one may be only a short time to another. Who am I to decide?" As she speaks, ripples race across her skin, like a pebble disturbing the water's surface. She laughs when she sees me noticing. "Pay no mind. A lingering curse from a past life."

"Oh?" I raise an eyebrow, inviting an explanation.

"A story for another time. Just remember to always choose your words carefully when dealing with a jinn. No less than when dealing with a Fae, I imagine."

"You were cursed by a jinn?"

"I was the jinn. Now, let's dance." She grabs my arms and spins me into the clearing, where Eredin Glas has retreated to the sidelines and Jarild has been joined by three other hunters sporting a horn, a drum, and some kind of long stick that makes a low, dull sound when blown into. More hunters are clapping, and a circle of dancers forms around one of the bonfires.

The energy in the clearing is contagious. My pulse quickens as my heart speeds up to match the music. The liquid in my cup sloshes against the edge, sending a waft of fragrance at my face, beckoning me to drink it. I meet Eredin Glas's eyes and throw it back just like he did.

I lose track of what happens next. I dance. I laugh. I eat. I dance some more. At some point, Danen returns and I grab his hand, pulling him with me into the dance. He laughs like I've only seen once before, when I caught him unawares at a game with his Winter friends. Carefree. Unfettered. Tonight, I am, too. None of my troubles touch my mind. Not Danen, not the Realm, not the loss of Fae magic, not the scattering of my people. There is only the revel.

My resolve to be responsible and leave early vanishes. At some point, my feet find the path back up to the plateau, but I can't find a reason why I'm there and not still dancing around the fire. I turn to go back, but a nudge in my mind spins me right back around. As I reach the top, the sounds of revelry follow me up out of the trees. The hunters are still going strong, pulling my heart back toward the trees. Yet, I continue walking, until my feet carry me up the ladder of my palafito. I shut out the noise, crash into bed, and thankfully find dreamless sleep.

****

The next morning I'm too sore to move, my muscles protesting at every effort to rise. My head feels heavy from all of the junk I consumed last night, my thoughts muddled and fuzzy. One thing is clear, though. I need to get stronger. I've had food in plenty; now I need to focus on the strength of my muscles.

I finally make it outside to find Eredin Glas waiting once again by the fire. The sun is still low, touching the tops of the trees but not yet warming the ground. He turns at my approach. "Good morning, Eve. Are you rested?"

"I slept well." I'm not quite sure how to act around him this morning. At the revel, he was not the King I've come to know. And that's concerning. He keeps his eyes trained on me, even as I ignore his gaze and help myself to the breakfast he's laid out for me. A woodsman's fare, but I'm starting to look forward to the simplicity.

The King refuses to be ignored for long. "You rode with the Hunt yesterday."

"I did."

"You reveled."

"I did."

"You liked it."

"I did."

"Yet you still waver about whether or not you could make Hellequin Wood your home. Imagine eternity stretched out before you, the thrill of the chase, the call of the hounds, the simplicity of grass beneath your feet. You could wake every morning to a perfect sunrise and fall asleep beneath an ocean of stars, with the smell of the trees in your nose and the wind on your skin. We could dance under the moon together and never feel a moment of loneliness."

"My body would be at peace here," I concede,

finally meeting his gaze, "but how could my heart rest while my people still suffer? Even with their magic restored they would still be trapped in a land that's not their own. Would you house them here? Or leave them to devolve further into their factions, as they were before my family united the Houses into a cohesive whole? What would be their purpose in the human world? What would they live for?"

Eredin Glas answers with his own question. "Why do you think they need you, Eve? Look where your rule has led them. As it stands, they have the wisdom of their elders, each House led by those who understand them the best. When I give them their magic back, they will no longer be defenseless, as they are now. What do you bring to the table?"

It's a valid question. I can't pretend I haven't wondered the same thing. "I'm not wise. I'm not experienced. But I love my people. What do I bring to the table? I will fight for them. Until my last breath. I know what the Fae can be, what we deserve to be, and I will give everything I have to see it come to pass."

Silence falls while we breakfast, each mulling over the words of the other. I don't expect him to back off, but now he knows I won't be charmed so easily, either. For now, we're at an impasse.

"Do you have plans for today?" he asks when I set my bowl aside.

"I think I'll explore the Wood some more. Maybe go for a run."

"Would you like company?"

My eyes stray over his shoulder. "If you're offering yourself, then no. I have a different companion in mind."

## Chapter Seventeen

"Run with me."

"Pardon?"

My request takes Danen by surprise. Up until now, I've been docile and compliant, finding my footing, but I'll never move forward by staying where Eredin Glas wants me. Running with Danen in the Realm, learning from him, ignited our friendship there. Maybe it'll do the same thing here. Maybe it'll trigger some of those memories Eredin Glas claims lay buried deep inside.

"I'm going to go for a run. I would like you to accompany me."

The laughing Danen from last night is gone, vanished with the morning dew. Much like the dancing Eve, if I'm being honest. He fumbles at the strange request, but eventually says, "As you wish, Your Majesty."

I can't run in my riding leathers, but I'm saved the trouble of begging for more clothes by the appearance of yet another basket beside my bed. Whether it was there when I woke up, I can't say, but it leaves me wondering if Eredin Glas is picking out my clothes himself or if he has tasked one of his female hunters to do so. The idea of Eredin Glas doing it himself makes me chuckle as I sort through the various leggings and tunics available. At least the offerings are basic enough that I can figure them out without Tupi here to help me. *I miss her so much.* Once I'm dressed, I rejoin Danen outside, and he looks me over as if evaluating my ability to run at all.

"I will let you set the pace, Your Majesty." Not a bad judgment call, considering I'm still a malnourished waif without magic-enhanced abilities.

I move quickly through the warm-up stretches

Danen taught me. His body knows the movements, but his face doesn't recognize their significance. When I'm ready, I start off at a slow jog. My tight back and sore legs don't appreciate the motion, but my heart certainly does. I've always loved to run. Running through my Realm was such an intense experience, and I desperately want that back.

We descend the plateau, and it doesn't take me long to kick up the pace. My body remembers how to run, even though my strength is failing. It *wants* to run. Trees flash by as I go faster and faster. My bare feet leave the trail, taking us deep into the woods and away from the reminder that we're far away from home. I don't fight the beaming smile that crosses my face, and on impulse I look back at Danen. The far-off look in his eyes tells me his attention is elsewhere, and I'm so distracted I miss a step and tumble end over end.

Danen rushes to help me up, but I push his hands away. He's close, though, kneeling beside me, leaning over me, our breaths mingling in the morning air. I'm drenched in sweat and trembling, but he's barely breathing hard. My heart squeezes, and I blurt out the words before I can chicken out. "How can you not remember me?"

He scurries back, flopping onto his butt in the dirt. I've never once seen him possess anything less than perfect grace, and the sight brings out a chuckle. I sober quickly with his next words, though. "I know who you are, Your Majesty. You are the Queen of the Fae."

"And you're Fae. Surely you know that about yourself? How can you not think that we knew each other before you joined the Hunt?"

He shakes his head. "That doesn't … I don't know…"

"Listen to me, Danen. Know that what I say is

true. You have been a hunter for less than a year. Before that you were my ally. You were my friend. We trusted each other." Tears well up in my eyes and I don't hold them back. "You fought at my side the day Emain Ablach fell. You sacrificed your life to save mine." I swallow, hard, and reach for his hand. The same touch that was so easy last night now burns my skin as if with fire. "Please remember, Danen. Don't you feel anything at all?"

He stares at me. At the tears rolling down my cheeks, at the fingers wrapped around his, at the yearning in my eyes for him to believe me. "No. No, that can't be... I would know. I would..."

He stands up abruptly. A look of panic comes into those black eyes I know so well, eyes that I've seen angry, calculating, occasionally vulnerable ... but never so lost. "I can't..."

He doesn't finish the sentence. He tears his gaze away from mine and takes off into the trees, leaving me sitting alone in the dirt.

*Great. Way to go.*

Eredin Glas isn't going to be happy about this. He didn't specifically say I couldn't tell Danen who he was, but I can't see him taking it well, nonetheless. I flop backward onto the ground, the look in Danen's eyes burned into my retinas. Everything inside me hurts, and not from the exercise. I let a few more tears fall, then a few more.

A minute later, I'm curled into the fetal position sobbing into my arms. I never cried in the Fomorian fortress. Not really. Not like this. It wasn't safe. Now it seems like I can't stop. So, I cry for Danen. I cry for the Fae we lost in the battle. I cry for the scattered Fae, alone in the world somewhere. I cry for me, for feeling lost and alone and scared, and the impossibility of the task set before me: Give in to the King of the Wild Hunt, or find a way to save my people myself.

The tears eventually stop. I sit up and attempt to scrub the dirt from my face. I'm a mess. Again. As I fuss with myself, my fingers tangle around the golden chain hanging around my neck. My talisman of the last remaining vestige of Fae magic, the medallion testifying of my royal lineage. Hanging beside the medallion is the quartz Caspian gave me, filled with the light of the full moon. I finger the quartz, running my mind over everything that's happened since the night Caspian gave it to me. I'm not even supposed to be here. I'm supposed to be at home.

*Home.* I'm on my feet in a flash, weariness banished by sheer adrenaline. I run back the way I came, even though Danen and I left no visible signs of our passing. It was one of the first lessons he taught me, and a valuable one. When I get back to the main trail, I realize I have no idea where I'm going. But I do know someone who can help.

It isn't hard to find the clearing Danen took me to yesterday. Lella is there, still asleep, feet hanging out her open tent flap. I give one a kick, then jump back as she comes violently awake, cursing and flailing and knocking the tent half down.

She barrels out the open door with a snarl and a knife, pulling up short when she sees me. "Eve! What are you doing? I could have killed you." She appears to be naked, trying unsuccessfully to keep a blanket wrapped around herself.

"Where does the Hunt keep its mounts?"

She eyes me, her mind no less sharp for having just woken up. "Why don't you ask the King?"

"Because I don't want him to know," I say frankly.

She barks a laugh. "I am duty-bound to tell him if he asks," she warns. "But he hasn't asked. And he has made it plain that you are a guest here, not a prisoner. I see no reason I shouldn't tell you. He will know, though. You know that, right?"

I resist the urge to tap my foot.

She points. "Go that way. Take a right. Follow the path inland. You'll see hoof prints."

"Thank you," I say, giving her a grateful smile.

"Just bring him back in one piece!" she calls after me.

The Hunt has no reason to guard their horses. No one in this land is a threat, and no hunter would dare steal a horse from their King. Where could they go that he wouldn't find them? But I'm not a hunter, and I fully expect him to find me. He won't do anything, though. He still wants me.

Gent nickers at me as soon as I crest the hill. If I'd been expecting a barn and paddock, I'd be sorely mistaken. The mounts of the Wild Hunt need no such restraint. The open meadow stretches in all directions, lined by trees far off in the distance. Dozens of horses graze at their leisure, Eredin Glas's own behemoth standing watch from a hillock off to the side.

*He's going to be the one to tattle on me*, I think as he meets my gaze head-on.

Gent only takes a minute to trot up to me. He doesn't slow on approach, but slams his head straight into my sternum.

I backpedal to stay upright and gasp to catch my breath. "Hey, there. Happy to see me?"

Gent nickers again and lips the hem of my shirt.

"Okay, okay, you win. You can smell them, can't you?"

I unravel the handful of dandelions I picked on the way and offer them to Gent. He snatches the whole bundle at once and chomps them down, then starts nuzzling for more.

"Greedy, huh?" I scratch both sides of his neck, admiring the sleek dark brown hair shot through with strands of black. "I heard a rumor. I heard you can open a portal for me. Is that true?"

Gent turns his head to look at me fully with his left eye and grunts.

"Is that a yes?"

He shakes his mane.

"I'm hoping that's a yes, because I can't do it myself. I don't have any magic, so I'm going to trust you to know what you're doing, okay? I need you to take me to the Realm of the Fae. To Emain Ablach."

Gent prances in place, like a little happy dance.

*Here goes nothing.*

I don't bother with tack, and Gent holds still while I scramble up. "All right, boy. Let's go on an adventure."

## Chapter Eighteen

Gent races across the meadow, building up speed equal to when the Hunt descended on Atlantis. I clutch his mane for support, praying my exhausted body can hold on. A shrill neigh sounds out behind us, but Gent ignores the stallion, leaping into the air and pumping his legs. The rift opens as before, but not nearly so sharp or so bright. Gent sails through it and Hellequin Wood vanishes behind us.

What's left of Emain Ablach lays below us, and I nearly fall off Gent in my shock. I thought I had no illusions about the state of my city. I knew it was destroyed in the battle. I called the waters up from the depths of the earth myself. I unleashed the tsunami stirring in the lake. I watched as these forces combined to drown the city and everything in it. But the waters haven't gone down. Through the murky depths I can see outlines, rubble and pieces of buildings that couldn't withstand the pressure. There are bodies down there, I imagine. Definitely Fomorian, and probably Fae, too.

The valley which housed Emain Ablach is gone, filled to the brim with the deadly water. The land stretching in all directions is no less desolate. Halasuwa took pleasure in telling me how the Fomorians torched the Realm behind them, and I can see now that he didn't exaggerate. The lush forests are gone, reduced to stumps and ash. Not even the sun shines through the hazy yellow clouds overhead.

"Let's land," I whisper to Gent, unable to muster a stronger sound.

He circles, bringing us down on the same overlook where I watched the waters rise. I had an army at my back, then. I had a land and a people to fight for.

I slide off Gent and hit my knees, coughing in the billowing ash. The tears don't come, though. I spent them all already. Instead, a numbness steals over me, weighing me down, tethering me to the very ground. I don't know what I expected.

My eyes travel over the barren landscape before me. Even though the landmarks are gone I see what happened next like a scene from a movie playing out right in front of me. The sudden absence of Fae magic. The appearance of the Fomorians. The bravery of my warriors, and their deaths before the all-consuming enemy. I bury my hands in the ash as if it still holds the bodies of those I lost. Those I failed to protect. Their names come to my lips, every single Fae I saw fall. I whisper them to the still air, the only way I can think of to honor them in this moment.

"I'm sorry," I whisper when I run out of names. "I failed you all. But I have not forgotten you." I don't voice a promise to avenge them. I *will* avenge them, but here, in this moment, the words would feel empty without a way to follow through on such a vow. My chest constricts, like it always does when I dwell on how rotten of a queen I turned out to be. I'll give anything for the chance to somehow make it right again.

I sit for a long time, wallowing in the ash until the sheen of my golden skin no longer shines through the filth.

Gent doesn't rush me, and the utter silence doesn't seem to mind the intrusion.

*Hanathen.* If the Fomorians burned everything, is she gone, too? I only visited the queens' glade once, during her funeral, but I'm certain I can find it again. "Come on," I murmur to Gent. "Let's walk a bit."

I lead Gent across the scorched ground, navigating by my memories as no landmarks remain. We trudge on, leaving the waters behind, up and down hills and valleys that all merge together. Finally, I look ahead and see a vague darkness against the horizon.

*Is it possible?*

Emboldened, I urge Gent on, feeling a tiny spark fire inside my chest. Something up ahead reaches toward the sky. Something has survived. Another minute and I recognize the glade. It's the place in the forest where dead queens are laid to rest, only to sprout into living, towering trees. Against all odds, their essence still pulses through the ground here. My mouth drops open as we ride beneath the sparse canopy of branches. The Fomorians tried. The resting trees are bare of leaves, cracked and broken, and bearing the scars of gashes and burn marks on the trunks.

Still. *They survived.* I dismount and wander through the glade, Gent keeping close behind. If his twitching ears and tensed-up muscles are any indication, the Realm makes him nervous. Not encouraging signs from a battle mount.

The tiny spark in my chest flares a little as a tingle rushes over my body. A small wind stirs my hair, and a swirl of ash spins up in front of my eyes. It hovers a second, then drifts away, dancing here and there but never quite landing the way it's supposed to. I follow it with my eyes, drawn to its unnatural dance, my feet following when it moves too far away. It moves through the trees, until it finally alights on one I'll never forget. *Hanathen.*

The state of her tree brings the tears I couldn't find earlier. I collapse against the trunk, the rough bark tearing at my skin, and let all the emotions I'm feeling rain down on her. "Why?" I sob into my hands. "Why did you bring me here? Why did you do this to me?" I know the answers to those questions. My mother, in her limited vision of the future, believed I was the only one who could save the Fae from destruction. I let her down in the worst way, and every single one of my people with her.

"It's all gone," I whimper when my eyes once again run dry. "You trusted me. It took me a long time to accept that, accept my place here. Our people died while I fought against who I was. Did you see that, too? Did you see how I would fail them?"

Then I utter the words I haven't even been able to bring myself to think about. "Oberon told me your plan was for me to break Fae magic. He couldn't have lied. He said he told you no, that wasn't the way. But you saw it. You knew it would happen this way. Was it inevitable, then? I don't even know how it happened. But if you saw this … all of this … and still believed that I was the best one to lead our people through? I don't understand how that can be."

The confession takes all the remaining energy my exhausted body has to offer. The queens are still here, but they can't help me. They have no magic to offer. They will endure, bearing witness to the complete eradication of the Fae. Curled against Hanathen's tree, my body gives up and sleep claims me.

\*\*\*\*

A nervous whinny from Gent wakes me up sometime later. The sky is darker, twilight trending into night, though it remains cloaked behind its grungy mask. Gent stands over me, caging me in with his legs, and stares into the gathering darkness, ears twitching.

"What is it, boy? Something out there?" My own senses go on alert, but I don't see or hear anything.

He twists his head around and lips at my hair.

"I believe you, okay? Let's get out of here. Quickly and quietly."

In theory, nobody should be in the Realm. Without their magic the Fae cannot pass through the gate.

But I'm here, using borrowed magic. Eredin Glas hinted that some Fae survived the battle and escaped to the human world. The Fomorians got in, and maybe still roam these lands. Who's to say they were the only ones? Abandoned places tend to draw malicious forces.

"Stay on the ground," I whisper to Gent as I mount. "Go back the way we came. We'll leave from Emain Ablach." I want to see my city again. I need to remember.

Whatever threat Gent sensed is left behind as we leave the glade. Eventually, he stops twitching and grinding his teeth and settles into a steady pace. He knows the way back without needing me to guide him, so I settle in and watch the landscape pass.

By the time we reach the rim of the valley, the sun has fully set and utter darkness surrounds us.

*I still want to see it. One last time.* I lift my chain, exposing the quartz filled with moonlight. Light bursts forth, far brighter than it did in the Fomorian fortress, reflecting off the water and lighting the whole valley.

"Oh my." *There's something here.* Down in the depths, too far for me to realistically see, something reflects the moonlight back at me.

*Moonlight shows things for what they are.* There's something I need to see down there.

I don't even think about it. I'm on my feet in an instant, striding toward the water, when Gent bites my shirt and hauls me back.

"What?" I ask, rounding on him.

He just looks at me.

I sigh and rub his nose. "I know it could be dangerous. And there's still something out there that could find us before I get back. You're right. But I need to do this." I lay my face against his. "I have to go."

He nickers but lets go of my shirt.

"I'll try to be quick," I promise, dropping a kiss on his nose. Then, clutching the moonlight quartz tightly in my hand, I dive into the dark water.

I've always been a strong swimmer. I've even swum in this lake once, back when it was still a lake. Caspian chided me for it and said dangerous creatures lived in its waters. I never had the opportunity to test that claim, and my most recent swimming experience is not one I'd like to repeat. But I can't just ignore this. I have no weapon, so I'll have to count on getting in and out without being noticed. I swim hard and fast, straight ahead until I'm directly over where the light is coming from. Then with a deep breath, I plunge downward.

I don't make it the first time. My body fails me and I return to the surface in a panic, gasping for air. Once my heart rate calms, I try again, pushing my body to act like I know it knows how to. In the moonlight below me I see the remains of the palace. As the epicenter of the destruction, the only parts left are clumps of stone clinging to the island they were grown from. I kick harder, focusing on the point of light that seems to be hovering in midair. Or, midwater, rather.

As I swim, something passes above me, disturbing the water enough to send me sideways. My lungs are already burning, and knowing that something is in here with me has my heart racing. With a surge of adrenaline, I cover the last few feet and see moonlight reflecting off a glimmering rock ledge about three feet long and no wider than my hand. It hangs suspended with no visible support, but immovable. *What in the world?*

I touch the rock with my hand and get sucked forward. In my surprise, I open my mouth to yelp and water rushes in. Gagging and coughing, I splatter down onto hard stone and gulp sweet, precious air.

## Chapter Nineteen

My magic room. Only accessible to those with royal blood. I guess the queens' trees aren't the only things that survived, after all. Even as I think it, I feel a sharp prick on my finger and droplets of my blood splatter the ground, proving my heritage.

*Is it Fae magic keeping this place intact? This place outside of place, a little pocket of the Realm belonging only to me?*

The moonlight was showing me that this pocket still exists. Last time, I entered through the waterfall pouring down one wall of my bedroom. The waterfall may be gone, but the entrance remains fixed in the same place. Like before, I'm miraculously dry, and soft light fills the circular stairway.

The treasures of this room are untouched. Time itself could probably end, but this place would endure. The same scrolls and chests and jewels fill the alcoves leading up the spiral staircase. I doubt this time I'll find the answer neatly written out in a letter from my dead mother and placed on a table for me, though.

I climb the stairs. Something's up there. I can feel it. I'm not scared, though. This room is bound to me. No one else could possibly get in.

I reach the top of the stairs and enter the circular tower room. The lone table still sits in the middle, bare now that I've retrieved the letter Hanathen left for me. But the room is no longer empty. A figure sits on the floor, wrapped in a blanket and slumped against the wall. A tremor passes over me. *Impossible.*

I inch forward, well aware of how defenseless I am right now. *How did they get in here?* They're not a Fomorian. Too small. I'm not even sure they're alive…

I get close enough to reach the blanket. I grab a corner and give it a tug, enough to make it fall away from the figure's head. A shock of white hair pops free, followed by a face so sallow and withered it's almost unrecognizable. Almost.

"Oberon!" I drop to my knees, hands going to his face. "Wake up, Oberon. Wake up." *Please don't be dead. Please, please, please, don't be dead.*

He stirs, and with a pained moan his eyelids flutter open. "Titania?" he rasps.

"No, Grandfather. It's me, Eve."

"Eve." He says the name with some confusion, and his face scrunches up as he tries to remember who I am. "I think I was waiting for you."

"For me? How did you even get in here?" My eyes rake over the little of his body I can see. He's not in good shape. His skin is thin, stretched too tightly over bones that jut too prominently. *How long has he been in here? How is he even alive?*

"Titania," he says with a smile.

"No, Grandfather, I'm Eve, remember?"

"No. My Titania." He coughs, and his next words come out on a wheeze. "She gave me this. For an emergency." He shuffles around in the blanket and thrusts out his hand, fingers curled tightly around something red.

"She gave you … her blood?"

"To get me past the boundary." More coughs wrack his body, but barely any sound comes out.

"We need to get you out of here. I have a … well, not a friend, but I know someone who can help."

I reach for him again, but he waves my hands away. "My days are done. But I had to see you. Something … important." He trails off, and his eyes droop closed again.

"Oberon? What do you need to tell me? Oberon? Oberon!"

He doesn't wake. I touch his face again and his skin is cold to the touch. "Okay. You're coming with me." I unwrap Oberon, letting the blanket pool on the floor. It'll be easier to carry him without it. His body is shriveled and curled in on itself, resembling a child more than an adult. It's still a struggle to lift him with my own depleted strength, especially after the swim down here, but I manage to get him over one shoulder in a fireman's carry.

Hand on the wall to keep my balance, I inch my way down the stairs. I've never traveled more slowly in my life. My legs are burning when I reach the bottom, but I don't drop him. Now to get him to the surface.

"I'm so sorry, Grandfather," I whisper as I ready myself to step through the boundary. "You're going to have to drown a little, but it's the only way I know to get you out of here."

He doesn't respond. He hasn't made a sound since I hoisted him up. Not even a grunt.

I draw the deepest breath I can and step out into the lake.

I start kicking as soon as I feel the water. It seems to buffet me from all sides, pulling me downward, trying to keep me from reaching the surface. I'm not certain I'm making any progress at all. The quartz lights the water around me, but I still can't see how far it is to the surface.

Then something slams into me from behind. I tumble and spin in the water, scrambling desperately to hold on to Oberon. I kick again, fighting for the surface, but I don't know which direction it is anymore. In the light of the quartz, I see the creature again, circling just out of reach.

Teeth and scales flash across my vision, then

vanish behind me. Something hits me again, and I catch a glimpse of hair and webbed feet swimming away.

*The same creature? Or more than one?*

The next assault comes from the front, and I see our death coming straight for us. The creature is long and sinewy, resembling a monstrous eel, with white, blind eyes and overlapping pointed teeth. It rushes in and I kick backward, knowing it's no use. I can't outswim that thing.

Oberon moves. His body tenses against mine, and I feel his head lift up. A pulse explodes outward from where we tread water, and the eel creature is thrown backward. The water churns, surrounding us with bubbles, and I feel our bodies moving. Like a geyser we shoot out of the water, arcing through the air until finally splashing down again.

Oberon is limp once more, weighing heavily against me and threatening to drag me back under. Still, one thought pulses through my body like a heartbeat: *Oberon has magic.*

I flip onto my back and kick, letting the buoyancy of the water keep him afloat while I haul us both to shore. No other creatures bother us, and I drag a drowned, non-breathing Oberon onto dry land.

"No no no. Come on." I lay Oberon flat on his back and begin chest compressions like I learned in health class. Nothing happens. *It's too late. We were under too long. He's too old.*

I feel the King behind me as he approaches. He doesn't say anything, but his very presence has weight. "Please," I beg him, not even looking up. I keep pumping, until the weight behind me shifts and the King suddenly appears in the circle of moonlight bathing Oberon. He lays a finger on the old Fae's chest and a fountain of water erupts out of Oberon's mouth.

Oberon's lips flop open and shut like a fish, but he doesn't make any noise.

"Oberon?" I smack his face a little, but he doesn't open his eyes. He's breathing, though. Barely. I have to lay my hand on his chest to feel the slightest movement, proof that somehow his lungs are still working. I meet Eredin Glas's brown eyes. "Thank you," I say simply.

Eredin Glas doesn't answer, just stares back into my eyes as if he's searching for something. Before I can ask what, though, a shrill whinny cuts through the darkness.

I open my mouth to call for Gent, but Eredin Glas slaps his hand over my lips. His other hand goes for my neck but stops short and snags the quartz instead. With a flip of his fingers, he tucks the stone back into my shirt and the moonlight vanishes, plunging us into darkness. We wait, silent, ears straining for any sound.

Then Eredin Glas springs into action, tackling me to the ground as something heavy flies over my head.

A war cry goes up around us, from throaty voices I know all too well.

I freeze in my tracks as torches spring to life in the darkness, throwing shadows across the ground at the feet of massive figures with curling horns.
*Fomorians.*

"Foolish girl! Move!" Eredin Glas hisses in my ear.

I jump up to run, but freeze. I can't leave Oberon. Adrenaline pumping, I heave him up as Gent comes galloping up beside me. He's blowing and snorting in obvious distress, but I don't have time to calm him. I heave Oberon over Gent's back. "You have to get him to Hellequin Wood. As fast as possible, do you understand?" I smack Gent on the flank as he leaps into the air, willing him to get Oberon to safety.

That's all the time Eredin Glas affords me. "Morhogg!" he bellows, grabbing my hand and shoving me behind him. The stallion melts out of the darkness behind us as the sky roils with thunderclouds.

## Chapter Twenty

The Fomorians' torches have grown close enough to cast our faces into dim, shifting light. Their massive strides easily close the distance between us, and my body pushes me to run, run, run.

Eredin Glas doesn't run, though. It's not who he is. He plants his feet against the advancing enemy and faces down their torches.

The Fomorian flames can't compete with the ones flaring in the King's eyes. I haven't seen this facet of him yet. I've seen the staunch defender rescuing the damsel in distress. I've seen the simple hunter, tending his fire and roasting his kill. I've seen him on the chase, fixated on his prize. I've even seen him let his guard down and enjoy the company of his companions. But I've never seen him as the commander in battle, sizing up his enemy and executing his strategy. The advancing Fomorians do not concern him. They are no threat to him. Only to me.

Eredin Glas reaches inside his shirt and produces a tusk-shaped horn. With one blow, he sounds out the same ringing blast as he did for yesterday's hunt. The pure note echoes across the open land; nothing remains standing to hinder the sound.

Morhogg joins the call with his own ear-shattering neigh.

*He's calling the Hunt to the Realm.*

The Fomorian advance halts at the sound, and Eredin Glas seizes the opportunity. Releasing his scythe from his back, he whirls it in one hand and sends a blast of power that knocks three Fomorians off their feet.

They land heavily in the ash and don't get back up. Their fellows scatter, abandoning their torches and taking cover in the darkness.

"I thought you said you saw a Fae!" accuses one Fomorian, his voice oddly disjointed and hard to pin down.

"This is the Realm. What would it be if not a Fae?" The scout defends. "Besides, you saw the same thing I did. It shot out of the lake in a glowing ball of light."

*Oops.* I drew them right to me. I could argue it couldn't be helped, that I had no other choice, but it's a moot point anyway. They're here.

There's a metallic clang as one Fomorian hits another. "It has magic, you idiot. Fae don't have magic."

"Says the General! Who can say he's telling the truth? You were there when the queen escaped the fortress, same as me. Couldn't have done that without magic, could she?"

I lose track of the argument as Eredin Glas's hands wrap around my waist and deposit me on Morhogg's back. "Morhogg will take you back to the Wood. You are to wait for me there."

"What? No!" I wiggle and kick, but I may as well be fighting the air. "You can't send me away." Even as I say the words, I know how childish they sound. Still, being shuffled away from my own battle in my own land grates against every nerve I have.

The King's flaming eyes give his face a ghostly, menacing light. It's only a matter of time before the Fomorians regroup and come for us again. His voice is rough but not cruel. "How do you plan to fight the Fomorians, Eve? What weapons do you have at your disposal?"

I don't answer. I have none. My face heats in the darkness and I turn my head away, even though it's too dark for him to see. *Or is it? Can he see in the dark?*

"Exactly. The Hunt is coming. I do not need your help, and if the Fomorians catch you, they will take you, or worse. How happy do you think Halasuwa has been about your disappearance? What will he do to you the moment he gets you back?"

I sag on Morhogg's back. "You won't let him take me," I assert weakly. He's right. I can do nothing here, but fleeing goes against my Fae nature. He gives me no more of his time, turning his attention back to the enemy.

The sky splits open above us, the swirling lights heralding a portal in the hazy clouds. More horns announce the arrival of the Hunt. Hounds bay and harnesses jingle, the cacophony surrounding us and bouncing around the empty space. The storm overhead builds, melding with the whooping of the hunters and the baying of the hounds. Lightning splits the sky, illuminating the entire area, and Fomorian arguing breaks out again.

"The queen! I saw her!"

"I told you it was a Fae!"

"Seize her!"

Eredin Glas slaps Morhogg the same way I did Gent and the stallion rears. The sudden movement knocks me off balance and I throw myself against his neck, wrapping my arms around him to stay steady. "Don't take me to the Wood, please," I call to him. "Keep me close. I need to watch."

Morhogg prances forward then breaks into a canter, carrying me away from the rushing Fomorians. Eredin Glas roars behind us and I look over my shoulder to see him spinning the scythe as the Fomorians close in. They come from all directions, having spread out during the reprieve, and attack him as one entity. They must know who he is and the threat he poses. One tries to follow me, but the stallion quickly outdistances him.

129

Morhogg leaps into the air but has apparently agreed to listen to my plea. Instead of spiriting me back to the Wood, he circles above the action, keeping me well out of reach but allowing me to watch what's going on.

Eredin Glas fights like a madman. I was impressed watching him battle the Nix, but that fight may as well have been in slow-motion. His movements now are so fast they're hard to keep track of, but four Fomorians already lay dead and he's engaging another. *How many of them are there?*

More than I thought. It was likely a scouting party that spotted Oberon and me, maybe even the same threat Gent noticed at the queens' glade. They must have sent an alert before confronting us, though, because more Fomorians are on their way. I see them advancing in the distance, swarming across the ground like the sure-footed goats they are. Behind them I see the tunnels.

Gaping holes big enough to fit four Fomorians across mar the landscape. Halasuwa must have established an outpost here. That's the only way that many Fomorians could have responded so quickly. Eredin Glas told me Halasuwa was hunting the remaining Fae. Is that why he placed an entire garrison here? Or are they here for me? Did he know I would come back eventually?

The hows and whys matter less than the simple fact of the army's presence. They'll be at the lake in minutes, but I have no way to warn Eredin Glas.

The Hunt descends out of the sky, bringing the storm down with them. As if their presence energizes the King, he bellows again, causing an avalanche of ash to rise up and smother half a dozen Fomorians. Rain turns the ash at their feet to goo and bogs them down. The lightning dances around him, targeting his attackers while keeping those farther out at bay.

My mouth drops open at how seamlessly his combat and magic blend together. *There's so much I could learn from him.*

"Your Majesty! Are you all right?" Jarild rides up beside Morhogg and surveys the scene, his eyes zeroing in on his King.

No time for pleasantries. "Fomorians," I answer, pointing at the ground below. "And more are coming."

Jarild motions with his hand and the Hunt rides screaming overhead. I see faces I recognize—Lella, Danen, and Yaikhaa among them—as they descend upon the incoming Fomorians.

The Fomorians outnumber the hunters five to one but are no match for their speed and ferocity. Mounted and armed, the hunters sweep through the Fomorian ranks, laying waste to the massive warriors. I watch in awe as they easily do what my own armies couldn't once our magic was gone.

With that realization my anger flares. The Hunt was in the sky above Emain Ablach during the battle. It didn't have to end the way it did. Eredin Glas sat back and did nothing while my people were slaughtered.

"Land," I command Morhogg, and to my surprise he actually does.

Eredin Glas stands blood-splattered and heaving, wiping the blade of his scythe on the back of his sleeve. The Fomorian party lays in pieces around him, blood and ash mingling to make a grotesque paste. He turns at our approach and scowls. "You were supposed to leave, Eve."

I slide off Morhogg and march right up to him. My fist is clenched before I know what I'm going to do with it, and I punch him as hard as I can across the jaw. My scream is involuntary as the bones in my hand shatter.

## Chapter Twenty-One

"You could have stopped it," I growl, falling to my knees and cradling my hand. The power rolling off him makes the air feel molasses-thick, and his flaming eyes warn me to keep my distance, but my temper is too hot to care. "You were here. You were all here. I just watched the Hunt take out an entire Fomorian unit in a matter of minutes. You could have saved my entire race, and you chose to sit back and do nothing!" I spit on the ground in front of him. "At least you managed to scavenge the battlefield and steal my best warrior."

Eredin Glas grabs me by the shirt front and hoists me into the air. "Would you rather I'd left him to die? Your Danen lives today because I scavenged him from your battlefield."

"A battlefield that didn't need to be there!" I retort, still hanging. I can argue with him just as well from up here. The pain pulsing through my hand and arm only fuels my anger. "You could have stopped all of it!"

"I could have," he answers, his voice low and deadly calm. "Is that what you want to hear? That your people died for nothing? That is none of my concern, Eve. Do you expect me to fight in every war, to champion every leader who believes they hold the moral high ground? I do not entangle myself in affairs that have nothing to do with me."

I start shaking now, rage consuming every inch of me. "None of your concern?" My arms sweep out to encompass the Realm. "This is none of your concern?"

"Civilizations rise and fall, Eve. The Wild Hunt endures. I endure."

I kick him. Hard. Straight shot to the chin. He drops me, more out of surprise than pain, I think. "What about me, then? You said you wanted me at your side. Do you care so little for me that you would have let me be slaughtered, too?"

"I don't care for you, I care for your magic." Eredin Glas spits the words out like they're weapons. "You had no magic that day, and I had no reason to save you."

I stagger back like I've been shot. I gasp for air, clutching at my chest where very real pain squeezes everything inside. Oblivious to the situation, the Hunt rides into our midst, cheering their victory and waving their weapons in the air. Eredin Glas and I stand glaring at each other as an unspoken agreement falls. Our personal issue will be dealt with between the two of us, not in front of the rest of the Hunt. Still, I keep my distance, gravitating toward Lella as Eredin Glas morphs into the victorious King he needs to be right now.

The storm abated, Eredin Glas does the same glow thing he did while the two of us were lost in darkness in the Nix's cavern. The dull orange light spreads out, not from him only, but from every member of the Hunt, until the battlefield is awash with gentle light. The light is the only thing about it that's gentle, however. The bodies of dead Fomorians carpet the ground, blood and waste pooling around them. Already, flies congregate on the deceased, though where they came from I have no idea.

Eredin Glas contemplates the field, then raises his hands and closes his eyes. The ground begins to shake, then large cracks appear. One by one the ground swallows the dead Fomorians until only scattered stains and misplaced weaponry remain. "From beneath the earth they came, so beneath the earth I will return them." Then he looks right at me. "Five hundred years ago, when the Fae last defeated the Fomorians, their blood so poisoned the ground that it would no longer support life. The name of that place was Gasadalur. How many Fomorians does it take to foul the ground?"

I don't answer, and I don't like the implication. Did he bury them here intentionally to poison Emain Ablach? To ruin any chance I have at returning? At rebuilding?

"My liege," Jarild calls, striding up to the King and breaking the sudden tension. "We saved one alive, if you would like to question him."

At a snap of Jarild's fingers, two hunters drag a Fomorian into the circle. Blood seeps from a wound in his chest, a gaping maw he has no hope of surviving. The Hunt closes in while Eredin Glas kneels in front of the captive and gently turns his face upward.

"You are here for the Queen." It's not a question.

The Fomorian jerks his head away and says nothing.

The King is unfazed. He fastens his hand once more under the Fomorian's chin, wrenching the heavy head around to meet his gaze once more. The fire in his eyes flares and his fingers stroke the underside of the Fomorian's neck.

The Fomorian's eyes glaze over and I'm certain he's dying on the spot, but the King repeats the sentence.

"You are here for the Queen."

The Fomorian's voice comes out robotically. Detached and emotionless. "Not originally. Our parties hunt escaped Fae. But after her escape, General Halasuwa bolstered our numbers here in case she were to return."

My breath catches. It's as I suspected, but hearing it confirmed is troubling. A lot of warriors died trying to recover me. One single Fae.

Eredin Glas isn't done. "What do you do with the Fae you catch?"

No hesitation. "We kill them."

"And the Queen?"

"General Halasuwa wants her alive. The army is divided. Some would return her to him. Others would kill her."

Shivers run over my body at his words. I always knew the Fomorians would search for me. They hate me too much to let me go. My kidnapping, incompetent as it was, proved how bold Halasuwa's opposition had become, though I had no idea that opposition extended as far from Canowin Hollow as the scouting parties. Or that those same scouts would take my life into their own hands.

"You would defy your general?"

"I would. General Halasuwa is weak. His thoughts linger too much on the past and ignore our people's future. The Fae are part of that past. It is time to leave them behind and look forward instead, to the growth and glory of the Fomorian people."

Eredin Glas continues stroking the Fomorian's chin. Though his wound continues to bleed he has made no further move to escape, and he answers every question without objection. "I assume there is a new leader seeking to supplant the General?"

"Kharn."

"And this Kharn wishes the Fae Queen dead?"

"Yes. By any means necessary."

"Thank you. You have been most helpful."

"What of the goblins?" I interject, earning a scowl from Eredin Glas. "What happened after my escape?"

The Fomorian doesn't look at me. He doesn't acknowledge my presence, but he does answer the question. "The goblins no longer seek alliance with us. Baark escaped his assault on our fortress, though his companions were caught and executed. Kharn uses this failure as yet more proof that General Halasuwa is no longer fit to lead."

When the Fomorian falls silent, Eredin Glas looks to me, raising an eyebrow.

I shake my head. What else could I ask? Nothing else matters.

Eredin Glas brings his other hand up to cradle the Fomorian's head. Then, with a mighty heave, he snaps the great beast's neck.

Gaining his feet, he grabs my arm and pulls me off to the side. He examines my hand, bruised and swollen, then warmth surges through it as he heals the things that are broken inside. Then, like with the Fomorian, he places a finger under my chin and raises my face to look at his. His words are soft, meant for my ears only. "I hope this puts things in perspective for you."

## Chapter Twenty-Two

"What sort of mind magic does Eredin Glas possess?" I whisper to Lella. The King has moved away from me and wanders among his hunters, checking in with them and taking stock of their condition following the battle. Few hunters bear injuries, and the ones that do are soon whole.

"Would you ask someone what kind of breaths they take, or why their head sits upon their shoulders? The King is who he is." She doesn't even look at me. Instead, her gaze roves over her fellow hunters as her mount shifts uneasily beneath her.

Her defense of Eredin Glas takes me somewhat by surprise, since she's the one who let me subvert his authority and run off with Gent. *I thought we were friends.* As soon as I think it, I know the answer. Above all, the King prizes the loyalty of his hunters. Danen's amnesiac condition is proof enough of that. I do have a burgeoning friendship with Lella, but if I expect her to favor me over him then the error is mine.

Still, I don't want to let the matter drop. I know next to nothing about the King's magic, and it suddenly seems like a very important thing for me to understand. I try a different tack. "When he fought alone, the magic he used was minor. It wasn't until after the Hunt arrived that he used his full power. He didn't use much magic when he saved me from the Nix, either." I let the sentence hang, seeing how she'll respond.

She finally looks at me, and even in the orange glow from the hunters' bodies I can see the weariness in her eyes. "If you have a question, Eve, ask it. I do not like to play guessing games."

Do I have a question? "I don't even know," I

admit, drooping back against her horse. "There's so much I don't understand, and I don't know what questions to ask to find the answers I'm looking for."

Lella's hand lands heavily on my shoulder. "Admitting you need help is the first step." Then she chuckles.

"You're teasing me." *So our relationship is still intact.*

"You worry too much. What does the King's magic matter, so long as he is there to protect you with it? Try acceptance and see how it feels. You might find you like it as much as you like riding with us."

*Acceptance.* Of what, exactly? Does Lella know what the King has asked of me? Does she wish me to accept his offer? Or simply accept that I can't know everything, and I should stop trying to puzzle out the King?

Still without answers, I hear the horn blow once more and Morhogg thunders up beside me.

"Hunters! We ride!" Eredin Glas's arm snags me around the waist and deposits me in the saddle behind him. "You ride with me."

This close, I can smell the blood and sweat clinging to his leathers, the heat and musk rolling off Morhogg's flank. It isn't a pleasant smell, but comforting in an oddly familiar way.

Morhogg leads the way as the Hunt vanishes from the Realm, but he doesn't return to Hellequin Wood. Instead, I see the twinkling lights of a city far below me, a big one by the looks of it. A mountain range cuts straight through the lights, dividing the city in two.

"Where are we?" I shout to be heard above the wind.

"Does it matter?"

"I need to get back to Oberon."

"No harm will come to him in Hellequin Wood. He will be safe there until we return to him." His tone doesn't leave room for argument.

In seconds, we leave the city behind, racing across the night sky. Sparks from the horses' hooves fly out behind us like the tail of a comet. Eredin Glas releases the hounds from their tethers, and their joyful howls join the jingle of the harnesses and the whoops of the hunters to create a music that reaches way deep down in my soul. This is a different kind of ride. Not a hunt. Not a call to battle. Just riding for the ride itself.

Surely it's no coincidence that this ride comes on the tail of Eredin Glas's not-so-thinly veiled threat. Perspective. He wants me to fully understand the stakes of my continued existence in this world. It's no longer simple imprisonment that awaits me. Now it's death. Possibly a slow one. Alone and unaided, I have no chance. But if I ally myself with him…

Which brings me full circle back to our argument and the euphoria I feel in this ride dies out. He left us all to die. Because we had no magic, and therefore we meant nothing.

*There.* My mind snags on something I couldn't connect before. He says he stayed his hand because without my magic I was useless to him, yet he took Danen and stole his memories so he wouldn't be loyal to me. He waited to rescue me from the Fomorians until I was ready to fight. He didn't save me that day, but he made plans to do so eventually.

*Something doesn't add up.*

Unfortunately, that 'something' eludes me. The Hunt continues to ride across the sky, but I slump forward and rest my forehead against Eredin Glas's back. I bump into his scythe and scoot my head around until it shifts out of my way. He must notice but gives no indication.

*What are you thinking, Eredin Glas?*

We finally make it back to Hellequin Wood as dawn is breaking. The Hunt is subdued, their manic energy spawned by the battle burned off in the ride. The hunters disperse to their own tents as Morhogg veers toward the plateau. The thud of his landing jars me from my half-sleep, and I raise my head to see a lump on the ground beside the perpetual fire.

"Oberon!" I fall off Morhogg in my haste, landing hard on my right side. I scramble up quickly, ignoring the pain lancing through my shoulder, and hurry toward him. My panic lessens when I find his skin warm under my hand. *He's still alive.*

More than that. He's dry, his skin has been washed, and he's been redressed in something soft and fluffy. The blanket he's wrapped in is new, and his head rests on a pillow identical to mine. *Who took care of him?*

Oberon stirs and flutters open his eyes. His gaze goes straight to the sunrise, and his face looks about how I suspect mine did when I arrived here. Both of us were hidden away from the sky, a punishment too extreme for a Fae. His eyes finally find mine, but my face isn't the one he sees. "Titania," he sighs.

"No, Grandfather. Eve, remember? I found your hiding place." I don't want to give any details about the hidden room to Eredin Glas. He has no right to that information, and I don't know what he would do with it.

"Eve. I think I was waiting for you." His voice is so weak. His body so worn out. Even in Emain Ablach's final days his mind was breaking.

Unshed tears clog my voice. "You said that already. How long have you been waiting?"

He doesn't need to think about it. "Since the end," he says on a wheeze. "Morgan wanted me to flee, but I couldn't… You needed me to keep it … and then … and then…" He trails off, struggling to remember what happened next.

"Shh, it's okay. That part's not important. Just tell me why you were waiting for me. Did you need to tell me something?"

"Yes, I did." Then he passes out, and no amount of jostling rouses him. Defeated, I slump down and bury my hands in my lap.

I feel Eredin Glas behind me, even though I don't hear him approaching. He kneels down and places his hand on Oberon's forehead. I know what my words could cost me, yet I ask them anyway. "Can you help him?"

His voice actually sounds sad when he answers. "He is dying, but he is not injured or sick. Even my magic cannot halt his advancing age."

"But your hunters…"

"Are no longer bound by the regular order. Oberon will go the way of all those who have passed before him. He has lived an extraordinary life, and a longer one than most."

"Did you know him?" My anger is still there, but I don't reach for it. There's no room for it when I'm filled up with sorrow. Our argument will keep.

"Your grandfather and I crossed paths many times in his youth. At our last encounter, he gifted me this."

When I turn my head, Eredin Glas sits with his head tilted and his hair gathered in one hand. A thin white scar mars the skin along the side of his neck.

The bewildering sight draws me forward, my fingers reaching of their own accord to trace the line. "I've seen you heal from worse than this," I murmur, remembering the wounds he received from the Nix. They closed up in front of my eyes.

"Oberon was something else," he answers, his tone matching mine. His eyes are brown again, and he rests here with me no more than a mortal man. "I will be truly sorry to see him pass."

Again, that little voice niggles in the back of my mind. *Would it really be that bad to spend the rest of your days here with him?* Political marriages happen all the time. My people would be restored. I would be safe from the Fomorians. I would live the rest of my days in peace. My eyes fix on Oberon once more. The oldest Fae to have ever lived. I'm only sixteen. Seventeen, maybe, depending on exactly how much time has passed. I could have centuries ahead of me. Eternity, if I join Eredin Glas. How do I want to spend those days? Fighting? Afraid? Weak? Or at peace in a place I love?

Eredin Glas's eyes follow me as I scoop Oberon up into my arms like a child. I can't leave him out here on the ground. I feel the King's heavy gaze on my back until I disappear behind the gauzy curtains sheltering my bed. I snuggle Oberon into the blankets and curl up beside him, ears straining to hear the faint wheeze of his breath.

Eredin Glas knows what occupies my thoughts. Last night's attack only solidifies his position. Perspective. I have it. Now what do I do with it?

## Chapter Twenty-Three

The sun sits high in the afternoon sky when I wake. My head aches, foggy from the shift in my schedule and last night's ride. One thing is certain, though. I know what I need to do today. I've put it off long enough.

Oberon still slumbers beside me, although his color is better and his chest visibly rises with each inhale. I don't know if he'll wake up this time, but the improvement gives me hope. He's not the only one in my palafito, though.

I've woken up next to Danen a handful of times, in the days when we were trapped in the human world and unable to cross back into the Realm until the new moon. This isn't like that.

Danen's eyes are fixed on Oberon, concern screwing up his features so tightly he looks made of stone. It's the first time we've been in direct contact since he abandoned me in the woods. Was that really just yesterday? For a moment I just watch him, aware that anything I say may send him running again.

Finally, I can't help it. "Do you recognize him?"

He starts as if unaware I was there and stares blankly at me. After a minute, he switches his gaze back to Oberon and mutters, "I've heard some things."

I hold my tongue so hard I bite it.

"Who is he?"

"The oldest living Fae. A formidable warrior. A legend in more worlds than one. And my grandfather."

Danen's voice drops even lower. "Why is he here?"

"Because I need him. And he needs me." I pause, but Danen has gone back to studying Oberon like he's going to be tested and doesn't respond. "The better question is, why are *you* here?"

"I wanted to see him. He's a Fae." The answer comes so quickly I don't think he meant to say it. Once the words are out there, though, they can't be taken back. Danen's eyes shoot to mine, hurt and confusion clouding his expression.

"And you wanted to know what another Fae looked like," I whisper, finally untangling my legs from my blankets. I reach for him, but he recoils.

"I shouldn't be here." All vulnerability drops from his voice in an instant. "I apologize for my invasion of your privacy, Your Majesty, and for disturbing your rest."

"Please don't go." I lunge for him, but he's faster than I am, springing up from his crouch and dropping silently off the edge of the palafito. By the time I make it to the edge, his shadow is slipping between the trees. There's nothing else to do but swallow my feelings and officially get out of bed.

*Compartmentalization, that's the key.*

Eredin Glas tends the fire, a simple hunter roasting his latest kill and whistling a forlorn melody. I never see him build the fire, or even skin or spit the carcasses, yet some new animal appears every day. Come to think of it, I've never seen him sleep, either. Two hounds lounge in the sunlight, thumping their tails when they notice my presence.

Last night's argument is still fresh in my mind, along with the emotions that go with it. Just looking at him now makes betrayal knife through me, knowing that he let all of this happen. None of it was his fault; the Fomorians would still have invaded and I would still have somehow broken Fae magic. But he had the power to save all of their lives, and he didn't, and I don't think I can ever forgive him for that. That doesn't mean I've decided not to stay. Just that I'll never be able to fully trust him if I do.

"Are you planning to join me? Or just stare a hole through my back?"

With that kind of opening, he must not have noticed Danen's visit.

Deep breath. Here goes. "I thought I might ask you to take me somewhere instead of stealing a horse again."

He stills but doesn't look up from the half-burned log he's in the process of flipping over. "I would appreciate that, although if you truly think you could steal Gent, then you have much to learn. Gent is young and headstrong, pushing boundaries, but he will always first and foremost belong to the Hunt."

I wave his words away, but I don't join Eredin Glas at the fire. My legs are too antsy, my mind too muddled, my emotions too raw. I can't sit there like this is any other day after the words that passed between us.

"Are we to continue our discussion, then?" he asks, his voice deceptively mild. He finally looks up at me, chocolatey brown eyes meeting my own silver ones with an intensity that is becoming all too familiar. I know how quickly his temper can turn, how close to the surface his pride lurks. "Or would you like to ask me what you came to ask me?"

It has to be one of the two. We can't scream and rage, then ride off together like nothing happened. And I suspect the things I would learn would drive me from Hellequin Wood entirely. He would be up for either scenario. The choice is mine.

I don't hesitate. I'm a queen, and it's time I start acting like one instead of like a petulant child. "You told me the Fae were scattered and broken in the human world. Is that true?"

"It is."

"Do you know where to find them?"

"I do."

"Will you take me to them?"

He considers. "Is that what you really want?"

*Of course it is.* My mouth opens to say the words, but something else comes out instead. "Why wouldn't it be?"

"You know your desires better than I," he says, his tone implying exactly the opposite. "If you say that is what you want then I will believe you. But it has been several days now since I pulled you from a watery grave, and you have not yet asked me to take you to your people."

"I have spoken of the Fae many times." I keep my voice level, but the quip is too quick. Too defensive.

"You have spoken of them. But you have not asked me to take you to them. To my knowledge, they don't even yet know that you live. Someone else might wonder why that is."

I bite back my excuses. I don't have to defend myself to him. And excuses I have. My first day here I was barely capable of walking down to the waterfall where I bathed. My body is only now rebuilding itself. I've needed this time to heal, to clear my head, to find a way to deal with the situation we all find ourselves in. But the real reasons run deeper than that.

I'm the one responsible for all of this. I made the decisions that led us here, and it was my actions that broke our magic and left us defenseless before our enemy. I still don't understand what happened; I'm afraid the only one who does may never wake up. How can I face them after everything I've done to them? Eredin Glas's proposal makes a degree of sense. *You're no good for them. Cut them loose, give them over to someone who is better suited than you.*

Eredin Glas nods his head. He sees the thoughts play out across my face, leaving me wondering how much he is able to read and how much he is guessing. I can't hide things from him. He's too old. He understands the world in a way I can only hope to reach someday. Of course he knows why I haven't gone to the Fae. He doesn't say any of that, though. "The sun is already far spent. We will go in the morning."

"Thank you." I've said a lot of that lately. I owe the King of the Wild Hunt a great debt. A debt I don't know if I'm capable of repaying. We eat in silence, but not an uncomfortable one. This stalemate of sorts can't last, but for now it's nice to not engage in strategic power-play.

****

"Who were you, before you became the King of the Wild Hunt?" I ask sometime later, laying stretched out on a bench enjoying the late afternoon sunshine on my face.

"What makes you think I was anyone?" he asks, not looking up from the slip of wood in his hand. He's spent the last half an hour chipping away at it with a narrow blade, focused on his task with a brooding, silent intensity.

I crane my neck to see him better, wincing as the wood of the bench digs into my shoulder. "You told me, the first time we met, that your mother named you Eredin Glas. If you had a mother, you weren't always a king."

He chuckles. "That is interesting logic. You are not wrong, though. I was born, like any other child, before I grew to be a man."

I sit up and give him a deadpan look. "Is that it? You were born, and then you grew up? That's all you'll tell me?"

He heaves a sigh and sets his woodworking project aside. "What do you wish to hear? Do you want me to tell you about when this world was new? When people had yet to discover they could take things from each other, and magic flowed freely between all living creatures? What about when those illusions were shattered, and the days grew cold and dark? When the mother who had birthed me and nurtured me and protected me was taken away from me and I was left all alone in this new, scary world?

"Do you wish to hear the tale of how I hardened my grief and my despair, turned them into weapons I could wield against the one who took her from me? That man they called the King of the Wild Hunt, though he was hardly a king, and the Hunt was hardly a hunt. Little more than drifters and thieves. He took everything from me, so I took everything from him in return."

"You killed him and assumed his title and position?" It's the basic story of conquest, but with a heartbreaking emotional twist. The idea of Eredin Glas loving anybody enough to avenge them like that is unexpected. And unsettling.

"That world had nothing left to offer me. This one" —he sweeps his hands to the sides— "was full of possibility. I elevated the Wild Hunt into legend, crafted a place for us that history will not soon forget."

"And earned yourself immortality in the process. How did that happen?"

Eredin Glas sits back and crosses his arms. "My secrets for yours, Your Majesty? Or perhaps we'll save that tale for another time."

I make a show of laying myself back down on the bench. "I'm not interested enough at the moment to trade a secret. You can keep that knowledge to yourself for now."

He chuckles. "Another time it is, then. I look forward to many such conversations as this."

His comment jars me, but I hold myself expressionless. If he thinks this is an indication that I am planning to stay I will not disabuse him of the notion, but I am far from ready to make that decision. Though I suspect if I continue to waver the decision will be made for me.

# JESSICA GOEKEN

## Chapter Twenty-Four

As sunset approaches, a horn rings out in the valley below the plateau. My eyes shoot to Eredin Glas, but he hasn't moved. "Someone else calls them to the Hunt?" I ask, my puzzlement plain in my voice.

"Not a Hunt as you know it," he answers, sounding almost bored. "There is no magic to be captured tonight. The hunters hunt in the Wood for sport."

"Do you hunt for sport?" I can't help asking.

He grins wickedly, his canines flashing in the evening light. "Often. Not tonight, however. Tonight, my mind is preoccupied and will not be settled in the company of others."

"I often find running through the trees to be quite settling," I respond, my eyes going to the tree line.

"Join them. They will always welcome you among their company."

*I just might.* No sooner do I think the words than I'm running for the path off the plateau, desperate to catch the hunters before they move too far into the woods and are lost to me. I needn't have worried. Halfway down the path I collide with Lella. The difference in our bulk means that she merely grunts while I ricochet into the dirt.

"Eve! I was just coming to collect you. Hurry, the hunt waits for no man. Not even a queen."

She doesn't give me the chance to respond. Grabbing my elbow, she heaves me off the ground and drags me into the trees. The path hasn't leveled off yet, so we scrabble down the rocky incline, sending pebbles and shale raining below.

"Where are we going?" My heart pounds at this sudden adventure, all trepidation and doubt vanishing into thin air. The bottom of the incline ends in a ten-foot drop, and without hesitation I follow Lella off it.

"Into the wild," she says mischievously, then takes off at a run.

I'm two steps behind her, dodging roots and leaping fallen logs. When she whoops, I whoop with her, sending my voice up into the sky. We break out into a clearing where Gent and Lella's dappled mare wait for us. Already winded, I'm glad to see Gent and greet him with a nose kiss before scrambling onto his back. He needs no urging to follow Holiday's gray rump as she gallops out of the clearing and onto a narrow game trail.

After a few minutes of hard riding, we catch up to the rest of the hunters. Compared to when the Wild Hunt rides, this adventure is ghostly silent. Not even a single jingle, since none of the mounts wear their harnesses. The game trail winds between trees that grow increasingly taller, up and down valleys where scores of creatures flee at our passing, and finally splashes down into a wide, shallow creek. Even here I can't properly see the sky, the canopy is so dense.

"What are we hunting?" I finally ask Lella as Gent and Holiday pause for a drink.

"Anything we find," she answers with a shrug. "Hellequin Wood is populated with many prey beasts and no predators, so game is always in abundance."

"No predators? Really?"

She shrugs. "The King built Hellequin Wood to be a haven for his hunters. Surely you've noticed the bounty it provides you? Nothing here will harm us. You would be hard pressed to even find a sprig of poison ivy." Hellequin Wood *is* a haven. It would be the perfect home for the Fae if we are unable to reclaim the Realm. *Maybe Eredin Glas would let them live here if he and I—* No. I refuse to let my thoughts go there. Such weighty matters have no place in this adventure.

With a flurry of hand signals, the hunters break into small parties and melt into the trees. I spy Danen for the first time, unsurprised that he's here. These are his people. Of course he's here. I stare at him so long I pull his eyes to mine. He meets my gaze then deliberately turns away, joining Jarild as the lieutenant's party climbs the opposite bank. I'll give him this: He looks at home here amongst the Hunt. Welcome. Accepted. Happy. Though how happy can he be if he doesn't know who he truly is?

Something squeezes too hard inside my chest, but I don't have time to dwell on it before Lella and I are joined by her campmates, Farooq and Nes-Unnefer. I haven't spoken to them much, but now isn't the time. Lella leads our silent party into what I soon recognize as 'the wild'.

The terrain shifts abruptly from the temperate woodland I've become accustomed to. Jungle creepers hang from a canopy so thick I can't see the stars. The trees on the other side of the creek are easily fifty feet across, shedding long strips of bark that coil amongst the undergrowth and form meandering half-tunnels filled with clusters of bright yellow flowers.

Lella sees me noticing the flowers. "Bacopa Rosea," she murmurs, keeping her voice low so as not to startle the game. "Hellequin Wood is one of the few places it grows in the wild. It's said to have rare magical properties."

This wild place reminds me so much of my first sight of the Realm that painful tears spring to my eyes. The depth of color and the purity of the Realm's wildness will forever be unmatched, even by this haven housed in Hellequin Wood. My memories of that first night in my homeland will forever be etched into my brain. My body will always long to return to the place it calls home.

I don't have time to sink into all that I've lost, however. Farooq gives a shout and a great horned beast leaps clear across our party. In unison three bows unleash twanging arrows. Two hit their mark, with the third glancing off the left antler. The beast bellows, crashing back to the ground and charging off into underbrush taller than I am. The tunnel left in its wake is dotted with blood and looks almost ominous in the darkness.

"We're on foot from here," Lella announces, sliding off Holiday.

I take the rear as we advance, watching the hunters do their thing with fascination. This mundane hunt, so different from the manic ride across the sky, boasts a simple and primal beauty. I've never hunted for the sport of it. Never tracked an animal for the singular purpose of killing it. This isn't an activity I would be likely to do in the Realm. We track the beast for half a mile before finding the spot where it finally succumbed. It isn't dead yet, though. It blows and heaves, struggling vainly to rise.

Nes-Unnefer puts it out of its misery by slitting its throat, and my eyes lock on its eyes as its life drains away. I can see now that it's a stag, taller than Gent and heavily muscled, sporting three different sets of interlocking antlers. Lella, Farooq, and Nes-Unnefer make quick work of field-dressing it, and it takes all four horses to drag it back to the beach.

Our party was not the only successful one. Several fires dot the sand as the night's prey is spitted and roasted. The instruments come out and a chanting song begins, though the energy doesn't come close to that of the revel. The air feels more subdued, more personal. I feel suddenly like an impostor and am considering making a quiet exit when Lella notices.

"Not leaving, are you?" she hollers, drawing the attention of half the hunters my way. She makes a beeline for me and thrusts a cup into my hands. It's different than whatever we drank last time, smelling of lemons, honey, and some flower I don't recognize.

"I was just going to—"

"Just going to split and make us carouse by ourselves? You did the work, you share in the spoils. Stay. Dance. Eat!"

I could argue that I did no work at all, but the festival atmosphere is too enticing. It doesn't take much coaxing on Lella's part. If anything, I'm dying to know what makes this celebration a 'carouse' and the last one a 'revel'. Tonight is definitely tamer, although there is still plenty of laughter and dancing.

I catch sight of Yaikhaa and start making my way over to say hi, but before I make it, she's gone again. The next time I see her she's dragging another hunter off into the trees, and I decide whatever they're up to is decidedly none of my business.

Danen is another hunter I can't seem to catch. Every time I sight him, he vanishes before I can get close, and after his dismissal on the hunt it's clear he's avoiding me.

I don't carouse long, though the night is far spent by the time I go looking for my bed. I haven't forgotten my plans to track down the Fae with Eredin Glas tomorrow. I half expected him to make an appearance on the beach, but if he did, I didn't see him. He isn't at his fire, either, but before I can climb the ladder to my palafito I finally see him. He's standing so still as to be motionless, at the farthest tip of the plateau, his profile stark in the weak moonlight.

At the top of the ladder, I find a small wooden carving sporting impressive antlers. At first, I think it's the stag from tonight, but then I notice the dragonish features and the overlapping half-moon marks down all four legs. *Keshi*.

I whip my head back around to stare at the silhouette of the King. *Is this a gesture of kindness? Or is he screwing with my head again?* I consider going to him but instantly dismiss the idea. He wouldn't appreciate me interrupting whatever is brewing in that head of his. I shake my head, put the King behind me, and crawl beneath my covers.

## Chapter Twenty-Five

I'm foggy and sore the next morning, but I roll out of bed with the sunrise anyway. The moon had already passed its zenith when I dragged myself to bed last night, but nothing could keep me there if it tried. Eredin Glas is taking me to the Fae today.

I'm disappointed to find only the hounds at the fire this morning, but the basket of fruits and pastries is a welcome sight. I eat and walk down to the waterfall to bathe, and Eredin Glas is waiting when I get back.

"Are you ready?" he asks, his eyes skimming over my outfit. I've chosen to dress simply today for a reason. My riding leathers would be a visible show of alliance with the Wild Hunt, while any show of authority or power on my part will surely drive the remaining Fae away from me before I can even begin to mend fences. I've imagined this scenario thousands of times, drafted thousands of scripts that never quite felt like enough. Even at this moment I'm still not certain which words I'll choose to say in the moment.

"Is Danen joining us?" I ask, apprehension making my voice wobble.

"No. His presence would only complicate things."

"I agree." The words are too formal for the immense relief I feel. Explaining his situation will be difficult enough. They don't need to see their strongest brought so low. "Let's go."

Gent and Morhogg wait for us at the edge of the plateau. Riding a horse across the sky has already become second nature, and I don't even blink at the portal ripping open before my eyes. On the other side waits the human world and all of the memories of my upbringing. That world isn't my home anymore, though. My parents were the only thing still tying me there. They were the first thing the Fomorians directly took from me.

"Where are we?" I ask Eredin Glas, the sharp coldness of the air dragging my mind out of my memories. Snow-covered mountains stretch out below us with both ocean coastline and city lights in the distance, making it impossible for me to pinpoint our location.

"Nagano, Japan."

I look at him in confusion. Japan is nowhere near Ireland, where the gate spits out those crossing from the Realm into the human world.

"They lost everything," he continues quietly, almost to himself. "They tried to stay close, to wait for you, but it soon became apparent that you weren't coming. Without their magic they could not hide from the humans like they used to and began to draw attention. That was the first chink in the alliance that held them together."

I can see the scenario playing out in my head. "They decided to split up. Blend in."

"Then they kept going." Eredin Glas sweeps his arms out. "Winter House ended up here. Perpetual snow, hot springs, good fishing. Access to the city but easy to stay hidden in the mountains when need be."

"Winter House?" My heart flips over.

"I knew you would want to tell them about Danen."

*Is this one of his games? He's been exceptionally straightforward with me lately, but this has a feel of manipulation about it. Maybe he thinks I'll keep Danen a secret? Maybe he wants me uncomfortable and off balance?* I don't say any of that. "Let's get closer."

The air off the mountains is cold, slicing right through the pants and shirt I'm wearing, though it doesn't seem to bother Eredin Glas. It won't bother Winter

House, either. They're born for this kind of weather. Eredin Glas gives Morhogg his head as we descend into a narrow ravine separating two peaks. No storm follows us today.

My teeth are chattering and I'm shivering uncontrollably by the time we land, sinking knee deep into fresh powder. No signs of life greet us. If Winter House is here, they're well concealed.

Eredin Glas looks at me expectantly.

Guess I'm up. I clear my throat and call out, "Hello? Is anyone here?" The wind snatches away my words as soon as I say them.

Our arrival hasn't gone unnoticed, however. Movement catches at the corner of my eye and I spin to find a completely white figure extricating itself from the snow. Fur lines its face and cascades down its neck like a mane, and yellow eyes in a human-looking face meet mine. Fae.

"Hello."

The Fae bares its teeth in a growl, but no sound comes out. It stalks toward me, hunched over with arms dangling like some kind of wild animal. *It probably is,* I realize. Having spent most of my time in Emain Ablach I met very few of the wild Fae, and certainly none belonging to Winter House. I hold perfectly still as the Fae gets right in my face, fur tickling my nose, and keep my breathing calm and controlled.

It huffs out a breath smelling of fish and licks my cheek.

"Enough, Liri."

The command comes from ahead, where a cluster of red pines act as a bulwark against the freezing wind. This time it's a voice I recognize. "Ellis." My voice comes out strong, belying the sudden palpitations of my heart. *They're really here.*

"Your Majesty." The cold acknowledgment sounds strange coming from my former guard's lips. Ellis's coloring is so like Danen's that his change in demeanor hits extra hard. "You should come inside."

"Thank you." I move forward, but his raised hand stops me in my tracks.

"The stranger stays out here."

I look at Eredin Glas, who seems unperturbed by either this development or the harsh conditions. I quickly turn away before he can acknowledge me so it doesn't look like I'm asking his permission. Without another word, I follow Ellis into the red pines, which form a sort of corridor around us. The deeper we move into the trees the more they shift until I find myself standing in a structure that seems to be made entirely from the interlocking trees. The ground is the rocky mountainside swept bare, and even though the top is open to the sky the temperature is only mildly chilly. "This place is beautiful."

"Winter House has enjoyed recreation here for generations. It is little wonder we would choose to seek refuge here again after the losses we have suffered."

The bitterness in his voice reaches deep into my core, but I don't respond. Nothing I can say will make any of this better. Now that we're on level ground I can see that Ellis is limping, favoring his left leg. I press my lips together to avoid commenting on it.

Ellis leads me into a cleft in the mountainside, where homey comforts suddenly abound. Modern furniture crowds the space while shaggy rugs cover the floor. More Fae than I've seen in a long time huddle together and whisper, but the state of them! There are palace staff and guards, like Ellis, who oversaw the evacuation, but the rest are the old, the infirm, the ones unable to stay behind and fight. This is not the future of the Fae, but the past. The young, healthy Fae make up the minority, but even they are not whole. Like Ellis, they sport the ghosts of injuries sustained in battle but are unable to be healed without Fae magic. These Fae healed like humans, and they bear the scars to prove it.

In the middle of the room, reclining on a chaise lounge, sits a severe-looking Fae with straggly white hair. Her normally alabaster skin is sallow and gray, her ageless face wrinkled and drooping. Her eyes, however, remain as piercing and filled with hate as they've ever been.

"Master Virosa?" I can't keep the confusion out of my voice. I last saw her slaughtering Fomorians at Emain Ablach. *After* the magic failed. "How are you here?"

"The borders of the Realm are not what they once were," she replies, her voice low and gravelly. "The better question is, how are *you* here?"

The whispers in the room stop as every Fae waits to hear my answer. "During the battle, I was taken prisoner by the Fomorian General, Halasuwa. I have spent these last months entrapped in their fortress and only recently escaped." I look around at the gathered Fae, allowing their sorrow to wash over me. "Tell me, is this all that remains of Winter House?"

Virosa's eyes flash. "You have the audacity to ask me that? You, who have been the ruin of not just my House but our entire race, come walking in here like you belong and wonder at how few of us made it out?"

Her words hit me like a lash, not just because of their ferocity, but because I deserve them. In all of my mourning, all of my guilt, I have not faced repercussions for my actions. Even my imprisonment was not justice enough for the destruction I caused. With that thought, I drop to one knee, lowering my head until my eyes find the floor. I let every emotion I've felt in these past months bleed out into my voice.

"Your judgment of me is well deserved, and I am truly sorry for the ones you have lost. I cannot hope to make you whole, even were I to dedicate the length of my life to doing so." I raise my eyes to meet hers. "I failed you, and I failed the Realm, and I failed the entire Fae people. But if it does take the rest of my life, I will do everything in my power—"

"Power? You have no power. Not there, and certainly not here."

"—to see the Fae restored. I cannot bring back the dead, but I can save those who remain, and I can save the Realm—"

"You were never capable of saving the Realm." Virosa comes out of her seat, staggering at the sudden change in position. I scramble to my feet as she teeters over to jab a finger in my chest. "You were a weak, ignorant child from the beginning. I pleaded with Vogelein to rally the synod to depose you, but so blinded by love for your mother was he that my warnings went unheeded. I am alone because of you. My brother and my nephew are dead because of you, and—"

"Danen lives," I interrupt, stepping out of her reach and holding out my arms to brace her in case she falls. *Has grief done this to her?*

Virosa lurches toward me again, wrapping her skeletal hands in the fabric of my shirt. "Say it again," she orders.

I pour every ounce of sincerity I can into my eyes, into my words, into my hands as I cup her shoulders. "Danen lives. I have seen him, spoken with him. He was taken from the battlefield by the Wild Hunt."

The hope that blossomed in Virosa's face shatters. "The Wild Hunt?" she spits. "A fate worse than death. How dare you tell me that he lives?" Then she slaps me.

I stagger back, more in surprise than in pain. "Please, believe me. Danen is just as alive as you or I, and—"

"Begone from here, child. You are not welcome in this place."

"Master Virosa, please—"

"Leave! If I ever see your face again, I will kill you. I swear it."

# JESSICA GOEKEN

## Chapter Twenty-Six

Virosa's vow hangs heavily in the air. I know she'll keep it. The oath of a Fae is unbreakable.

I scan the crowd, which has only grown larger as word of my presence has spread. As raw and heartbreaking as Virosa's actions are, I can see she's not alone in the way she feels. There is no absolution for me here. It was naive to think there might be. Winter House is lost to me.

*For now.*

The Fae have long memories indeed, but the years will pass quickly enough. With Fae magic restored and a Realm to go home to, Winter House will thaw. I have to believe it.

"It's time to go." Eredin Glas's voice speaks softly in my ear. I'm not even surprised that he followed me in here.

The Fae, however, are another story.

"You dare bring that creature in here?" Virosa screeches, having lost whatever vestige of control she still held. The distinctive sound of blades being drawn circles the room.

I hold my hands up in a conciliatory gesture. "The King is here as my escort. It was he who plucked me from the darkness and returned me to the light."

"Then he should have let you die and rid us all of your incompetence," Virosa spits. "This is who you choose to ally yourself with? This vulture, skulking about the carrion and gorging himself on the flesh of the dead? How far you have fallen, how ashamed your mother would be to see what you have become."

A strangled cry bursts from my lips and I lunge toward Virosa. I don't know what I intend to do and I never get the chance to find out.

Eredin Glas blocks my way, bodychecking me into an elderly Fae behind me. We both go down.

"How dare you put your filthy hands on me!" Virosa's voice screams out above me. Eredin Glas has his hands on her shoulders, keeping her from following me to the floor. She thrashes like a wild animal, clawing at his face and snarling. Her guards leap to her defense, but Eredin Glas is too fast for them. With a shove, he sends Virosa back to her chair and spins to face his attackers, knocking them back with a burst of energy.

I find my feet and race to his side. "Don't hurt them," I plead, grabbing onto his arm as he reaches for his scythe.

But the damage has already been done. Virosa devolves entirely. "You see? He taunts us with his magic! He glories in the fall of Winter House! Kill him! Kill him!"

Chaos breaks loose. Fae rush us from every angle. I see Ellis in their midst, the fires of hate stoked behind his eyes.

Eredin Glas's arm wraps around my waist and suddenly we're airborne, sailing straight up through the open canopy and back into the cold mountain air.

Screams ring out below us, but we're no longer within reach.

Eredin Glas releases me, but I only fall a few inches before Gent glides up beneath me, catching me neatly on his back. I sink forward, ignoring everything else as I bury my face in Gent's mane and cry.

"Do you see now?" Eredin Glas asks sometime later.

After crying myself out, I expected some kind of comment from him, but he held his words until we reached warmer weather. If I were to guess I'd put us somewhere in the South China Sea. Now, with humid air pressing in on us and endless water in all directions it seems he's ready to make his point.

"See what?" I ask, refusing to cede any ground to him. I'm not in the mood to be lectured, especially about this particular topic.

He pins me with a glare, well knowing the game I'm playing. Unfair, since he's playing games, too. "See the attitude of the Fae. Their bitterness. Their hostility. Virosa herself, the head of Winter House, cursed you." He pauses, but I don't respond. "They have no faith in you. They will not follow you. Why not give them what they want and step away?" His tone is neither cruel nor persuading. If I didn't know he had ulterior motives I would believe he was asking sincerely.

But he isn't asking sincerely. My first impulse is to snap at him, but I shove that down and take some deep breaths instead. I know how I am seen: a child playing at being queen. And, I'll admit, my actions have sometimes been childish. That's part of the learning process. But I can't afford to be childish here. Not anymore. Not if I want to win back Winter House's loyalty. And not just them. The rest of the Fae, too, which surely don't hold me in any higher esteem than Winter House does.

I knew this wouldn't be easy, which is part of the reason I put it off for so long. My mind couldn't even imagine the decrepit state in which I would find them. I see now why Eredin Glas took me to Winter House first. It wasn't to tell them about Danen, although I'm glad I did. Much as the news pained her, Virosa needed to know, and I had to be the one to share that news. No, he took me there to make me lose heart. And I understand their position, I really do. How else should I expect them to feel? They've lost everything, and it's all my fault. Those kinds of wounds don't heal easily, if they ever heal at all.

But Eredin Glas miscalculated. If anything, my resolve is stronger, not weaker.

*Restoring our magic is the only way to begin the healing process. Even then, nothing I do can bring back the ones we've lost. If, when my people are whole once again, they choose to depose me ... I'll step aside and let them. I owe them that much.*

And Virosa's curse … I'm going to have to deal with that before all is said and done.

Eredin Glas has stopped waiting for my answer, but I give him one anyway. "I am not yet ready to concede defeat." He doesn't even look my way. I sit up straight and swipe my sleeve across my eyes. "Where to next?"

He sighs, but to his credit he doesn't push. "West," he mutters, kicking Morhogg out of range.

I can't hold back a vindictive grin. The King of the Wild Hunt—timeless, ageless—stymied by a teenage girl. How many people in history have ever held this kind of power over him? I have something he wants, and he can't just take it from me. I have to agree.

That being said, at least he has a plan. He will demoralize me until I admit that I need him to step in and fix everything. I don't have a plan. I have a goal: restore Fae magic and reclaim our homeland. It's ambiguous and grandiose, and I don't know what steps I need to take to get there. I have clues. Eredin Glas knows, but he won't tell me. His hunters won't go against him, so even if they know anything they wouldn't tell me, either. Oberon still has magic, but is incapable of telling me. If I broadcast my ignorance and weakness, I will open myself up to manipulation and deception. And if I leave the protection of the Hunt, I will be scooped up by the nearest Fomorian patrol or rogue goblin, and my life will end quickly and painfully.

*That about sums it up.*

My efforts up to this point suddenly feel weak in comparison to the enormous task before me. My body is mending, but now I don't know what to do with it. I've made progress with Danen, precious little though it is, but he still remains out of my reach. And I've contacted the Fae, with nothing but disastrous results to show for it.

*I'm not done yet, though.* Winter House was a disaster, yes, but three more Houses remain. I can't believe I missed the opportunity to ask Virosa if she knows what happened to break Fae magic. She probably wouldn't have answered, considering how our conversation did go, but it was a wasted opportunity nonetheless. *Not again. No more wasted opportunities. I can't do this on my own, and I'm tired of trying.*

My new resolve makes my spirit lift. I have a job to do, and I need to be better about doing it. The next House visit will be better. It has to be.

When Eredin Glas said "west" he wasn't kidding. Morhogg and Gent race across the sky, carrying us across Asia and into Europe before turning north. Eredin Glas can't help himself. He has to let the world know he's here. Rumbles of thunder now follow us, and the horses' hooves send black clouds skittering in all directions.

When lush green mountains and jagged, rocky cliffs overlooking mirrored coasts come into view, I think I have an idea where we are.

"Ireland?"

*I thought he said they all moved away from this area.*

"Close. Scottish Highlands. Spring House has taken up residence on the Isle of Skye."

# JESSICA GOEKEN

## Chapter Twenty-Seven

*Spring House.* Tingles erupt across my skin and a familiar ache squeezes my chest as I urge Gent to go faster. Loneliness and emptiness rise up to battle the hope those words spark.

*Tupi's down there.*

Morning is well advanced by the time we land, having circled the island at my request to get a sense of what we're walking into. And what we're walking into is strange; I'm just not sure how strange yet. The little I know about Scotland is enough to tell me that the Isle of Skye is a popular tourist destination, yet we saw no signs whatsoever of human activity. That can't be a coincidence.

Neither can the ranks of Fae lined up along the walkway leading up to a magnificent castle. We've obviously been spotted, but whether this is a welcome or a hostile reception remains to be seen. Winter House's blades leap into my mind, and I struggle to see past them and observe this scene for what it is. Spring House is not a violent people. It isn't in their nature. They're subtle when they need to be, and if this were some kind of attack they wouldn't be lined up out here to jump me. I probably wouldn't even see my death coming.

Still, nervousness washes through me as I dismount. They may not be out here with clubs and pitchforks, but they have no reason to love me any more than Winter House does. Their grief and pain is just as real. I try to respect that as I pass between them, meeting the eyes of any Fae who will look at me and giving them a solemn nod.

They nod back, faces expressionless. No one moves. No one speaks.

Until I'm standing in front of the castle. Then, the doors swing open and a tall, stately Fae emerges, sunlight highlighting her daffodil hair and a wide smile showing off her teeth.

"Eve!" she gushes, pulling me into a tight hug. Though her welcome is warm, her body is tight and unyielding against mine.

"Master Ailie," I respond, sticking to formality until I understand the situation. "I am pleased to see you well."

She holds me at arm's length and looks me up and down. "I was worried," she says. "No one knew what happened to you."

Fae double-speak. She means for me to believe she was worried about me, but that's not what she said. I feel a shift in my head, reverting back to when I had to listen to every word twice to catch the implications and hidden meanings. The hunters speak without deception; it's part of their charm. I'm out of practice.

My reception is so unlike that of Winter House that I decide to shift gears. Humility was the right call at Winter House. It was what they needed from me. But the energy here is so different. If I cower here, I fear I may never rise again.

I make a show of looking around me. "It looks like Spring House is managing itself well. There is much I wish to discuss with you." Then, without asking permission, I bypass Ailie and mount the steps to the castle.

Her surprise is palpable, but she recovers well and escorts me inside.

The castle is incredible. Vaulted ceilings, stunning architecture, portraits, tapestries, and furnishings that pull the eye in a hundred different directions at once. I allow myself five seconds to marvel at it before returning my attention to Ailie. Against the grandeur of the castle her navy-blue power suit is a jarring aesthetic.

"This is beautiful," I say, waving my hand to encompass our surroundings.

"That it is," she agrees, leading me down a hallway and into a formal drawing room. "Have a seat."

*I can't let Ailie control this meeting.* Ailie was always my ally, always ready to help me, and I don't understand the power dynamic that's suddenly sprung up between us. But it's there, invisible but pressing. I speak as soon as I'm seated, oozing assumption that I'm the one in authority here. "Tell me what happened after the evacuation. How did all of this come to be?"

If Ailie is annoyed she doesn't show it. "We waited. Outside Leprechaun's Gold. We all felt it when the magic failed. I remembered your edict: to protect and lead the Fae in your absence. More Spring Fae evacuated than any other House, and they were distraught. Lost. So, I gathered them together and brought them here. I have guided them, just as you requested, and against all odds we have prospered."

*Clever.* "Here? This island, specifically?"

Ailie smiles. "Yes. My ancestors were quite fond of the Isle of Skye, and Dunvegan Castle, specifically." She rises and crosses to the far wall, where an ornate frame holds ragged scraps of brown silk. "My grandfather was a close friend of the MacLeod clan, and gifted them this artifact. In their ignorance they named it the 'Fairy Flag', but my grandfather forgave the slight in light of their devotion. They believe this flag protects the clan and grants them help in battle."

"And does it?"

Her eyes twinkle, and the corner of her mouth lifts in a half-grin. "It is just a length of silk. A Fae trick. But, when the Fae arrived helpless on their doorstep, the

MacLeods were easily convinced to help."

Ailie resumes her seat and clasps my hand. A tone comes into her voice as if she's carefully explaining something to a child. "Day by day, Spring House began to create a home here. To rebuild. We tend the gardens, and we feed our families, and we heal."

Her skin on mine makes my hand itch. "What of the other Houses? Do you have contact with them?"

She shakes her head, and a sorrowful expression crosses her features. It's an expression I can't trust, because she is allowing me to see it. "When the Realm fell, we went our separate ways. Without your line to unite us, it was easier to return to how things were before."

*How things were before.* Independent Houses. A fractured, fighting Fae. Putting them back together again may be harder than restoring all of Fae magic in the first place. That's a problem for the future, though. First, I have to ensure that future can become a reality.

After only that brief report, Ailie's done talking about herself. "Now, what of you? I have heard stories of the battle, from ones who escaped after the borders fell, but no one knew what became of you. Most thought you dead, but I was not willing to believe it. Not without proof."

I tell her. I tell her about General Halasuwa, about my imprisonment in Canowin Hollow, about the degradation I experienced. I gloss over the details of my escape, particularly the moonlight quartz and Caspian's role in the whole thing. Why I'm shielding him I can't say, but Caspian isn't something I want to discuss with anyone. I want to leave him firmly in the past where he belongs. I give a few lines about recuperating with the Wild Hunt but leave out my visit with Winter House.

"What an ordeal," she says after I've finished,

patting my hand. "Of course you need time to recover and to heal, just like we all do. Is there anything Spring House can do to help you?"

"As a matter of fact," I begin, watching her expression closely. She seems a bit perturbed that I actually have a request, but I can't be certain. "I am trying to understand what happened that day, and since you were chosen to instruct me in magic in the first place, I hope you can help me puzzle it out." The flattery can't hurt, though I doubt she's so vain as to be swayed by it. "Do you know what mechanism broke Fae magic? Because I don't."

Ailie sighs and lets me see that fake sorrowful look again. "I wish I did know. If I had been there, beside you, maybe I could have stopped you from doing it."

The door opens and a burst of redbuds precedes Ailie's sister, Fanta, into the room. Fanta holds a tray with a kettle and an array of cups and bustles over to set them down on a nearby table.

Ailie's expression shifts, but I can't read it before it vanishes. If I were to guess, things between the sisters aren't as cohesive as they used to be.

"I thought you might like a refreshment." Fanta serves me first, pouring a steaming cup of tea and offering it to me. As I lean forward to accept it, she meets my eyes and opens her mouth wide. Her back to Ailie, she moves her lips in slow, exaggerated fashion. *Don't believe Ailie. She can't be trusted.*

## Chapter Twenty-Eight

I keep my expression neutral. What else can I do?

Fanta serves Ailie her tea as if nothing is amiss.

*Why would she say such a thing? She obviously believes it.* I never spent much time with Fanta. I found her quiet and service-focused, concentrating more on the duties of the synod than on the political games at play. Ailie was the one tasked with being my keeper. She was always quick to support and encourage me. But she also sent Tupi to spy on me and report on my movements.

After Fanta leaves, I pin Ailie with a look. We've been small-talking long enough, and I haven't missed the subtle aspersions Ailie's been tossing my way. Might as well address the issue head-on and see how things shake out. "Now that we're both caught up, let's discuss the future of our people."

Ailie doesn't react. I didn't expect her to. She can't help but feel the shift in the conversation, though, and it's only a matter of time before I say something that she *will* react to. I plow on. "I'm in no position to resume any kind of authority at the moment. That's obvious to both of us. Spring House appears to be safe and cared for under your leadership, and I thank you for taking such good care of them in my absence."

She doesn't respond, just sits motionless, waiting for the other shoe to drop. She knows how this game is played. "But this situation is temporary. The Fae can't exist as refugees in a world that's not their own. We aren't built for that."

"What else do you expect us to do?" she asks, ice filling her voice in a way I've only ever heard from Winter House. "We are stranded here. No home. No magic. We've done the best we can with the situation that's been dealt us." She doesn't say it's my fault, but her voice is heavy with implication. No matter.

Then I make her my promise, words I have yet to voice, words that will bind me as surely as Virosa's vow to kill me binds her. "I will see the Fae restored," I vow. "I will bring back our magic and I will return us to our home. Despite our circumstances, I am still the Queen of the Fae, by right of my lineage, and I will not abandon my responsibilities so easily."

Ailie stands, all pretense of welcome gone. "You are not our queen any longer, Eve. After what you've done, you hold claim over Spring House no more. I rule this House as I see fit, and I do not see fit to return *my* people to your inept and careless leadership." She steps closer, staring down at me and wafting wintergreen breath into my face. "It is only by the capriciousness of fate that your head ended up under a crown instead of mine, *little sister*."

Ailie ends her tirade with a sneer, and I almost miss the last words. Those incredible, life-changing, world-ending last words. "Little sister?"

"No one told you, did they? After you appeared in Emain Ablach the synod launched an investigation into your birth. We had to know how Hanathen hid such an event from so many for so long. Hanathen's consorts were all a matter of public record. I know you were sired by Zephyr of Spring House."

I am Hanathen's only child. I know that for a certainty. Royal blood wins out, and neither Ailie nor Fanta bear the golden skin and silver hair of the royal line. So that means...

"Zephyr was your father."

Ailie's lips press so thin they become invisible. "Do you know how he died? Neither do I. But it isn't hard to figure out *why*. Hanathen killed him to keep her secrets. He died because of *you*."

"Plenty of Fae have died because of me," I answer, meeting Ailie's icy stare with a fiery one of my own. I refuse to let her guilt and intimidate me into backing down. "And you were no nearer the crown than any other Fae in the Realm. It grieves me that you did not share this information sooner. It would have been nice to have a sister."

My temperate response only incenses Ailie more. "I should have been queen!" she roars, her voice echoing through the posh but empty castle.

"You will never be queen," I breathe, intentionally pitching my voice low in contrast to hers. "I *will* restore Fae magic. And then I will come back here and take my people back. And if you stand in the way of that, I will take you out. Sister."

Without waiting for a response, I brush past Ailie and head for the door. She doesn't follow, but I feel her eyes boring fiery holes into my back.

*How many more enemies can I make today?*

Fanta is hovering in the hall. "Thank you," I tell her earnestly. "I hear we're sisters."

"That is true," she answers, "though the situation is not as fraught as Ailie would make it seem. She is an entire decade older than I am, and neither of us had spoken with Zephyr for fifteen years at least before he joined with Hanathen's company. Even the two of us do not share a mother. Our emotional connection with our father was, in essence, nonexistent."

"How do the Spring Fae fare, truly?"

They looked healthy enough outside, but looks can be deceiving.

"Truly? You were right in your assessment. Ailie is a fair and just leader. She cares for the wellbeing of Spring House above all. We will be in good hands until you are ready to resume your duties."

"When that time comes, do you think Spring House will return to me? Or will they choose Ailie?"

Fanta shakes her head slowly. "I cannot say. We are hurting. You know that. But the Fae loved you, and I believe they want to love you still." She hesitates, then adds, "When that day comes, I will support you, Your Majesty."

Sudden tears spring to my eyes. "Thank you, Fanta. I look forward to growing closer with you in the years to come." We clasp hands, then I force myself to turn away. After leaving Ailie the way I did it won't do for me to linger.

Outside, the sun has tipped into afternoon and a wave of exhaustion washes over me. Far down the road I can see Morhogg and Gent grazing contentedly on the lawn, but Eredin Glas is nowhere in sight. The congregated Fae have returned to their tasks, some in the gardens, some coaxing animals into wagons, some launching boats out on the loch. The absence of humans baffles me. The Fae aren't even using human technology like phones and cars, with the exception of electric lights. *What kind of place is Ailie running here?* A safe one, by all accounts, and today, that's all that matters.

I'm halfway back to Gent, intending to explore the island a bit more intensely while searching for the next person on my priority list, when a high-pitched squeal brings me up short. "Your Majesty!"

"Tupi!" I call, spinning in a circle as I search for my friend.

There she is. Running across the lawn as fast as her little legs can pump, wings flopping around behind her in a pathetic impersonation of flying. Then I'm running, too, and seconds later we crash into each other full speed.

"You're alive! I was so worried! And you're

here!"

"I'm so happy to see you. I've been so scared and lonely. Just wait until I tell you everything that's happened!"

Our words tumble over each other as we talk at the same time. Then we just laugh and hug and collapse on the ground like the teenage girls we really are.

When I finally catch my breath, I sit up and look at her, really look. Her face is too pale, her cheekbones too prominent, her wings too droopy. "What's wrong, Tupi? Has Ailie been unkind to you?"

She sits up straight, shaking her tangled hair out. "You gave me a job to do, Your Majesty, and I have been doing it to the best of my ability. A lot of Fae need help, though, and I am just one person."

My last words to her float through my head. *I want you to watch over them, Tupi. The synod will be there to make the big decisions, but a lot of people are going to be confused, scared, and hurting. Maybe even angry. They're going to need to someone to care for them.*

"Oh, Tupi." I sniffle, pulling her into another hug. "I never meant for you to take on so much alone."

"I would have done it anyway," she says. "To keep my hands and mind distracted." Her eyes rove over me, seeing every injury my imprisonment and malnourishment has inflicted on my body, no matter how clean Eredin Glas has made me. "What happened to you?" she whispers.

I want to tell her. But more than that, I want her with me. I want her friendship, I want her confidence, I want her wise words that keep me on track and always show me which path I should take. "I have missed you more than words can say, my friend. I'm not giving up yet, and I am in need of your friendship once more. Will you come with me?"

"My duty is always to you, Your Majesty," she answers on reflex. Then she pauses. "Come where?"

The boom of thunder is all the answer she needs as lightning strikes the ground not ten feet from us, revealing Eredin Glas in all his kingly glory.

I stand and bend down to offer her my hand. "Come, Tupi. I ride with the Wild Hunt."

## Chapter Twenty-Nine

Tupi needs a little convincing. I don't blame her.

Eredin Glas stands before us in all his kingly glory, and the power radiating off him is enough to drive all the Fae in the area to their knees. I've been there. Just because I no longer quail before his presence doesn't mean I don't feel it.

Tupi, on the other hand, is frozen to the ground, quivering and covering her eyes.

"It's okay," I murmur as I pull her to her feet. "He's with me."

And he isn't alone. The wind picks up and clouds cover the sun as hunters circle above us.

It's a mark of Tupi's trust in me that she puts her hand in mine and shoves herself to her feet. Gent is a welcome distraction from the King, and she clings to him gratefully as I boost her up.

"Where to?" I call out as I clamber onto Gent's back behind Tupi.

"Fomorians," he growls. No manic energy lights his eyes, as with his other hunts.

At the word, my blood runs cold. Eredin Glas has no quarrel with the Fomorians, and their magic isn't strong enough for him to seek out. So that must mean...

"Are they coming here?"

He gives me a brisk nod.

*They followed me.* I know it. The chances of them choosing to attack Spring House the same day I showed up are too great for it to be a coincidence. *How did they know?*

I'm not the only one at risk, either. If they arrive at the island, they'll slaughter any Fae they find. "Hold on tight," I whisper to Tupi as I kick Gent forward. Not to the air, though. Not yet. His legs make short work of the distance to the castle door.

"Ailie!" I call, as loudly as I can without tipping into hysteria. "Fanta! Ailie!"

The door finally cracks open, but I don't see who's on the other side. "Fomorians incoming," I bark. "Pull the Fae back. The Wild Hunt will meet them." Without waiting for a response, I nudge Gent, who leaps straight up into the air. Two strides and he's sailing over the castle, whirling to chase after Eredin Glas and Morhogg.

Tupi squeals as we climb higher, her fingers clenched white around Gent's mane.

I can't help but laugh at her. "You have wings, Tupi. You can't tell me you're scared to fly."

"This is a bit different, Your Majesty," she mutters breathlessly. She begins to relax, though, and soon is comfortable enough to look down and all around. "I've never been so high before."

"It's incredible, isn't it?" Our moment of levity only lasts a moment, though. Then we catch up with the Hunt.

"Hail," I call to Lella as we draw alongside. "Where are they?" Eredin Glas rides at the head of the Hunt, fully ensconced in kingly duties.

"Look." She points to a tiny island off Skye's southwestern coast, where the ground appears to be bulging outward in the shape of a dome.

"Canna," Tupi supplies, leaning over to get a better view. "The island is a bird sanctuary, but otherwise uninhabited." Lella raises an eyebrow at me over Tupi's presence but doesn't say anything. As we watch, the dome bursts open and Fomorians spill out like roaches, scattering to all sides to let the warriors behind them out. *They must be trying to take Skye by surprise. They don't know they're found out.*

"Here we go."

Then the Hunt is descending, and Lella is screaming, and the hounds are baying, and the sky erupts into torrential rain. Gent keeps us steady and well above the fighting, though his body tenses with desire to follow his fellows into battle. I don't see or hear much of it through the darkness, but after the Hunt's last encounter with Fomorians I'm minimally concerned. Sure enough, the whole thing is over in minutes, and the sky clears as hunters swarm us, whooping, hollering, and making a ruckus.

Eredin Glas rears up in front of me, flashes me a grin, then tosses me a horn. "Sound the all clear. Alert the Fae."

*Me?* I've never blown a hunting horn in my life, but the smooth surface feels right under my fingers. I take a deep breath and give it all I've got. The sound that bursts forth is clear and ringing, and it brings tears to my eyes. It's a sound that speaks of safety and home, of return and good fortune. How one sound can say so much is beyond me, but I dare not question it.

"Hunters, with me! We ride!"

The thrill of the Hunt races through me and I kick Gent faster to catch up with Morhogg. In this, I belong at the King's side. Hounds race around us, howling and baying, reaching deep into that primal part of my brain that yearns to claim this for my future.

In front of me, Tupi feels it, too. The thrill of the Hunt. Racing across the sky, free of our worries, our burdens, and our responsibilities. When I ride with the Hunt I *want* to choose it.

Then something crashes into us from above and sends us hurtling out of the sky. I lose my grip on Tupi as she is knocked away from me. *She'll be okay, she has wings.* I have to believe that.

Gent is screaming, out of fear or pain I can't tell. I wrap my legs around his belly as tightly as I can to keep from flying off myself as he flails his legs to get his footing back. And the *thing* is sitting where Tupi should be, hunched and hairy and reaching for me…

Danen's hand-to-hand combat lessons rear up in my memory and I lash out with a fist, landing a blow squarely in the middle of the writhing mass. Pain shoots up my arm, but I raise my fist again, ready.

"Ow!" it screams, hurrying to cover itself. "Stop, please, stop!"

*What in the world?*

Gent finally recovers, pulling us out of freefall and snapping my neck with the abrupt shift in motion. The horse is trembling, though, and can't keep himself steady. The *thing* falls over but doesn't have the grace to tumble off Gent's side. I'm reaching forward to help it when the lump of hair suddenly writhes and parts, revealing a bloodied face beneath it.

"Caspian?" I would recognize that brown face, those budding horns, anywhere. The hairy covering appears to be some kind of blanket that he throws to the side and lets fall to the ground.

He gives me a sheepish grin. "Apologies, Your Majesty. My aim was not as precise as I wished it to be."

I hit him again. Right in the nose. This time, I feel the bones in my hand give way for the second time in as many days and let out an involuntary yelp.

Then an untamable wind whips around us and Morhogg crashes into Gent's side.

Eredin Glas launches himself across the horses, tackling Caspian and dragging him out into open air.

"Eve! Are you all right?" Lella pulls me off Gent and onto Holiday.

Gent gives a grateful whinny and vanishes in a flash of white light.

Lella spins me all around, looking me over. "Where did he hurt you?"

"He didn't hurt me. Where's Tupi?" Between the fall and the whiplash, my head feels three sizes too big and like it's spinning around inside a pinwheel. I don't even know which direction to look for her.

"The pixie?"

"Yeah."

"I am here, Your Majesty." Tupi appears at my side, her gossamer wings buzzing furiously to keep her aloft. "Are you injured?" Her eyes go straight to my hand, zeroing in on the weakness there.

"I am, but it'll keep. Lella, take me to Eredin Glas."

Lella is no subject of mine, but she obeys the order anyway, turning Holiday into a steep dive. The rest of the Hunt trails us as we make for the ground.

We land only a minute behind Eredin Glas. The King stands upon a windswept outcropping of rock, the ocean crashing below him and salt spray in the air. We didn't even make it out of the Scottish isles, though which one we've landed on eludes me. Caspian lays in a heap at the King's feet.

Tupi gasps when she recognizes him but doesn't try to stop me.

The hunters hang back as I approach alone. The lump that is Caspian stirs and moans, so at least I know he's not dead. I ignore him for now, though, training my eyes on Eredin Glas.

"Who is he?" Eredin Glas doesn't miss much. Caspian is obviously Fae, but I wonder if the King can sense the Fomorian blood in him. If nothing else, surely he recognizes him as one of the Fae who had my back during our first encounter. He may have even heard me say his name, but that doesn't mean he knows who he is. Or what he's done.

"He is the one who betrayed me to the Fomorians."

Eredin Glas growls.

"He is also the one who enabled my escape."

"My Lady, please, I—"

"Shut up, Caspian."

He shuts up.

"What do you wish me to do with him?" It's a sincere question, but a dangerous expression lurks in Eredin Glas's eyes. I can't read it, so I don't know what he would prefer I say.

There's only one thing I can say, though. "Take him home. I should talk with him."

"You wish me to release him?"

"Goodness, no. Tie him up. Keep him close. He can't be trusted."

## Chapter Thirty

Caspian sits at the fire, hands tied behind his back, a strip of cloth keeping his tongue in check. Dried blood still covers the lower half of his face from where I broke his nose—a nose which Eredin Glas graciously healed, right after healing my hand, tending to Gent, and seeing the hunters settled for the night. No less than six hunters guard the plateau tonight. I can't see them in the darkness, but I know they're out there. Danen isn't one of them. I didn't ask, but I suspect Eredin Glas is keeping Danen far away from Caspian. To be fair, I haven't sought Danen out, either. It hurts too much, and I feel too helpless to change it.

Caspian can wait. Tupi still has more questions than answers, but the second she saw Oberon all other concerns vanished. He still hasn't woken, although his breathing is even and his color is good. When she heard he still has magic, her eyes grew large enough to cover half her face. As a Spring Fae, she is gifted in healing, and the pain her helplessness is causing her makes my own heart ache. Magic or not, Oberon will be in good hands as long as she's tending him.

"If your attention is needed elsewhere, then you should go," Tupi says, nodding toward the fire. "I am not a pressing need."

"Not pressing, no, but neither is he. I've missed you, Tupi, more than I can say." I let emotion color my words, but no tears come to my eyes this time.

"Tell me what happened." It's not a command, but a simple plea from someone yearning to make it all better. So I do. I tell Tupi everything, from the moment I sent her away from Emain Ablach until I saw her running across the lawns at Dunvegan Castle. It isn't a short tale, but she listens attentively, gasping and, on occasion, crying. I leave nothing out, not about Caspian, or Baark, or the fear I felt, or the times I considered throwing myself out my tower window and ending my suffering once and for all. I tell her about my conflicting feelings about riding with the Hunt, and the bargain that Eredin Glas is offering me. I tell her about Winter House, Danen's stolen memories, and Virosa's curse. This is the first time I've told it in its entirety, and with the release comes a feeling of lifting weight. Finally, I'm not carrying all of the emotional load anymore.

I talk so long my throat grows dry and scratchy, and my butt gets numb from sitting in the same position on the floor. When I'm done, Tupi throws her arms around me and holds me tightly for a long time. Then, without prompting, shares her own experiences.

"Those first days were awful," she says, her voice growing dim and her eyes catching the faraway look of someone lost in a memory. "The evacuation was chaotic, Fae from all Houses crossing worlds without a plan, without supplies, many cut off from their families. We tried to hold glamours, but there was so much activity it was impossible to not draw notice. The synod did a great job of making contact with the Fae from their Houses, but no one knew what to do after that. We stood outside, in the rain, trying to be quiet so the humans wouldn't hear us, and waited for news of the battle.

"Then the magic failed. It hit everyone at once, and the screaming, oh, the screaming. It felt like the air was suddenly ripped from my chest. I couldn't breathe. I could barely stand. I couldn't even fly."

"But your wings are a part of you. They don't require magic to fly." I can't help interrupting. Her story cuts me to my core, hearing about all the ways I hurt the people I was supposed to be protecting.

"My wings worked, but my balance was off. I had to relearn how to fly, relying on my own strength without the added buoyancy of my magic. I was lucky, though. I'm young. The elder Fae? The ones who have possessed their magic for centuries? Many could not handle the loss. They fell and did not rise again."

"They died?"

She shakes her head, but the denial holds no joy. "We didn't let them. They live, but their existence is an empty, painful one." She takes a deep breath, as if bracing for the next part. "Then the warriors came."

"From Emain Ablach?"

"Yes. The borders of the Realm fell with the magic, and when it became obvious the Realm was lost those remaining chose to flee. They arrived broken and bleeding, from all directions, as the gate no longer connected the Realm to the Leprechaun's Gold. They knew where we would be, though, and they made their way to us. They told us of the Fomorian victory, and of the loss of the Realm."

"Fleeing was the right choice," I whisper, staring down at my hands. It is a comfort that not everyone who followed me into battle died, but it is a very small one. I saw some of my warriors with my own eyes. Since winter and summer are the more volatile of seasons, Fae from those Houses made up the bulk of my army. Those Winter Fae who returned did not return whole.

"How long did it take for the Houses to split?" I ask.

Tupi returns her attention to Oberon, stroking his hair absentmindedly. "Days. Everyone had an opinion. Where we should go, what we should do, whether you were alive or dead, and who should lead in your absence. All four premiers stayed in their territories, fighting to get their people out, which left the synod as the ranking leadership in the human world. They bickered over every detail, drawing things out until the Fomorians discovered the weakness in the borders and came after us."

I gasp. Neither Ailie nor Virosa told me that part. "Did they…?"

Tupi shakes her head again. "We had warning. The Fomorians made enough of a fuss in the human world that word of their presence reached us. That was the final straw. The synod split, collected their own Fae, and left, destroying the unity your ancestors created."

I wave that part away. "The division is the least of my concerns right now. If I have to deal with each individual House to win back their allegiance I will gladly do so. Ailie, for her faults, is taking care of her people. I trust Virosa to be doing the same. I still need to track down Autumn and Summer Houses, but I have suspicions about how well I will be received."

"I do not envy you," she murmurs.

"What about Spring House? How did you end up on the Isle of Skye?"

When she tells me, her story mirrors Ailie's, except for one horrifying detail.

"She ordered them off the island?" *I knew the lack of humans was suspicious.*

"Yes. I did not hear the exchange, but Ailie knew of the MacLeods from her family history. The clan holds some kind of pact with the Fae. One of Ailie's ancestors tricked the head of the clan into making a bargain with him, a bargain that, as you know, he had no choice but to keep. Ailie entered the castle and announced that we were taking over the island. She gave them two days to collect their things and evacuate to the mainland."

"And the humans let her?"

"What could they do? It is a pact with the Fae."

We both fall silent.

Still, I'm struggling to wrap my head around this whole scenario. Ailie may have a pact with the MacLeods, but surely that doesn't extend to the entire island. And what about the Scottish government? They just ceded control of a portion of their own land and a major tourism hub without a fight? Nothing makes sense, but the answers aren't here for me to find. The idea of so many Fae loitering around Ireland hits me strangely, too. An incursion of such magnitude should have drawn global attention, but my people seem to have passed through unseen.

"Fanta was right to warn you against her," Tupi continues, unaware of the direction of my thoughts. "Ailie is one of the most conniving Fae I have ever known. She will not release her hold on Spring House easily."

"When the time comes, she won't have the power to stop me," I promise.

Another moment passes, and Tupi once again nods toward the fire. "It is time."

"I know."

She resumes stroking Oberon's hair, her expression turning wistful. "I'll watch over him for you."

"Thank you."

# JESSICA GOEKEN

## Chapter Thirty-One

Outside, the half moon overhead casts the plateau in a gentle light. I see the two men I expected to, and a third I didn't.

"I thought Eredin Glas sent you away," I tell Danen as I come up behind him in the darkness. On impulse, I reach out and touch his shoulder, the hard muscle tense and unyielding under my hand.

He doesn't even startle. "My King gave me duties elsewhere."

"Then why are you here?" I edge around him so I can see his face. We're too far away from the light for me to see his expression properly, but I can tell that his eyes are fixed on Caspian. The intensity of his stare makes me think of when he came to see Oberon, like he's desperately trying to understand something, but he doesn't know what. "You feel something."

"Who is he?"

It's a different question than Eredin Glas asked. The King wanted to know who Caspian was to me. Danen wants to know who Caspian was to him.

"In the beginning, a rival. You feared his influence over me and the repercussions that could have for your House. Occasionally, allies. The two of you stood with me the first time I faced Eredin Glas. And in the end, enemies. Do you see that scar on his cheek? You gave that to him."

"I have no memory of that," Danen whispers, the sound echoing like a drumbeat through my body. I don't mention the vow Danen made to kill Caspian if he ever saw him again, so similar to Virosa's now that I think about it. He doesn't seem compelled to fulfill that vow, and I don't dare prompt him. Not when I still need

Caspian alive.

I step closer to Danen, my hand reaching for him again. I want to pull him to me, but this connection between us is too fragile for that, so I rest my hand on his arm instead. "You're searching, Danen. I can see it. You know that what the King has told you isn't true. I have the truth you're looking for, and I will gladly share it with you. My strongest desire for you is for you to know who you truly are. Because I know who you are, and you are so much more than the King has turned you into."

Danen finally wrenches his gaze from Caspian and settles his eyes on me. "Or it could be a trick."

"A trick?"

"The Fae cannot lie, Your Majesty. Everyone knows that. But neither do they tell the truth. You could be playing a Fae trick upon my memories, convincing me that I am someone I am not."

I will my pulse to steady. I can't take his words personally, and I certainly can't show how much they hurt me. "And what would be my purpose in doing that?"

"To make me forswear my oath to my King. To seduce me into choosing to follow you instead. It is no secret that you are in need of allies."

*Calm. Stay calm.* "Is that really what you feel is true?"

He hesitates long enough that I know he doesn't really believe what he's saying, but he's spared having to answer by the arrival of another shadow. "You are not where you are supposed to be, Danen."

"Hail, Jarild. As you say. I will return to my duties at once."

"See that you do."

Jarild keeps his peace while Danen vanishes yet again into the darkness. Then he turns to me. "I believe you have business to attend to also, Your Majesty."

I turn back to the fire. "Yes. Yes, I do."

"Are you hungry?" I ask Caspian a moment later as I remove his gag, then take a seat near him. I hold a skin of water to his lips and he drinks furiously. This close to him, I'm once again surrounded by his familiar smell of rain and fireflies, but this time it stirs no emotions in me. I just don't have the energy to feel anything for him anymore. I don't apologize for letting him stew for so long, and he doesn't ask about my absence.

Eredin Glas sits across the fire, a menacing presence that threatens bodily harm if Caspian makes the slightest false move.

Once again, I find myself questioning his motives. *Is he here because he actually cares? Or just protecting his investment?* By his own admission it's the latter, but with the way he looks at me sometimes I'm not entirely sure I believe him.

Caspian looks between the two of us, trying to read the relationship there. "I will admit, My Lady, I did not expect you to end up here."

"How did *you* end up here?" My question is neither friendly nor hostile. I'm neither his ally nor his captor. But I do need information, and he's the one who always has it.

He decides to ignore Eredin Glas and focus only on me. His gaze settles on mine, and the weight of history passes between us. He takes a deep breath. "Fomorian magic," he answers. "When you fled the fortress, I anticipated you would make for the tunnels. I did not anticipate you choosing to go downriver, and I was unprepared to track you along that route. You vanished with the water, and I did not know if you survived the fall.

"Then you reappeared in the Realm and caught the attention of the scouting party. I was able to pick up your trail there and I waited for the right opportunity. Today, I led the Fomorians to you so that your allies could kill them."

In the silence that follows I hear the crickets unnaturally loud in my ears. "You're speaking in absolutes." It's the only response I can think of. *What does he expect me to say? He just admitted to leading the Fomorians right to me!*

"I am telling you the truth. No more riddles from me, My Lady."

"What of Halasuwa's compulsion? The restraints he placed on you to keep you from divulging his secrets?"

"General Halasuwa is dead."

The words hit like a blow to my chest. *Dead?* He has to believe it to be true to state it so bluntly. Still, I struggle to wrap my mind around it. The General has been my bogeyman for a long time. My hunter. My captor. My … nemesis, if I could be so bold as to claim him as such. I had assumed the two of us would meet in battle again someday, and next time, I would prevail. To have him gone without warning echoes hollowly in my core.

Caspian isn't done talking, however. "I belong to you, My Lady. I always have. My actions may have been dictated by the curse of my birth, but I have never desired to betray the Fae. I have done so much that you do not know. I started a rebellion for you."

*The rumblings in the tunnels.* I think of Caspian at the goblin dinner, whispering in the ears of the same Fomorians who later kidnapped me. The memories feel so far away, and my mind is scrambling to catch up to all of the twists Caspian is throwing at me. "The Fomorian sect rising in opposition to Halasuwa? That was you?"

"As much as it could be. Per his edicts I could not act against him, but whispers and rumors in the right ears spread quickly enough. Baark's ability to sneak into the fortress under Halasuwa's nose showcased the General's weakness. Losing you was the spark the rebellion was waiting for."

"How did he die? When?" *I have to be sure.*

"A day ago. After losing you the second time. He knew you would return to the Realm, and he focused all of his energies there. Neglected his duties at home. Defied his advisors who counseled him to let you go. When you reappeared, he sent all available warriors to bring you back. Alive."

"Last time he came for me himself." The quip is out before I think about not saying it. It certainly doesn't match the somber mood of the conversation.

"The limp you gave him kept him grounded. Yet another sign of his weakness. With the slaughter of the garrison by the Wild Hunt, Halasuwa lost the last scraps of his credibility. But you know the nature of the General. He wasn't one to back down from a fight. When it became apparent that the spirit of rebellion was more than just whispers in the dark, he called Kharn out. Dared Kharn to challenge him in front of the remaining Fomorian army."

"And?" I prompt when Caspian falls silent. He needs to say the words before I can believe them.

"Kharn put a blade between his ribs. I saw his body go still with my own eyes."

I mull this over. Halasuwa's death is important for me to know, but ultimately it changes nothing. We already knew that some Fomorians were trying to kill me instead of just capturing me. Shifting that assumption to *all* Fomorians is easy enough. My course of action remains the same. Restore Fae magic. Retake the Realm. Restore the Fae.

I resist the urge to glance over at Eredin Glas. I

can't read his silence, but I also can't let it seem like I'm taking my cues from him. Caspian is, for better or worse, my subject, and mine to deal with as I see fit. Not his. "And what do you want from me? You have to understand by now why I can't trust you."

"I do understand. I hoped that by helping you escape I would have earned back some measure of your regard, but I understand why that is not the case. You have every right to kill me for my betrayal, and if you choose to do so I will accept your judgment. But before you decide, allow me one plea.

"My task, as you now know, was to convince you to willingly break Fae magic. Doing so would make the Fae easy prey for the invading Fomorian army."

"Get to the point," I nearly growl. I don't need the reminder of his failings, let alone my own.

I hear Eredin Glas shift his weight behind me, suddenly attentive to our conversation. Not that he wasn't listening before, but even he can tell that the conversation is about to shift dramatically.

"Did you ever wonder how you would have accomplished such a thing? And, once it was done, how it could be undone?" Caspian's voice turns urgent, almost desperate, as if afraid I'll sentence him to death before he gets all the words out.

"Speak plainly, Caspian."

"Of course, My Lady. I can tell you how to repair the broken Fae magic."

## Chapter Thirty-Two

"Eve? A word?" It sounds like a question, but it's not. I consider ignoring the King altogether and pressing Caspian for this one, final answer, but I doubt I would get the words out before Eredin Glas suddenly portaled me to Timbuktu. He won't let Caspian spill this information lightly, not when it's the same bait he's been dangling in front of me since he pulled me out of that cursed underground lake.

I hesitate long enough for it to appear to be my decision to follow Eredin Glas outside the flickering ring of firelight. Caspian says nothing as I go, making me wonder just how much of the dynamic between the King and myself he's picking up on. More than I would like him to, no doubt. He's always been able to read me better than anyone, even Danen.

Eredin Glas wastes no time. "You can't trust him."

"I know that. But that doesn't mean he isn't telling the truth." Can Caspian tell me how to fix Fae magic? I have no idea, but I have to at least hear him out. The possibility is too important to dismiss.

"He knows that's what you want more than anything, and he will hold it over you until you give him everything he wants."

"Like you?"

Eredin Glas says nothing.

"You made me a similar offer, and all it would cost me is everything I am. How are you any different than he is?"

He snarls, so low I barely hear it. I can't trust Caspian, but I can't trust Eredin Glas, either. Especially now, when his tentative grasp on my future appears to be slipping out of his hand.

"I have never betrayed you, Eve—"

"But you have lied to me. Manipulated me. Played on my emotions. You have yet to reveal how you would accomplish everything you've said you will, yet you expect me to blindly accept your assurances and leap forward into the unknown. If I follow Caspian, at least I know what I'm getting into."

I turn to go and Eredin Glas's hand closes around my arm. Hard. "Am I someone you want to make into an enemy? We've stood in that position before. I have healed you. Sheltered you. Spilled blood for you. Would you turn your back on my generosity only to later find a knife in it? Is he worth that?"

With a wrench, I escape the King's hold. "No, he isn't. But my people may be. They deserve for me to hear him out." And I walk away without looking back. Despite my harsh words, I have no intention of running off with Caspian and abandoning Hellequin Wood. But I can't commit to choosing the King, either.

Caspian's been paying attention. "Are you still your own, My Lady? Or do you take orders from the King of the Wild Hunt?"

*What harm would it do to tell him?* "Your offer is not the first of its kind I've received. Eredin Glas claims he can restore Fae magic."

Caspian raises his brows. "And his price?"

"The renunciation of my crown and the subjugation of my magic."

Caspian doesn't hesitate. "He would destroy you."

Neither do I. "But the Fae would be whole."

Contemplation steals across Caspian's expression. "I understand your dilemma. I know you, My Lady, better than most. You love your people with all your being. Their suffering pains you greatly. If you could end that suffering … no cost would be too high."

"You do know me. And here you sit, offering me the very thing I want most in the world. Since you know me so well, how do you expect me to respond to that?"

Caspian's voice is soft but sure as he answers. "Your heart yearns to believe me. You don't trust me, but deep down you wish you still could. And you are desperate for an answer that doesn't leave you stripped and vulnerable before one of the most powerful beings in existence. You will save the Fae, in whatever way you must, but you would prefer to return to them as their victorious Queen, not sink into oblivion."

He does know me. Caspian has succinctly put into words everything I'm feeling. He knows exactly the choice he's placing before me. "I will give you one chance to earn my trust back. Right this moment. Tell me how to fix it, Caspian. Lay it out for me now, step by step, and I will welcome you back with full forgiveness and open arms."

Caspian's eyes fly wide open and his mouth parts in surprise. He wasn't expecting that, which was kind of the point. It's a test, a chance to prove himself. One moment to decide his entire future.

"I will not tell you here, My Lady, not when that information would put us both in danger. Allow me to take you—"

My expression slams shut. I expected as much, but he was right. A very tiny part of me still had hope. I stand, and panic flits through his eyes.

"Wait—"

"You failed, Caspian. You gave a pretty speech, and I know you believed it, but your loyalty isn't to me. It's to yourself. It always has been."

"I am not lying, My Lady—"

"I'm done listening to you. If you decide to help me, *truly* help me, alert one of your guards. I'm going to bed."

Caspian protests as I walk off, but I tune him out. I can't do it anymore. It's late, and I'm exhausted. Not only exhausted, I'm *drained*. Drained of hope and spirit, which is far more taxing than the physical fatigue.

*And it's not over yet.* Because sitting on the bottom rung of my ladder is Eredin Glas. I stop a good ten feet away from him, keenly aware of how our last conversation ended.

He stands, and his imposing size seems somewhat diminished. "I care for you, Eve," he says, his voice softer than any other time I've heard it.

Adrenaline surges and I'm suddenly wide awake. "What?"

He steps closer and blows out a heavy breath. "I spoke roughly to you earlier, I know, but I want you to understand why. You think I only want your magic, and I have only myself to blame for that. I haven't told you how much I've come to care for you in these last days."

My mind spins. I don't know this Eredin Glas. "So, now that my acceptance of you is under threat, you're declaring your love for me?"

He chuckles. "Nothing so dramatic. The choice is your own, as it has always been. I don't think Caspian is the right choice, but I can see how you would favor him over me given the things you've learned about me. But it is important that you know these things, too. I enjoy your company. You make this plateau feel less lonely. I desire someone in my life that is not subservient to the vows of the Hunt, someone that can ride beside me as my equal. Given free reign, you are my equal. I would enjoy spending my eternity with you."

I step closer cautiously. "And you're telling me this hoping it'll convince me to trust you over Caspian?"

He sighs. "Always looking for the ulterior motive,

aren't you?"

"Because you usually have an ulterior motive." Confessing his affection for me is a desperate play, and I don't see how he thinks I'm going to fall for it.

"I don't expect you to believe me. I've given you plenty of reasons to think I'll tell you anything to get you to do what I want you to do. But, please do this. Think good and hard about the life you could have here. I've seen the joy in your eyes riding with the Hunt. Would it really be so bad to spend your days with me? As my partner, my confidante, my equal? Is there any part of you that can see yourself here?"

There is a part of me that can see myself here. I haven't kept that a secret. "It's late," is all I say, though.

"It is. Sleep well, Eve." He vanishes into the darkness without further comment, leaving me to make my befuddled way up into my palafito.

Tupi is asleep in my bed, one hand curled protectively around Oberon's as he slumbers on. *I need to prioritize you, too, Grandfather, but I don't know how.* I have a feeling all of my problems would be solved if he would just wake up and tell me everything he knows.

****

I wake with the first blush of sunlight. My bed has become strangely crowded, and it takes some maneuvering to get past Tupi and Oberon without waking up my friend. Outside, the grass is still dew-wet and while the tops of the trees shine in the morning sun, the depths still lie in shadow.

Caspian is still by the fire. Hands still tied. At least Eredin Glas gave him a blanket before leaving him to sleep in the dirt. I don't go near him, though. Just looking at him is enough to send my head spinning anew. *I need ... I need ... guidance, that's what I need.* But the

207

only people capable right now are the ones who have something to gain.

"Your Majesty?" Tupi's sleepy voice reaches my ears. She's standing behind me at the top of the ladder, looking ready to take on the world if I tell her to but that, if given the choice, she'd rather be sleeping instead.

"Go back to bed, Tupi."

"Do you need something, Your Majesty?"

*She always knows*. "Just someone to help me sort out this whole mess," I mutter.

She hears me. "Then go find him." I spin to meet her eyes and she gives me a knowing look. I bared my soul to her last night, and besides that, she knows the direction my heart lies. There's only one person she could be talking about.

I run. Down the plateau, through the woods, into the smattering of tents where most of the Hunt chooses to camp. The hunters grumble at being roused so early, but I harass them until someone tells me where I can find Danen. Turns out his nature hasn't changed much. He's already awake, doing stretches down on the beach.

For a moment I just watch him. My eyes follow the lines of his body, knowing every move he's going to make before he does it. We've been through this routine dozens of times.

"I can feel you."

"Run with me." I don't give him a chance to refuse. I take off at a jog down the beach, bare feet sinking deeply into the powdery sand.

He follows. Of course he does.

Danen and I haven't been alone for a long period of time together since the last time we ran. Since I failed to make him remember who he was. Eredin Glas buried those memories deep. Last time he left me lost and confused, but the encounters we've had since then make me certain that he feels the truth. He's been lost inside himself too long. It's time to get him back.

## Chapter Thirty-Three

"Where are we going, Your Majesty?" It took Danen half an hour to ask, half an hour in which we fled together with nothing but the sound of the waves in our ears.

"Far away," I answer. I've never been this far down the beach, but still I push myself harder. I want to put as much distance between myself and everything behind me as I can. My body protests, telling me I'm not strong enough for this, but I ignore it. This is where I need to be right now. This is where I *want* to be right now.

Finally, we run out of sand. The beach gradually slopes upward until the ground gives way to craggy rocks and shoreline cliffs. A lone limber pine tree stands watch at the top, holding out against the assault of the wind and the waves. It's beneath this tree I finally stop, leaning against the scratchy bark to catch my breath. The sun is still in the process of rising, weak light spilling down through the spindly branches.

Danen ducks beneath the boughs but keeps his distance. I can't read the look in his eyes. "What are we doing out here, Your Majesty?"

"Enough with the 'Your Majesty's. You never called me that, and it sounds wrong coming from your mouth." I face him head-on and catch a shocked expression crossing his face.

He recovers quickly. "What did I call you?"

"You've chosen to believe me? What if it's just a Fae trick?" I step closer. I can't help myself.

"Truth cannot be denied," he starts, then seems to lose his train of thought. "I still do not remember... I want to know..."

Every encounter we've had has been building to

this moment. All of his questions, his doubts, the King's lies, weigh down the air between us. But this time there's nobody around to interfere.

Danen's finally stopped running, and I'm the one left standing with the answers. "You called me 'Eve', because you held high standards and did not believe I was worthy of your respect. I fought hard to earn it, and you strove to teach me how to act like a true queen. When I did, you called me 'My Queen'." I take another step.

"My Queen," he whispers, testing the words. "What else?"

A shudder passes through me at hearing those words once again fall from his lips. "We ran together. In the mornings, like this, when the world was just waking. You showed me how to trust my body, to move with the same strength and grace you yourself possess. You taught me secrets of the Realm no one else bothered to tell me." I take another step, and our faces are only inches apart. "You were the one I ran to when I discovered the Fomorian in the catacombs. I stood by your side when you carried your father's body out of the ground and bore him home. And when I was taken by the enemy, you came for me, sword flashing, and severed Halasuwa's hand. He broke your neck for it." A single tear falls at the memory. I've replayed Danen's death so many times I'm not in danger of losing control, but recounting it to him still clogs my voice with emotion. But then, he didn't really die, did he?

Danen bumps his forehead into mine. "Tell me," he breathes.

My voice drops to a whisper. "A tornado came down from the sky. The Wild Hunt, watching over the battle. The King chose you. He took you away, and I didn't know if you were alive or dead." I utter a whimper. "I didn't think I'd ever see you again."

Time slows. Danen's vulnerable eyes bore into mine. My hand moves on its own, drawing the cord from beneath the neckline of my shirt. The quartz pops free, filling the breath of space between us with moonlight. *Moonlight shows things as they truly are.* It's the missing ingredient. On impulse, I lean forward and press my lips to his.

The kiss sends shockwaves through my body.

Danen gasps, shoving his mouth against mine so hard it hurts.

I don't break the kiss, though, willing it to be enough, calling Danen, *my* Danen, back to me. From behind my eyelids, I can see the moonlight flare up, shining bright as the noonday sun here in our little alcove by the sea.

Danen abruptly breaks the kiss, crashing to the ground and wrapping his arms around his head. A pained groan escapes him, and I drop down beside him. At the slightest touch, he collapses into me, burrowing his face into my neck and crushing my body with his strong white arms. He groans again like a wounded animal, heaving and panting against me. After a moment, his body goes still and I freeze, scared to disturb him in this state. *What did I do to him?*

"My Queen," he rasps, his voice raw and filled with anguish. He raises his head and once again rests his forehead against mine. "My Queen, I've been so lost."

"Danen?" I can barely get the name out. "Is it really you?"

"It is me, My Queen. Somehow you have dragged me out of the darkness and back into the light." Then he's kissing me again, lightly and hesitantly.

I kiss him back, tears streaming down my face, hands clasped against his cheeks. "I've missed you so," I whisper against his lips.

Danen ends the kiss again, pulling back and studying my face, tucking a stray strand of hair behind my ear. "I have missed you, My Queen. These last months have been … dim. Trying to remember them now feels like looking through water." His eyes rake over me, assessing me, noting the exhaustion, the weight loss, and the weakness. He frowns.

"Do you know where we are?" I ask him.

"I have knowledge," he answers, eyes once again locking with mine. "I know that I have pledged myself to the Wild Hunt. My oaths bind me, My Queen, regardless of the person I was before. Regardless of my desires now."

"I know. But you are alive, and that is infinitely better than the alternative. I can handle Eredin Glas. I will find a way to release you from his hold. I will wrench you out of his hand if I must."

"In time. There are more pressing matters. Tell me, how did you do this? Do you have magic still?"

"No magic of my own, but the moon still holds sway. It cannot be tricked and does not abide hidden things." I hold up the quartz, which has dimmed now that its task is complete.

Danen fingers the rock. "Where did you get this?" *Deep breath.* "Caspian gave it to me."

"He is here, isn't he?"

"He is."

Danen's eyes harden.

"He is under the protection of the King of the Wild Hunt, and you cannot touch him. Besides, he claims he can help me to restore Fae magic."

He scowls. "And you believe him?"

"I believe he believes what he says. He may even know how to do it, but he refuses to tell me how, and I refuse to blindly trust him again. We are at an impasse, and in entertaining him I have ostracized Eredin Glas."

Danen closes his eyes and rubs his temples. "Tell

me everything I've missed."

I do. Just like with Tupi, I leave nothing out. Not even my encounter with Virosa and the curse she placed upon me. I've never been able to keep things from Danen, but more than that, I don't want to. He's my right hand, my confidante, my closest adviser. My friend.

The tale takes a long time to tell, but Danen listens with rapt attention, occasionally interrupting to ask for clarification on some detail. When I tell him of Eredin Glas's proposal storm clouds gather in his eyes, and if he still had magic, I know we'd be fighting off frostbite. After I finish, he sits in silence, processing the suffocating amount of information I just inundated him with.

"Oberon," he mumbles, drumming his fingers against his legs. "That tricky old bastard. He is the key to all of this."

"How so?"

"He has magic. And he knew we would lose it, so he hid in your secret room to shield himself from its loss. He was supposed to evacuate with the rest of the elderly Fae, but I'm not surprised he refused to go. What does surprise me is that Morgan let him."

"If he set his mind against her, she would not be able to change it. Do you know what happened to her?"

"I do not. My focus was on the battle. The synod oversaw the evacuation. But Morgan cared for Oberon for many years, and she was an experienced witch even when she still walked the human world. If anyone knows how to wake him, it would be her."

"And if Oberon wakes, and is able to help me, then I can bypass both Caspian and Eredin Glas entirely."

Danen grins. "Precisely."

I smile wide to match him. "Your insight is always exactly what I need." My smile fades quickly, though. "Eredin Glas is not going to be pleased."

## Chapter Thirty-Four

Eredin Glas knows.

"Did you think I would not know when magic is being done in my own home?" His voice is low and dangerous, and distant thunder rumbles across the sky. The plateau is deserted. Eredin Glas cleared it of witnesses the moment we returned. "This Wood is a part of me. Nothing happens here that I don't know about."

The little girl in me wants to cower in the face of his rage, but I shove that part aside and stand toe-to-toe with the King. "It wasn't a secret," I answer, keeping my own voice calm but edged with authority. "Using Danen against me was a cruel game, so I decided not to play anymore."

"Your pet belongs to me now, Eve, and I will do with him as I will. If I choose to obliterate his identity forever there is nothing either you or he could do to stop me. I hold his very life in my hands."

I can feel Danen simmering behind me, but he holds his tongue. I didn't have to ask him to let me deal with Eredin Glas alone. He, more than almost any other, knows how these political games are played. Any interference from him will destroy the image of power I'm trying to project.

I step closer and lean in to Eredin Glas. "If you deal with your hunters so capriciously, how long do you expect the rest to stay loyal? Loyalty is what you value them for, yes?"

The loyalty angle strikes a chord. I see it in his eyes. I press further. "Is Danen really worth losing everything?" I ask him quietly. "If I am willing to take his side over yours without regard to the cost, are you willing to do the same?" The implication is clear. If he forces his will upon Danen, he loses me. I won't say the words, though. I can't. I can't commit to that course of action until I'm certain I no longer need Eredin Glas on my side.

Thankfully, he doesn't press for me to say it. Complacency or oversight I don't know, but either way, he backs down. For now. I know him too well, though. The issue is far from forgotten. Danen and I will both pay.

Eredin Glas growls. "You have no magic. This I know. How did you accomplish such a task?"

I tug out the quartz. I glossed over the details of my escape when I recounted the story to him, choosing at the time to keep the moonlight a secret. I have to give him something now, though. He can't leave this confrontation empty-handed. His pride won't allow it.

"I saw you wearing this in the Realm. What is it?"

"Clear quartz containing light from the full moon."

Eredin Glas whistles. "The moon reveals the true nature of things. Clever. Where did you come by such a trinket?"

I take a step back, now that the aggression portion of this discussion is over. "Caspian gave it to me."

"Caspian," he hisses. "He is suddenly everywhere. If you are finished with the traitor, I will gladly escort him out of this place." The threat in Eredin Glas's words is obvious. I'd better be done with Caspian, because either way he has worn out his welcome.

"Caspian stays," I answer, waving off Eredin Glas's words. "Until the matter of Fae magic is resolved. 'The traitor' claims he can fix it, but will not tell me even with a promise to restore his position in my counsel."

"A dangerous promise."

"Yet a well-placed one. I will put the same

question to you, oh King, for you have made the same claim. How would you restore Fae magic?"

A knowing look comes into the King's eyes. "Do you think to circumvent me and restore your people by some other means? That is not something I will allow to happen. Caspian cannot help you, despite his deceptive claims. Your Danen, talented though he is, cannot help you. Only I can help you, but I am not so foolish as to part with the very knowledge you seek. You know how to get this answer, Eve. Join with me. Become my queen, and I will fulfill every promise I have made to you."

"Then I can trust you no more than I can trust Caspian," I assert, raising an eyebrow.

For the briefest second, a glimmer of hurt flashes in his eyes and I'm reminded of his words from last night. His admission that he cares for me. In this moment, I believe those words were true. Clumsy as they may have been coming out, and the obvious timing issue aside, I do believe he has come to care about me to some degree. He doesn't want just anyone at his side. He wants *me*. And in different circumstances I could be happy with that life. It would be a marvelous, carefree adventure. But that isn't the life that I want.

Eredin Glas's vulnerability passes as quickly as it came, and I sense with it goes any chance of this ending in goodwill between us. I can't help feeling we've passed the point of no return, even though I haven't officially made my mind up yet. A heaviness settles in my heart and stays there.

The King doesn't take the rejection well. His anger is a palpable thing, and it takes visible effort for him to rein that storm in. Flying off the handle at me won't help his cause, and he fights that urge for only a moment before turning on his heel and stalking away.

I take a deep breath and let it out slowly.

"Are you all right?" Danen asks now that we're alone.

"That could have gone better," I hedge. In truth, I'm not completely all right. Eredin Glas is not a bridge I wanted to burn just yet, especially since my victory is so uncertain and I may still have to come crawling back later. The worst thing that could happen is him pulling out completely, leaving me alone and extinguishing my last hope of saving my people. "Oberon better be able to fix this, or I'm in a world of trouble with the King."

"What do you want to do?" He knows what I want to do, but I appreciate the submissive gesture.

"I want to find Morgan Le Fey. I need to know if she can help Oberon before things between Eredin Glas and me come to a head. His patience had already worn thin before Caspian crashed into his world, and now all of his carefully laid plans are under threat. I can't forestall him much longer."

"I can't help you, you know that, right?"

"I know." I give Danen a tender smile. "You don't serve me anymore, and I doubt Eredin Glas will grant you leave to escort me on a mission to subvert him." Despite the lightness of the comment, the seriousness of the situation is not lost on me. "Danen?"

"My Queen?"

"What was it like?"

He pauses so long I think he's not going to answer. When he does, a certain vulnerability I've only seen on rare occasions peeks through. "Quiet. Not in the way you'd expect, since you've seen the Hunt in action. But the sense of looming threat, the pressure to keep everyone alive, they were quiet. There was only the Hunt. Exciting. Carefree." He shrugs. "Fun."

I get it. I've felt it.

"I love him," he admits. "As much as a subject

can love a king. He is a good king. I agreed to join him to get myself back to you, but once you were gone … I was happy here."

"I'm happy here, too." Danen's gaze snaps to mine. "It sneaks up on me in the little moments. Waking under the sky. Sitting by the fire. Riding with the hounds."

"The call of the Hunt."

"The call of the Hunt." No more needs to be said. There's a reason Caspian warned me of the hounds the first time I heard them. He knew I would ache to join them. But he underestimated my ability to pull myself back.

"Is there someone who can go with you? To find Morgan?"

Danen's question jars me back to the present problem. He's no longer looking at me, but he doesn't have to be for me to sense his need to change the subject. His complicated feelings about his time with the Wild Hunt are his own. As are mine. I will never ask him for them again.

"Maybe." I would love to take Lella, because I know she would be fierce and I would be safe. But she is loyal to the King, and taking her would present the same problem as taking Danen. I can't take any of the hunters. And I refuse to take Caspian, which leaves me only one option. "Tupi will go if I ask her, but that would leave Oberon unprotected. With Eredin Glas's temper, I'm afraid he's no longer safe here."

"I won't let anything happen to your Grandfather." Danen tries to offer reassurance, but I'm already shaking my head.

"You can't promise that."

"I already did." Danen tilts my chin back so I'm looking into his cold, black eyes. They are a sight so familiar, yet slightly off without the chill of his Winter magic radiating off his skin.

"And when Eredin Glas orders you to stand down? What will happen then?"

"Hurry back and we won't have to find out." Without hesitation, Danen presses his lips lightly against mine. "You gave me myself back, My Queen. Whatever happens, I will face it in full possession of my faculties. No greater gift has ever been given. No matter his orders, my heart will always choose you."

## Chapter Thirty-Five

*Hurry back.*

Danen's words echo in my head as I go hunting for Tupi. Eredin Glas chased her off the plateau along with everyone else, and I'm not quite sure where to find her. My eyes search, but Danen is the one occupying my thoughts.

Danen and I never got around to confessing our feelings for each other. I had feelings, at least. Many times, I thought he did, too, but we were never each other's priority. The Realm came first. And the nature of those feelings? I can't be sure it was love.

Tension, sure. Connection, definitely. And a single kiss, which was disrupted when he tasted Caspian on my lips. Our bond was unquestionable. Something that can only be forged by facing down an invasion, desperation to save our people, and complete trust in one another. Any notions of romance took a necessary backseat.

And now? What do I feel for Danen now? I have no idea, and once again, it's not the time to figure it out. I still have people to save. But that was one heck of a kiss...

"Tupi?" I find my friend down at the waterfall, splashing the cool water up over her face and neck. She looks peaceful in a way I've rarely seen. Her first impulse, always, is to see to my needs first. I don't get to see her taking care of herself.

"Yes, Your Majesty?" She instantly rights herself, professionalism and service falling into place.

"How is Oberon?"

Her voice drops. "He sleeps, Your Majesty. All I can do for him is be near."

*And I'm going to take her away.* "I'm leaving for a bit, and I could use your help. Will you come with me?"

"Anything you need, Your Majesty." Her words are fervent, but with the slightest hesitation.

"I worry for Oberon as well," I say, trying to ease her concern. I step closer so I can lower my voice. Who knows how much this island hears. "It is for Oberon that I must go. I seek Oberon's caretaker, Morgan Le Fey. I hope she will have some insight into how he can be revived."

The sudden tension in Tupi's shoulder relaxes. "That is well. I am not enough to care for him, not without my magic." Her eyes widen as she realizes what she just said. "Your Majesty, I did not mean to imply... It's just, I—"

"It's all right, Tupi. I know the situation. Intimately." I give her a tender smile. "So, will you come with me?"

She smiles back. "I will."

We don't return to the plateau. I lead Tupi through the tangled woods until we find the meadow where the Hunt's mounts graze. Morhogg is nowhere in sight, but that doesn't necessarily mean the King has left Hellequin Wood. I keep my eyes peeled as I approach Gent.

"Hey, boy," I coo as I wave a handful of dandelions under his nose. "You up for another adventure with me?"

He lips at the flowers and pushes his head into my chest.

"I'll take that as a yes."

He appears to be fully recovered from being knocked out of the air by Caspian. More than recovered. He dances when I mount him, eager to be off.

I pull Tupi up behind me and Gent takes off at a

run before she even settles. The trees whip by in a blur until he suddenly launches into the sky. For the next several seconds, he's moving too fast for me to get my bearings. We're still in Hellequin Wood, or rather, above it, but in his haste to burn off energy Gent isn't letting me get a good look at anything.

"Is this normal?" Tupi asks from behind me, wrapping her arms around my belly and squeezing way too hard.

"He'll settle," I assure her with a wince, hoping it's true.

It is. After his initial burst of manic energy, Gent finally calms to a steady pace. He's still racing, but he's stable enough to let me see the ground stretching out below me. And stretch it does. I've seen Hellequin Wood from the air before, but I'm usually too tired or anxious to pay much attention. I've never noticed how incredibly massive the island is. I can only see the slightest twinkling of blue water on the far side.

Even riding with the Hunt through the wilds only showed me a small percentage of explorable land. My body tingles with excitement at the idea of everything to be discovered down there, but my mind stays firmly fixed on the task at hand.

"Do you know where to find Autumn House?" I ask Tupi. "We'll start looking for Morgan there."

"I do not know for sure, but Ailie believed them to be located in a region called the Pacific Northwest. She has been in communication with Dermot and Grielle, but they have not divulged their exact location."

"Gent?" I call out to the horse. His ears prick back. "Are you able to find Autumn House of the Fae in the human world?"

In response, his muscles bunch beneath me. A portal flashes in front of us and we go soaring through.

The other side meets us quickly, blazing afternoon sun reflecting brilliantly off the ribbon of water stretching out below us. Gent emerges right above the treetops, his hooves sending cascades of leaves and pine needles to the ground below.

"Are we here?" Tupi asks into my ear as Gent slows.

"I don't know," I answer honestly. I don't even know where *here* is. The scenery is gorgeous, dense pine forests lining the river as far as I can see in either direction. The roar of a waterfall reaches my ears, but I can't see it. And the colors. Flaming red, orange, and yellow interspersed among the stalwart pines sings of Autumn House. A chill in the air contradicts the heat from the sun. If we're really in the Pacific Northwest, then autumn has indeed come, helping me place just how long I was trapped in the Fomorian fortress. If autumn is in full swing, then I was captive nearly a year and my birthday has already passed. I'm seventeen years old.

I shake off the realization and sharpen my focus to the present moment.

Gent slows to a trot, then to a walk, landing along the bank of the river and veering off into the trees. His feet follow a barely visible game trail, and I have to trust that he knows where he's taking us. We pass silently through the forest, which is anything but silent around us. Birds rustle and squirrels chatter in the branches overhead, while ground critters scurry through the fallen leaves and yap at each other. Winter preparation is happening all around us as if we aren't even here.

"The animals are familiar with the presence of Fae." Tupi's observation sharpens my focus. "From what little I've seen of humans, the wild creatures are not comfortable in their presence."

*Is that what's going on? Maybe Autumn House is here.*

Twenty minutes we pass through the trees until finally stopping before a magnificent douglas fir. The fir tree partially obscures a broken crevice in a cliff face that appears seemingly out of nowhere. A tingle rushes over my whole body. *They're here.* I can't explain it, but I can feel it. The feeling is so reminiscent of my magic that for a brief second I think it's spontaneously returned. I reach for it impulsively, just like when Caspian taught me how to find it, and leave myself gasping instead.

"Are you all right, Your Majesty?" Tupi asks with concern.

"Not really." I do my best to compose my features. "Let's see if anyone is home."

I release Gent to graze and approach the crevice. "Hello?" I call into the depths.

"You are not wanted here." The answer comes not from within the crevice, but from above. The branches of the douglas fir shake as a weight moves through them, and then a Fae drops to land lightly on the ground in front of us.

"Master Dermot." The red hair and beard are easy to recognize, especially coupled with the permanent scowl etched across his face.

"Your Majesty." My formal title has no sincerity behind it. With a rush, I realize just how much I don't want to do this dance again. My reunions with Winter and Spring Houses still leave a bitter taste in my mouth, and time is pressing.

"I'm going to speak plainly, Master Dermot, and I hope you will appreciate that. I know my own failings, and I understand the current state and mindset of my people. I am not here to convince you of anything, and I understand that my presence is neither needed nor wanted. The big issues can wait for future discussion, but I am on an errand of utmost importance. I seek the human witch Morgan Le Fey. Do you know her whereabouts?"

My frankness takes Dermot by surprise. His expression doesn't change, but I see it regardless. "You come here uninvited and demand this information of me?"

"It is not a demand, but a request I hope you will honor." In the next breath, I make a hasty and possibly stupid decision. "I will share a piece of information with you, and I hope you will understand the sensitive nature and will choose not to share it further." Dermot eyes me but doesn't interrupt. "Oberon lives. More than that, he has magic."

Dermot's mouth drops open. "How can this be?"

"I do not know. Oberon sleeps unnaturally, and I seek Morgan Le Fey to wake him."

Dermot doesn't question my need of Morgan. While she has never possessed Fae magic, as a human her magical proficiency was legendary, and she has walked the Realm of the Fae longer than most who now live. His mouth turns downward, though, and sorrow fills his eyes. "I cannot tell you where to find Morgan Le Fey, for I do not know where she is."

My heart sinks, but I can't give up yet. "Did she not evacuate with Autumn House?"

"So far as I know she did. But Morgan is human and is not bound by the rules of the Fae. She may not have chosen to continue with Autumn House once she was returned to the land of her birth."

"Can we look?" I don't bother to hide the hope in my voice.

He gestures at the trees around us. "You are standing in the Columbia River Gorge, which encompasses hundreds of thousands of square miles. Autumn House has spread throughout the Gorge and beyond, blending in to more than a dozen national parks and forests in Oregon and Washington states. You may look, but you will not find her."

# JESSICA GOEKEN

## Chapter Thirty-Six

My stomach drops into my shoes. "But … how? How is Autumn House spread so thin? Surely you know that what remains of the Fomorian army continues to hunt Fae?"

Dermot shrugs, a very human gesture. "Autumn … endures. Like our season, my people are isolated by nature, shedding our outer layers and patiently waiting for winter to come. The Fae people are in a time of winter, and Autumn House has chosen to hunker down and wait for the thaw."

I raise my eyebrows. "Are you suggesting that Autumn House is … hibernating?"

"In a sense. You yourself felt our power of hibernation. We no longer possess that magic, but our nature remains unchanged. We have spread throughout this land, blending in and awaiting the next stage of our existence."

"So Morgan could be anywhere in the surrounding several million acres?"

"If she even still remains with Autumn House."

That's it, then. My last hope of reviving Oberon. My last chance to restore Fae magic.

Dermot isn't done, though. The eyes he turns to mine are solemn. "Oberon holds my utmost respect. I will keep his secrets, and should he wake, Autumn House will perform any task he requires of us." Then he says something I don't expect. "Autumn House waits, Your Majesty. Give us something worth waiting for, and we will stand behind you once again."

The sudden oath sends my emotions roiling, but I don't let any of them show on my face. "Thank you for your candor." Without another word Tupi and I return to

Gent, much more dejected than we arrived not long ago.

"Where do we look next, Your Majesty?" Tupi's small voice still holds onto hope, despite Dermot's words.

"I don't know." I swing myself up onto Gent's back and scratch behind his ears. "We can't just wander through the woods calling her name."

*Think! Where would she go?*

I don't have an answer. I didn't know Morgan that well on a personal level. I always knew I could find her with Oberon, but that was when she was at court in Emain Ablach. Besides her time shepherding the collection of humans in the Realm known as The Blessed, I have no idea how she filled her days.

A rustle in the brush ahead of us sends Tupi squeaking into the air. Her pixie wings hold her just out of range as a creature emerges into the open. Gent doesn't react, which convinces me such a strange-looking creature is not a threat, despite the oversized eyes and pointed ears. It also only comes up to Gent's knee. Whatever it is, it certainly doesn't belong in this world.

"Your Majesty?" the creature pants. Before I can even answer, it falls prostrate on the ground, arms outstretched in front of it in a gesture of obeisance. Its back continues to pulse as it gasps and wheezes.

"Rise. What is your name?"

The creature doesn't rise, but mumbles its name from the ground. "Knippit, Your Majesty."

Tupi lands beside Gent, her alarm quickly dissipating. "He is a brownie, Your Majesty. They often enter themselves into the service of Fae in leadership positions."

"Do you serve Master Dermot?" I ask the brownie, who still lies with his face on the ground.

"No, Your Majesty. I serve Master Feufollet. My

master witnessed your passing and sent me to intercept you before you were once again lost."

*Feufollet?* My mind fills with the image of my history instructor, so old and fat he had essentially melded with his own chair. "Master Feufollet is in the vicinity?"

"He waits only a mile downriver, Your Majesty. I ran as fast as I could to catch you."

"Then lead me to him."

The brownie doesn't hesitate. He scrambles to his feet and disappears back into the brush without bothering to dust himself off. He doesn't go far, though. Once Gent clears the undergrowth and emerges once again by the river, Knippit is waiting for us. He's clutching his side as if in pain, but straightens once I notice him.

"Should I invite him to ride with us?" I ask Tupi. "He seems to be in pain, and is exhausted at the least."

She shakes her head no. "He would refuse. His pride will not allow him to be borne when he is capable of walking."

And so we follow Knippit downriver, shoving our way through where we can and flying over where we can't. Gent doesn't seem to mind the rough terrain, although he consistently balks at the slow pace.

Knippit leads us as best he can, choosing the most passable routes.

Finally, Knippit turns inward at some landmark only he knows. He leads us to a grove of ponderosa pine trees growing so close together as to be nearly indecipherable from one another. The space inside is dim and gloomy even with the sun burning brightly outside.

"Master Feufollet." Knippit grovels like I've never seen, bowing his head low as he ducks into the grove. "I have returned with Her Majesty, Queen Eve of the Fae."

"Show her in," a familiar voice rumbles.

Once inside the grove, my eyes take a moment to adjust to the dim light. Once they do it still takes a few seconds for me to find my instructor on his cushion of moss and needles. His position is no different than in the classroom, though the accommodations lack the same comfort.

"Master Feufollet. It is a pleasure to see you again." And it is. Despite the monotony of his lectures, I learned much at his hand, and he never made me feel as though I didn't belong. At this point, finding any Fae I once knew alive is a pleasure.

"Your Majesty," his deep voice rumbles. "I am pleased to see you as well. I will not waste your time, for I surmise your errand requires haste. Tell me what you seek from Autumn House, and I will provide what aid I can."

It takes me a minute to answer as my mind races, trying to figure out how much he knows, and how he knows it. Finally, I decide he's right about not wasting time so I come right out and ask. "What do you know, Master?"

In response, he unravels one massive hand, revealing a small rectangular piece of plastic. I gape at it. "A cell phone?"

"Indeed. We live in strange times, Your Majesty. I have a contact in Spring House who has kept me abreast of your situation and your plans to restore Fae magic. If you are here, then you are still searching and require assistance."

"Fanta?" She's the only one besides Ailie who would know that information.

He doesn't confirm. He doesn't have to. "How may I be of assistance, Your Majesty?"

"I seek Morgan Le Fey."

"Ahh." He folds his hands and rests them on his

protruding belly. The dappled coloring of his skin blends them in until I can no longer discern their outline. "Then you have recovered Oberon."

"Indeed."

"A powerful piece to have back on the board."

"That is my hope."

"Master Dermot does not know where she is." It isn't a question.

"He does not."

Feufollet considers me. "Morgan Le Fey cannot be found in this world. She was here, but she has long since returned to the Realm of the Fae."

"That isn't possible," I say before I think it through. It's already been well established that the borders of the Realm no longer hold. Who can say what is possible and what is not?

"And yet, that is where you will find her. She seeks her own answers for questions she does not share, but I suspect she has returned to her own quarters in Autumn House. Perhaps she believes there are still secrets there the enemy failed to unearth."

Feufollet falls silent and I sense that he's said everything he's going to. Which is a lot. "Thank you, Master Feufollet, for your continued guidance."

He waves my thanks away. "It was my lot to instruct you in Fae history. Now that we are living our history, I will not stand in ignorance."

We make our exit, Knippit having vanished once his task was complete. As we emerge back into the sunshine, I hear his squeaky voice once more, asking Feufollet if he requires any further service. We're out of earshot before I hear my instructor's reply.

Gent is, once again, waiting right where I left him. He's almost as perfect a mount as Keshi. "Tupi? Do you know what happened to the quilin?"

"I do not, Your Majesty. They were released before the evacuation, but I do not know if they were still in the Realm when it fell."

*If the Fomorians found them, they would have killed them all. If they weren't in the Realm, where else would they have gone?*

Tupi breaks into my thoughts as we mount. "Can we really return to the Realm?" She asks me in quiet voice.

"We can. We can go anywhere we wish. But I must warn you, you will not like what you see."

## Chapter Thirty-Seven

Gent finds the Realm easily. Despite my warning to Tupi, I'm not prepared to see the Realm again, either. She sucks in a ragged breath as I shake my head violently to clear the fog threatening to overtake me. *You have a job to do*, I remind myself. *Do it, and you can fix this.*

I haven't allowed myself to think much about the Realm itself. This quest to restore Fae magic has been all about my people. I haven't been able to think about what happens next. But Titania was strong enough to summon the island of Emain Ablach out of the depths of the lake and crafted the palace with her magic. Might I be able to restore the Realm itself? Even if I'm not strong enough, perhaps the combined strength of the Fae could pull it off. I don't voice these hopes to Tupi, though. I keep them buried deep inside where they belong. *One impossible task at a time.*

During my brief time in the Realm, I never made it to the Autumn Citadel. Any of the citadels. In fact, my only time in Autumn Territory at all was combating the natural disasters spawned by my own indecision and lack of faith in myself. Still, I know the general direction, and between Gent and Tupi we soon find ourselves flying over what used to be Autumn Territory. Not that we could tell by looking, since the ground is covered in the same ash and detritus that covers the rest of the Realm.

*The glade of the queens survived,* I remind myself. Maybe something survived here as well.

Darkness falls quickly, due to the lateness of the hour and the ash still clogging the sky.

"What do we do now?" Tupi asks.

"Just wait," I whisper. "Keep us steady," I add to Gent, who doesn't need the direction. My eyes strain against the darkness, searching for something, anything…

"There," I point out sometime later, though neither of us can see my outstretched arm. "A fire."

"Morgan?"

"Let's find out."

I'm not weaponless. Since my last trip to the Realm and Eredin Glas's warning about the Fomorians, I've kept a blade on me at all times. I didn't ask when it appeared by the ladder of my palafito, just like everything else I've been mysteriously gifted. It isn't a large one, but I have to hope it will be enough if the situation calls for it.

Gent soundlessly circles the fire, slowly dropping lower as we try to see who lit it.

Before we can get a visual, however, a rough voice reaches our ears speaking a language I'm all too familiar with.

"Fomorians. Pull back."

Gent glides back into the sky and we land a safe distance away. "We have to be very careful," I say to Tupi. "Fomorians can track Fae with their magic. If they notice us here, they will come for us, and they will kill us."

I can feel her eyes even through the darkness. "The wise choice would seem to be to leave the area, but you are not unwise, Your Majesty. You have some plan. Otherwise we would not remain this close to danger."

"I have the beginnings of a plan. But I do not know how to work it."

"Tell me."

"With their magic, the Fomorians are capable of tracking Morgan Le Fey. She may even be the reason they are here, if they have become aware of her presence. If we could capture one and force it to do our bidding, it could lead us to her, even in this darkness."

"But we are not strong enough to overcome Fomorians, Your Majesty."

"Hence my hesitation." I mentally review our assets. My blade, inexpertly wielded. My moonlight quartz on its chain around my neck. Tupi's wings. Gent, battle-trained and our only hope of escape.

"How strong are your wings?" I ask Tupi.

"Umm…"

"Strong enough to lift a Fomorian?"

Her voice goes up a pitch. "Maybe?"

I lay out the thoughts in my head, and Tupi helps me refine them until we have a semi-sensible plan. And if it all goes wrong, Gent will snatch us away from here. It's as good as we're going to get without calling in backup in the form of the Hunt, and I want to keep Eredin Glas as far away from this as possible. I don't flatter myself in thinking that I'm pulling a fast one on him. He knows where I am. And if I don't sort this out quickly, he'll come looking for the reasons I'm here.

My palms are slick with sweat as Tupi takes to the air. The soft hum of her wings is barely noticeable, but I have to trust that she'll keep pace. Our timing has to be perfect or this isn't going to work.

Gent needs no encouragement to barrel toward the Fomorian campfire. As a mount of the Hunt, he's bred for this. It's a small fire, so hopefully the scouting party is small as well.

My pulse races as the fire draws closer. Gent's hooves crash soundlessly against the thick ash and I stop breathing altogether. My hand clenches the chain around my neck, ready. Before I know it, we're upon the fire. Gent looses a shrill whinny and leaps the fire, muscles bunching powerfully beneath me. At the same time, I unleash the quartz. Light fills the space, sending the startled Fomorians cowering away from the sudden harshness. I see three Fomorians in the brief seconds Gent is airborne. Then he crashes back to the ground and I stifle the moonlight, plunging the world into darkness once again.

As the light vanishes, a guttural scream rings out behind us and I know Tupi has found her mark. I have to trust that she's able to handle the scout until I can get there to help her. The Fomorians we left behind scramble to respond as Gent leaps back into the air. By the time they register what's happened we'll be too far away to catch.

The campfire is still a prick in the distance when we catch up to Tupi. I have to risk the moonlight again; otherwise, we'll never find each other in this blackness. Our time on the ground will be short, though. Short enough to keep us ahead of pursuit.

Tupi is struggling. The weight of the Fomorian drags her down, made all the worse by his flailing and thrashing. When she sees the light, she sighs in relief and lets him go.

I watch the Fomorian drop. I would love to skip seeing this part, but I can't do that. This is my doing, and I will see what I've brought to pass. It must be a hundred feet at least. Not high enough to kill him, not with the natural armor his horns and hide provide, but the snap of his legs is audible even up here.

I send Gent to the ground without delay.

The Fomorian is screaming, a beacon even the densest hunter could follow. From the looks of him more than his legs are broken. His left arm lays awkwardly at his side and blood dribbles from his nostrils.

I leap off of Gent and stuff the strip I tore off my shirt into his mouth, muffling the noise and earning a bite for my troubles. I shake my hand as Tupi lands, visibly shaking and looking nauseated.

"Are you all right?" I ask her, my eyes searching for obvious injury.

"I am unharmed." The subtext is clear: *But I am not all right*.

Neither am I, but I don't have the luxury of admitting that. Not at the moment, at least. I approach the Fomorian once again, who despite his pain tries to swipe at me anyway. Hate fills his eyes as recognition strikes. Even if he doesn't know me personally, my golden skin and silver hair couldn't belong to anyone else.

"You know who I am." It isn't a question. "You see what I'm capable of, even without my magic. There is something I want from you. Give it to me, and your suffering will end."

He doesn't move, just locks eyes with me and sends every evil thought he can think of through that gaze.

"Stalling won't help. Your comrades won't reach us. If you don't answer now, I'm going to load you up on my horse and fly you out of here, somewhere a bit more … private." I fill my words with implication and let his imagination do the rest. "I can only imagine the pain such a maneuver will cause. Will you speak with me?"

He still hates me, but after a moment he nods.

I draw my blade, more a knife than a sword and roughly the length of my forearm, and approach. "I'm going to remove your gag. Scream or attack, either one, and you'll bleed."

I tug the gag out and the Fomorian spits on the ground. "What do you want?" he growls, pain lacing every syllable.

It doesn't matter how much information I reveal. "I seek a human hiding in this territory. I cannot find her on my own, and I wish for you to assist me."

The Fomorian's expression remains guarded, but

his eyes flicker away from mine.

"You know of whom I seek." Again, not a question. Still, he nods in affirmation. "You seek her, too." Another nod. "How fortuitous, then."

"What do you want with Morgan Le Fey?"

"Our time here runs short, so I will ask this once. Will you track her for me?"

"No," he spits, then bursts into cackling laughter.

I shove the gag back in so far he chokes. He gasps when I seize his useless arm and wrench it behind him, tying it to the other with yet another piece of cloth. At this rate, I'll be returning to Hellequin Wood topless. A whistle brings Gent in close, and he lays down at my request. Tupi and I drag the Fomorian across Gent's back, doing our best to ignore his moans and muffled screams.

"Follow close enough to hear us." I climb up behind the Fomorian. "We can't risk the light."

"Where are we going?"

I don't like the things I hear in her voice, but I'll have to address them later, when this whole episode is behind us and we're once again on safe ground.

"Somewhere far from here, where I can get him to give me the answers I need."

## Chapter Thirty-Eight

Gent has no problem carrying the weight of the Fomorian, and over the next hour he carries us deep into what used to be Autumn Territory. In all that time we see no further indication of either campfires or Fomorian activity. My stomach churns over what just happened, and what else I may have to do before this night is over. I've killed before, but this is something different. Something … inhuman.

I finally decide we've traveled far enough when I hear Tupi struggling to keep up. My own fatigue threatens to rear its head, but my adrenaline keeps it tamped down. I can sleep when all of this is over.

"Here." I nudge Gent, and he leads us gracefully to the ground. I spend a couple minutes snuggling his neck and rubbing his face. "Sweet boy. You've done everything I've asked of you, so can you do this, too? Keep an ear out. If anything approaches, anything at all, whether by land or by air, let me know?" Gent pushes into my chest and, taking that for assent, I give him an ear scratch. "Thank you."

Tupi hits hard and stumbles before finding her feet. I fumble for her and find her elbow in the dark. "Lie down and get some rest."

"But—"

"No, Tupi. I don't need you for this part, and you don't need to see it."

"Yes, Your Majesty." Is that only exhaustion, or do I hear disappointment in her voice as well?

Our captive passed out long ago. With a pat on the butt, Gent wiggles all over and dumps the Fomorian to the ground. He wakes with a hiss and a grunt, scrabbling around in the ash until he remembers why he's bound and in so much pain.

I let the realization settle before taking out the moonlight quartz. I don't hold it high this time, though, broadcasting its light for all to see. Instead, I clutch it in my fist, keeping the light muted and intimate. I can see the Fomorian, and he can see me, and his hate has not lessened.

"I'm going to approach and sit you up so we can talk." I do just that, heaving him up by the shoulders and taking out his gag. "We are far away from your comrades, so be assured no help is coming to you."

"Do you think we are the only creatures lurking in your precious Realm? You have no idea the dark things that have spawned in your absence."

My pulse quickens at his words, but I let no apprehension show on my face. He's looking for a reaction, and he isn't going to get it. I need to be emotionless. I need to be cold. I need to be Danen. I pull my blade once again and let it shine in the moonlight. "You are hunting Morgan Le Fey. Why?"

"Why would I tell you?"

"Because I choose when you die. And how."

He thinks this over.

While I implied earlier that I would torture him I have no intention of doing so. That's not a line I'm willing to cross. He still needs to think I will, though. Information is an easy thing for him to give up. Getting him to perform the tracking may be harder.

"The human witch has something that belongs to us. We want it back."

*Interesting. And unexpected. What business does Morgan have with Fomorians?* "Where is she?"

He shrugs and grins.

I step forward. "Let me make this plain. Track the witch so I can find her, and I'll put you out of your misery. Refuse and I will leave you here, broken and bound, for whatever creature finds you next."

His eyes widen and I can almost see the thoughts racing through his head. He knows I can't lie. I will do exactly what I said I would. I couldn't change my mind even if I wanted to. But what are the chances he'll be found by allies before any other 'dark things' he claims have taken up residence?

He waffles in stubborn indecision for several minutes so I decide to spur him on. "Okay, then. I'll respect your decision." And I start walking back to Gent.

"Wait!"

I stop walking and pause, drawing out the moment before I turn around. "Yes?"

"I can't do tracking magic. Only The General's line can."

"I'm sorry about that." I make to turn back around.

"But-but I can tell you where she is. Or at least, where she was."

"Where she was?"

"Last report was two days ago. Scout had eyes on her before she vanished again. I'll take you there." The Fomorian tries shifting his weight and hisses in pain.

I need to wrap this up and stop prolonging his agony.

"She can cover quite a distance in two days."

"She won't have gone far. Not with the baggage she's carrying."

I let the qualifier slide. I can't afford to let him distract me with rabbit trails. Whatever link exists between Morgan and the Fomorians I'll find out when we locate her. "Lead me into a trap, and I'll drop you out of the air and leave you there."

"Understood."

Waking Tupi is the last thing I want to do, but I gently shake her shoulder anyway. "It's time to go," I murmur as she slowly stirs.

"Hmm?" She stretches hard before remembering where she is. "Your Majesty?" she half-shouts as she bolts upright.

"It's all right. You haven't been asleep long. The Fomorian is going to lead us to Morgan, and we need to get moving."

Her eyes search my face. "What did you do to him?"

"Nothing I regret," I answer truthfully.

I ride Gent behind the Fomorian. Tupi is still tired but insists she can fly. The Fomorian studies the starless sky, reading things there I can't understand. "Turn east," he finally says. "You bore too far north, I assume aiming for the Citadel."

"How can you tell?" I ask him suspiciously.

"It is my job to know such things. My people are bred in the darkness; your world has become much akin to ours."

His words make my skin crawl, but I direct Gent to the east regardless. "Where are we going?"

"An area your people called the Red Mountains. Morgan Le Fey has been evading our scouts in their shadow."

"Why would she be there?" I wonder softly to myself.

The Fomorian answers anyway. "Because the mountains are still standing. The General could not burn through rock."

*He can tunnel underneath it.* He actually did, in his first incursion, using the bulk of the mountains to hide his advance. I guess when he finally won, he didn't see fit to reduce the mountains to rubble.

Even I can see when we finally approach the mountains. They rise before us like a solid wall, darker than the night. I hate that my first time seeing them is like this. I follow the Fomorian's directions between two peaks to what he says is a valley on the other side. Gent lands in the darkness and Tupi lands heavily beside us. I hear her collapse to the ground, but she doesn't get back up.

I risk the moonlight. I have to. "Tupi?" The light shows her crumpled on the ground, her back moving slightly with her breaths. *Exhaustion.* I've driven her too hard.

The Fomorian breaks out into laughter. "Stupid queen. Do you honestly think you can make it out of here alive?"

I whirl on him. "What did you do?"

"Nothing. I've brought you exactly where you asked me to. But Morgan Le Fey is the least of the creatures haunting these mountains." Punctuating his statement is an unearthly howl echoing between the peaks overhead. Gent snorts and stomps as enormous wings rustle and snap, and a vicious wind circles around us.

"What is it?" With a snarl, I grab the Fomorian by the shirt and dump him onto the ground.

He doesn't answer, just screams as his body bursts forth into a fresh wave of agony.

I turn my attention to Tupi instead, hefting her slight weight over my shoulder and flopping her across Gent's back. "Get her out of here!" I slap Gent across the rump.

He responds instantly, leaping forward and opening a portal back to Hellequin Wood. Deja vu floods my brain, but this time I don't have Eredin Glas at my back.

The creature above me cries again, driving spikes into my skull. I draw my blade and advance on the

Fomorian, who still writhes in the ash. Halasuwa may not have been able to burn the mountains, but he didn't leave them untouched, either. The Fomorian knows what is coming, but his hands remain bound behind his back and he is powerless to stop it. With one clean sweep, I slice the skin of his throat and send his blood burbling to the ground. Then I run.

Whatever is hunting me descends on the fresh blood, the sudden displacement of air strong enough to knock me off my feet. Before I can regain them the ground around me erupts into motion. It bucks and shifts, splitting open with a resounding crack. The creature cries again and wings whip the air into a cyclone. Fire sparks at the edge of my moonlight, then flares bright as the sun as the flames rush to engulf me.

## Chapter Thirty-Nine

I do not burn. I don't know how, but the flames roar to life around me and spread outward, leaving me trapped in a three-foot circle of burning heat. The skin on my arms blisters and I rip off what's left of my shirt to cover my mouth and nose. Spinning, I search for an exit, but there's none to be found.

Above me, battle rages. The winged beast against … something. I can't see anything through the smoke in my eyes. Neither creature is targeting me, though, and I need to make the most of their distraction. Picking a direction away from the cacophony, I steel my nerves and race into the flames.

Now I'm burning, but I can't stop. If I stop, I die. The fire eats away at my hunter's boots and I push myself to put on speed. I finally reach the other side of the fire and suck in the clear air. It isn't enough, though. My body is failing, and falling, until I crash into the earth and am unable to rise again. I roll over onto my back, registering the sudden silence as the light from the fire fades away.

A hazy outline appears in front of my face and a cool hand lays itself on my forehead.

"Oh, Eve. Whatever are you doing here?"

Then I'm lifted and borne away as I finally pass out.

**** 

When I come to, I'm underground. Stone surrounds me on all sides and a soft light diffuses through the air. I'm not bound in any way, and other than a pounding headache and a pressure in my chest I seem to be fine. I examine my arms and find no trace of burns. I even have new clothes, with soft slippers covering my feet.

*Someone's been doing magic.*

"Morgan?" I ask tentatively to the room. It's a small space, but hanging coverings speak to branching tunnels that could lead anywhere.

"You're awake," she says from somewhere in the darkness. A moment later she appears from behind one of the coverings, wiping her hands on a towel. "Good. I worried the damage in your lungs was too severe to recover from."

"We are under the mountain?" The notion is not a comforting one. It takes a great deal of effort to keep my heart at a steady pace at finding myself trapped underground once more. I can't keep the emotion hidden in my eyes, though.

Morgan reads my panic and drops to her knees in front of me. "You are safe here, Eve. You may leave whenever you wish, but I have a feeling you didn't come all this way just to say hello."

Her words reorient me to my task. I grip her outstretched hands and meet her eyes. "You are right. I have many questions for you, not the least of which is what you are doing under this mountain, but I came seeking you for a reason. I require your aid, and I am afraid time is of the essence."

"Stop speaking around the issue and tell me. What has happened?"

The earnestness in her expression fills me with warmth. Morgan was always a friend to me, even when we disagreed. "I discovered Oberon in a secret place in the drowned Emain Ablach. He retains his magic, but he sleeps unnaturally. I need your help to wake him."

Morgan sits back on her haunches and blows out a breath. "So that is what he meant," she mutters.

"He told you this would happen?"

She shakes her head, unruly waves flying. "Not in

so many words. You know how he was near the end. He said a lot of things about magic and secrets and one final thing he could do for his family. I tried to convince him to leave with me, but he refused and locked himself in his room. By the time I forced the door he was gone."

"I believe Oberon is the key to restoring Fae magic. He tried to tell me after I found him, but he was so weak and confused I couldn't understand. Waking him is the most important thing."

"I agree. I will go with you, Eve, but it will not be an easy task. I am not alone and—"

"Mistress?" The voice comes from the same tunnel Morgan emerged from earlier. My head snaps up as a girl enters the room. Upon seeing me she drops her eyes to her feet. "I apologize, Mistress, I did not mean to interrupt."

Morgan waves the girl over but keeps her eyes trained on my face. "It is fine. Come, meet our guest. This is Eve, the Queen of the Fae."

The girl is human. I can tell that much. Tall, thin, with long dark hair that reaches past her hips. I know for certain I have never met this girl, but I can't tear my eyes away from her. Something in me calls to her, and I can't say what that something is.

She extends her hand without lifting her face. "Well met, Eve, Queen of the Fae. I am Rosalyn."

Our hands meet and my blood sings. I rise to my feet without intending to and step too far into her personal space. "Who are you?" I whisper.

She raises her head and her eyes meet mine. Hazel eyes that I looked into every day for sixteen years. My father's eyes. His freckles scattered across her nose. Her heart-shaped face and fine dark hair are Mom's. She's a perfect blend of the two of them. My heart stutters in my chest and I stop breathing.

She registers the look on my face and tears brim in her eyes. She doesn't say anything, though, and in her silence I know.

My voice cracks. "You know who you are, don't you?"

Now the tears spill over. Without hesitation, I pull her into my arms. When her knees buckle, I go down, too, and we collapse into each other on the bare stone floor. "I am so sorry," I sob into her hair. "I am so sorry for everything that's been taken away from you. I am sorry I couldn't save them."

Morgan discreetly backs away, giving us space. *She's alive.* Countless hours I spent considering the child Hanathen stole from my parents to make room in their family for me. Part of me feared she used the infant as her human sacrifice to cross back into the Realm. She could have even put the child up for adoption in the human world, lost forever in an anonymous system. I never asked, terrified of what the truth might be. But now the truth is here, in my arms, under this mountain. With Morgan Le Fey.

"You knew." My eyes find hers across the room. "You knew all this time, and you didn't tell me."

Her answer is soft but certain. "The time was not right for you to know."

Anger flares in my gut. Rosalyn stills beside me, our emotional connection severing with the turn of the room's atmosphere. "You had no right to keep this from me."

Morgan doesn't quail. She straightens her shoulders and tosses her hair. "Would knowing she was alive have helped you focus more on learning on how to be a queen? Would knowing she was in the Realm, no less, have driven you to focus more on knowing and understanding your own people?"

I open my mouth to argue but snap it shut as her words hit home. She isn't done, but her next words are gentler. "You were in over your head already, Eve. You were naive and inexperienced. The synod plotted against you. Your enemies moved against your land. You warred so strongly in your own mind that the entire Realm responded and broke itself. Rosalyn would have been a distraction, nothing more."

She's right, but I can't tell her that. I certainly can't admit such a thing in front of the girl herself. I switch my eyes back to Rosalyn, who has regained her composure and wears a decided expression I know all too well. And she has her own things to say. "I don't fault you, Eve. None of this was your doing, and Mistress Morgan has taught me that I am in the place I need to be for this time, even if I can't understand what role I am to play yet. Please, don't be mad at her. We all do our best with the hands we are dealt."

I look back and forth between the two of them, united against me but making too much sense for me to argue. I want to argue. I want to rage that none of this is fair. It isn't fair that I stole her family and her childhood. It isn't fair that Hanathen left me to stumble through my life blindly. It isn't fair that other people make decisions for me and decide what I get to know and what I don't. But raging is what a child would do.

Instead, I tell the most truth that I can. "I understand your reasons, Morgan. And Rosalyn…" I turn to her. "I regret that now is not the time for us to get to know each other. Your existence is important to me, and I want you in my life."

She smiles and clasps my hand. "I want you in my life, too, Eve."

For just a moment, peace reigns under the mountain. It can't last, though, not in the days we're living. "I do not like hiding things from you, Eve. So you should know that Rosalyn is not the only secret I am keeping."

Dread clutches at my newly-filled heart. "Speak plainly, Morgan."

She grasps my hand and hauls me off the floor. "There is something you need to see."

## Chapter Forty

Morgan leads me through one of the curtains, exposing the tunnel I suspected was on the other side. Rosalyn follows, carrying a meager light and keeping quiet. The walls and floor are rough, built entirely for utility and not at all for comfort. It turns sharply to the right, preventing me from seeing how far it stretches.

"Where did these tunnels come from?" I can't help asking.

"I don't know." Morgan's soft voice echoes strangely in the darkness. "They were here long before I came."

"Somehow that's not reassuring."

She doesn't answer, just stops in front of a heavy wooden door. It's the only door I've seen so far, the other entrances farther down the tunnel covered with the same curtains. Morgan produces a key and turns it in the lock. Without a word, she pulls the door open and stands aside, allowing me to enter first.

A gentle light suffuses the room and a strong smell of incense fills my nostrils. A low table holds various bowls and herbs that I instantly categorize as medicinal. Beside the table rests a bed much like the one I just woke up in, but the form occupying it is larger than mine. Much larger, and misshapen around the head. Rattling breaths echo in the small space as the form shudders and twitches.

It's a Fomorian in that bed. I feel it in my gut. *This is why they're hunting her. She has one of theirs, and they want them back.* A coldness washes over me that has nothing to do with the chill of the tunnel.

I step forward into the room. Neither Morgan nor Rosalyn follow me. The weight of death hangs in the air, but nothing can hold back my feet. I grab a corner of the blanket and tug it back, revealing the head and shoulders of the Fomorian on the bed. My heart thunders in my chest, matching the fury raging on the surface. "He's supposed to be dead."

"I know."

"You're saving him."

"Yes."

My hand goes to my blade, tied at my hip by a simple braided cord. Morgan doesn't try to stop me. I raise the blade, take a deep breath, and Halasuwa's eyes flicker open.

"I knew it would be you," he sputters, before a coughing fit wracks his body. "Just get it over with, will you?"

I drop my hand. "You died," I say instead, the words sounding stupid even as they come out.

"That's what the witch says."

I stare down at my enemy, the murderer of my people, and the hate I've been carrying for him drains away. He lies there broken, alone, and powerless. Defeated. Not by my hand, but defeated nonetheless. "How is this possible?" I ask Morgan instead.

"I am capable of a great many things, but I cannot restore the dead to life. I was led to him, pulled by an unexplainable force, and I found him barely clinging to life. I knew that he was important, though I cannot yet see how."

Halasuwa still stares at me, meeting my eyes, waiting for me to decide his fate. "I should kill you." He doesn't seem surprised at my bluntness. "For all of the evils you have brought upon my people. For the destruction of all that is good and beautiful. And for the breaking apart of my family, for without you, I would have known my mother." This singular Fomorian is the root cause of all that has gone awry in my life. He doesn't deserve to exist in this world any longer.

"So why haven't you yet?"

I look down at my hand, the blade now hanging limply from my fingers. "Because you are no longer a threat to me. If I kill you now, I am no better than you." I turn to go, wondering again at the strange emptiness that now fills the hole where my hate used to live. I don't know what Halasuwa's larger purpose is, but it no longer involves me.

"Little queen." Halasuwa winces as he pushes himself to an upright position. I can see the weakness in his body, the exertion such a minor move costs him. He waits for me to meet his eyes, and even though my hate may be gone, his still burns as brightly as it ever did. "You have cost me everything, and you will not turn away from me."

"You're not in a position to make such a demand," I reply without heat.

"If not a demand, then a deal." His eyes blaze, the sudden ferocity at odds with the weakness of his body. Even though he's sitting down, his sheer size still makes him tower over me. "Despite your friend's ministrations, I am not long for this world. I feel it. I would rather be cut down by an enemy than waste away in a sickbed."

"You want me to kill you?" I ask in surprise. "What are you willing to trade for such a thing?" For that is how Fae deals are made. Despite my words the wheels in my head start turning. *What does Halasuwa have that I want?* I can feel Morgan's and Rosalyn's eyes on my back. They're wisely staying out of this, but they're invested in the outcome nevertheless.

He grins, that same grin that has haunted my nightmares for the last year. "I can tell you the mechanism that turns off Fae magic."

My heart skips a beat and my shoulders tense.

Halasuwa sees it and his grin grows wider. He knows he has me.

Turning off Fae magic was his plan from the start. Caspian was supposed to convince me to do it, but I refused. It happened anyway, and not knowing what went wrong has been eating me away inside. I can't fix the magic if I don't understand how I broke it in the first place. But is that knowledge worth killing my enemy in cold blood?

I swallow past a sudden lump in my throat. "Not good enough." I turn away once again.

"No! Name your price, then. Whatever I have to give you, it's yours."

I let the tension drain out of my posture and take several deep breaths. When I turn back to Halasuwa, I'm ready. I choose my words carefully, knowing I will be bound to fulfill them to the letter. "I require three conditions. Once they are fulfilled, I will grant your desire to be slain by an enemy."

An intake of breath sounds behind me. It can only be Rosalyn. Morgan wouldn't be so moved by the turn the conversation has taken.

Halasuwa considers my proposal. "Name your conditions."

"One. You give me the answer you already offered. Tell me what you know about the failure of Fae magic. Two. I choose the time and manner of your death. Three. A favor to be named later."

Halasuwa bursts out laughing, which quickly turns to a cough so violent blood sprays out his mouth. "A favor to be named later? How much later do you intend for me to live? I will die on my own before I see the end of this deal."

"Those are my conditions. Do you accept, or

not?"

The deposed general grows sober, fingering the blood still dribbling down his chin. "I accept."

"Very well. Our deal has been struck. As to Fae magic?"

His eyes roll back. He's either trying to remember or about to pass out. "Fae magic is a delicate thing. Connected intimately to the royal line. It can vanish in a stray thought."

My heart pounds with the implication. "Speak plainly."

"How is this for plain? *You* did it. You got your people killed all on your own." He shrugs and slumps back, resting his weight against the wall behind him.

I advance on him, grabbing the front of his shirt. I'm not strong enough to lift him, so I don't even try, but I do push my face close in to his. "How do I turn it back on?"

With surprising delicacy, he plucks my hands free of his shirtfront. "My little queen, that answer was not part of our bargain."

Frustration races through my body, evident in my clenched hands and teeth. *Bungled that one.* The urge to strike him flits through me, but I shove it aside. I will not be that person.

"What next, little queen? What do you have in mind for my death?"

I can't look at him anymore. I spin on my heel and stalk back to the door where our audience still waits.

Morgan stops me with a hand to the shoulder to keep me from barreling through them into the tunnel. "What now, Eve?" she asks, echoing Halasuwa's sentiment. "I need to see to Oberon, and I can't leave him here like this."

I blow out a breath. I chose my conditions for a

reason. Morgan believes Halasuwa still has purpose, and I want to give that purpose a chance to make itself known. "Do what you can to get him on his feet and in fighting form. He's coming with us."

Then a peal of thunder cracks loud enough to make my ears ring and the mountain trembles, sending a deluge of dust and pebbles raining from the ceiling.

## Chapter Forty-One

"Eredin Glas." I would know his entrance anywhere.

"The King of the Wild Hunt?" Morgan actually seems surprised. I don't think I've ever surprised her before.

"Yes. He must have decided I've been gone long enough and come to retrieve me." Belatedly, I remember sending Gent back to Hellequin Wood bearing an unconscious Tupi. When I didn't follow, he must have believed the worst. From the sound of it he'll bring the whole mountain down if he has to.

Morgan shakes her head and ushers us out of Halasuwa's sick room, grabbing things off the shelves as she goes. "You will have to tell me how you came to elicit such a reaction from the King of the Wild Hunt, but first we must all survive his assault on my mountain. Rosalyn, show Eve how to get to the surface so she may calm His Majesty's anxieties."

"Yes, Mistress."

The tunnel twists and turns, but Rosalyn never hesitates. She navigates the dark corners with quiet efficiency until we land at a ladder leading up to a trapdoor. We finally gain the surface and find a howling storm waiting for us. Pouring rain blocks the peaks from view and vicious lightning strikes fuel the tremors we felt below ground. Eredin Glas flickers in and out of view, arms outstretched, channeling the lightning through himself as he targets different marks throughout the valley.

What's surprising is, he's not alone. Four Fomorians attack him in unison, while half a dozen more lie smoking on the ground. Our assumption that he was tearing the mountain apart looking for me was wrong. Instead, it appears the scouting party Tupi and I raided finally tracked Morgan down.

I pull myself through the trapdoor and help Rosalyn up behind me, the driving rain instantly soaking us through.

Morgan crawls up after Rosalyn, having caught up to us quickly.

"What of Halasuwa?" I call out to her above the raging wind.

"The herbs I fed him will land painfully. Better he experiences that in privacy." Morgan surveys the scene and frowns. "Why would the King come alone, knowing the likelihood of attack? At full power a single party would be no match for him. Why would he limit himself in such a way?"

A week's worth of observations click into place as Morgan gives me the final piece of the puzzle. I've noticed Eredin Glas's limited power but did not connect that with the times he was alone. In truth, he only shows his full strength when riding with the Hunt. When the two of us are alone, he is much more subdued. *Interesting*.

And possibly fatal. As we watch, one of the Fomorians lands a lucky hit and buries his axe deep in Eredin Glas's shoulder. Eredin Glas roars and swings wildly, missing the offending Fomorian and leaving his right side vulnerable.

I don't think. My blade appears in my hand as my body bursts into motion. I race across the valley, but I'm not fast enough to fend off the attack. Eredin Glas roars again as another blade hits flesh and the ground shudders beneath us. In the storm, no one hears me approach. I slam into the Fomorian with the axe, knocking him off balance and driving my own blade up under his chin. We go down together, drawing the attention of King and

Fomorian alike.

The distraction is just the opening Eredin Glas needs. He drops his scythe and, opening his arms wide, raises his face to the sky and bellows in a primal sound I've never heard from him before. Cracks appear in the ground around us, long-buried roots snaking out of the openings. The roots seize the remaining Fomorians and drag them screaming under the earth.

The rain ends abruptly and the world falls quiet. Without the lightning, the sudden darkness is thick and impenetrable, sending my fingers to my neck to dig the moonlight quartz out of hiding. A second later, the weight of the Fomorian pinning me to the earth is lifted and Eredin Glas stands scowling down at me.

"That was stupid." He wastes no time informing me.

"You needed help."

His eyes rove over me, filling with annoyance at finding me unharmed. "What were you thinking? Running off? Again? Stealing my horse? Again?"

I scoff at the accusation. "You knew I was gone. You knew where I went. Tell me you have no way to track either me or Gent."

His scowl deepens. "You know the dangers the Realm holds. I didn't think you stupid enough to venture here."

"And yet here I am."

"Yet here you are. Here you are, while your friend lies dying in a faraway land and with no way to call for backup."

"Tupi isn't dying. She just needs rest. And I have backup." I gesture at Morgan and Rosalyn, who are wisely staying out of this.

Eredin Glas eyes the humans with disdain, immediately dismissing their ability to be useful in any way. "And the Fomorians? They just happen to be lurking in this very spot upon my arrival? What was your plan for them?"

"I am not as defenseless as you think."

He ignores me. "And your backup? They look rather defenseless as well."

"Then you are wrong once again." My memories of the attack are fuzzy, but with the moonlight quartz finding the charred remains of the flying creature is easy. Eredin Glas grunts but holds his tongue as we move forward as a group to study the beast.

It's massive. And aerodynamically impossible, yet fly it did. "What is it?" I ask Morgan, who shakes her head.

"I do not know. But it is not the first."

Its body is long and slender, stretched tight with leathery skin. Its wings are even bigger, yet thin and membranous, and don't look capable of holding any kind of weight at all. The face is malformed, lacking eyes but with wide slitted nostrils that pull the skin into a grotesque mockery of a smile.

Doubt drips from Eredin Glas's mouth. "You slew this beast?"

"I did." She meets his eyes, no fear in her face or bearing.

"You are Morgan Le Fey."

"You've heard of me. I'm impressed." Her words are flat, emphasizing how little his recognition means to her. Her attention turns to the creature, analyzing it for uses I cannot imagine.

Eredin Glas also studies it, though with a more critical eye. Considering how it could be used, maybe? Before long, his gaze turns to me, evaluating me with that same critical eye. Taking in the drenched hair and clothes, the Fomorian blood, the blade still in my hand.

"You have changed."

"From?"

"From the helpless waif I saved from the clutches of the Nix." No judgment colors his voice. Rather, I hear a slight undercurrent of pride. "Do you know why I scold you, Eve?"

That's easy. "Because you want my magic, and if I run off and get myself hurt you lose out." That's not all it is, though, and I know it.

He shakes his head. "There is an element of that, yes. I have not hidden my desire for your magic from you. But I was not lying when I said I cared for you. I look forward to a future with you, you who can be my equal like no hunter ever could. I feared for your safety tonight. Not for the magic. For *you*."

I look at him out of the corner of my eye. "I wish that was enough. I really do. I wish I could count you as a friend, instead of a deceptive ally with ulterior motives. But no pretty words can change your actions. And your actions place your priorities on gaining my magic above all else. You have the power to make all of this go away, but you refuse to do so until you get something out of it. That's not someone I can tie myself to for eternity."

Eredin Glas's lips tighten. "This is why you came, then? In search of someone you can trust? Morgan Le Fey may be your friend, but the meager talents of a human witch cannot reclaim your magic for you."

"I will be the judge of that." I step away to put some distance between us. A metaphorical wall slams down between us at the gesture. Eredin Glas's confession was the closest he would ever come to offering me an olive branch, and I shut him down. Deep down, I know he will not offer again. Any goodwill between us has been effectively severed.

Still, I need to keep moving forward. I turn once

more to Eredin Glas, whose eyes now burn with menacing flames. I've fired his temper, and the blowback won't be pleasant. "We cannot linger here. Who knows what other creatures may be lurking in the dark. We need to get back to Hellequin Wood, and quickly. Will Morhogg bear us all?"

He snorts. My assumption is impertinent, but I'm not in the mood to dance around the subject. "You insist on bringing the humans to the Wood?"

"I do. And one other."

Eredin Glas moves swiftly, closing the gap between us in two steps. He growls his next words into my ear. "I am not a valet to do your bidding. Continue to order me about and you will not be pleased with the results. I have tried to win your loyalty, but I grow tired of your dalliance, *Your Majesty*. One more cycle of the sun and you will give me your answer. Accept your place at my side, or I will leave you in the human world with the rest of your doomed race."

Goosebumps break out over my entire body. This is the moment. I've finally pushed him too far. *It'll be okay,* I assure myself. I have Morgan now. Much can happen in this last day. Still, it can't hurt to play the part and salvage his dignity.

I take a deep breath to make sure my mind is clear and my face will show nothing of my thoughts. Then I pitch my voice high enough to carry over to Morgan and Rosalyn, who are still examining the creature. "Eredin Glas, King of the Wild Hunt, I find myself in need of your help. Would you be gracious enough to allow the use of your mounts to ferry the four of us to Hellequin Wood?"

He gives me a look that says he knows what I'm doing, but answers in kind anyway. "The pleasure of your company is mine, Your Majesty. But where is the fourth?"

I drop all formality from my voice. "Underground. Morgan Le Fey is tending the broken General Halasuwa."

## Chapter Forty-Two

Eredin Glas curses.

I beckon to Morgan. "It's time to get Halasuwa to the surface. Is he safe to move freely?"

She shakes her head. "I would never consider the Fomorian General safe. However, your bargain binds him. You have laid claim to his death. If he were to attack you, or force the King to rise against him, that would be a violation of his oath. The greater threat is that the King will kill him without provocation."

Eredin Glas has been listening. The hardness in his voice is foreign and jarring. "You hold a bargain with Halasuwa?"

I straighten my spine. "I do. As such, he is under my protection."

"An enemy and a traitor. You should give greater consideration to those you choose to protect."

A sudden horn blast knocks any further words out of my head. Eredin Glas winds the horn again, drawing out the note in a melody I'm all too familiar with. "He's calling the Hunt," I whisper to Morgan as my pulse races and the hairs on my arms stand straight up.

She notes the tremor in my voice and the visceral reaction of my body and raises her eyebrows. I ignore her. I don't owe her any explanations.

A moment later, the hounds respond, their baying voices echoing through the dark skies. I keep an eye on Morgan, but if she reacts to the call of the hounds, I don't see it.

"We need the entire Hunt?" I ask Eredin Glas instead.

"I always need the Hunt." His voice is cold. Emotionless. He's done with me, and he wants to make sure I know it. Still, he won't let anything happen to me. Not for the next twenty-four hours, at least.

I turn to face him, staring up into those flaming, alien eyes. Before tonight, I hadn't seen his flaming eyes in a while. As we've grown closer, he's diminished in my view, showing me more of the man and less of the King. Tonight, he's all King, power flowing off him like water. His wounds have already healed, leaving only rips in his clothing to show they were ever there at all. "Halasuwa is invalid in the tunnels. If he is to accompany us to Hellequin Wood he must be borne out."

Eredin Glas grunts but doesn't answer. Still, I know he's wondering the same thing I am, though his investment is somewhat less than mine. How Halasuwa lives remains a mystery. Caspian testified to his death, and his ability to share Halasuwa's secrets backed up his story. The General seems to have returned from the dead, but by what mechanism? And why?

Above us, the sky trembles with the arrival of the Hunt. I see flashes of them in the storm, not enough to make out individual hunters but enough to see terrible sights that have spawned thousands of years of stories. The lightning flickering off their hunting clothes could easily be mistaken for skeletal armor, and their manic battle cry for the voices of the damned.

Gent breaks from the fray and lands beside me. He greets me with a happy snort and I rub his nose in kind. "Hey, sweet boy."

"Let's go."

Eredin Glas's growl catches me by surprise. When I turn, he has a mass over his shoulder that can only be Halasuwa.

*How did he…?*

Then Rosalyn appears behind him, tiny and frail by comparison. She must have shown him the way into the tunnels.

Eredin Glas throws Halasuwa over Morhogg while Morgan and Rosalyn ride with me. Gent easily bears the weight, and within seconds we're airborne. Rosalyn screams as Gent races through the portal, while Morgan throws back her head and laughs from deep in her belly.

The sudden appearance of stars overhead fills my body with calm. A calm that lasts roughly ten seconds until Gent lands lightly on the plateau. Morhogg dumps Halasuwa in the dirt and snorts as if he's rid himself of something foul. Halasuwa moans and twitches but doesn't try to rise.

Jarild appears out of nowhere, having followed at Eredin Glas's request, along with two hunters I haven't met. "Take him away," Eredin Glas orders, waving at the General. "Keep him secure. Set a watch."

"Yes, my liege." Jarild hurries to obey, and Halasuwa vanishes from the plateau as quickly as he arrived.

I don't have the mind space to ponder the General's fate. Instead, I slide to the ground and grab Morgan's hand. "Oberon is over here."

Eredin Glas's eyes follow me like a hawk as I lead Morgan to my palafito. If he had any questions about Morgan's part in this, they've been answered. I feel the weight of his gaze with every step, but I refuse to turn my head and acknowledge him.

Tupi lies near Oberon, chest rising and falling in gentle sleep. It's what she needs after everything I asked of her. Morgan smiles at the sight of the peaceful pixie, but her expression falls when she settles on Oberon. She kneels next to him, careful not to jostle him, and runs her fingers through his disheveled hair. "Oh, my friend. What has happened to you?"

"Can you wake him?" I can't help asking.

"I need time." She's already distracted as she rummages through the bag slung around her hip. "Rosalyn, fetch me hot water."

"Yes, Mistress."

I can tell when I'm not needed. I back away, studying Morgan's face as she peers down at Oberon. She's murmuring something I can't hear, and her eyes are filled with such pain. I hit my own ladder before I know it and tumble over backward, bouncing twice before landing on my back on the ground.

No one rushes to my aid. Eredin Glas has retreated into the darkness, and the rest of the plateau appears empty. From across the island, I can hear the sounds of the Hunt in the beginning throes of revelry. *What I wouldn't give to go down there and forget myself for a while...*

It's a tempting concept.

"Are you planning to stay down there, My Lady?"

The voice comes out of the darkness, forgotten in the midst of chaos.

*I've been gone for hours. Most of the day. Half the night.*
"Who is watching you?" I ask Caspian as I get to my feet, rubbing my aching behind.

"It would seem my threat level has been downgraded in the wake of new developments."

"Eredin Glas sent your guard with Halasuwa?"

"So it would seem."

I find Caspian where I left him, sitting next to the fire, hands bound. "Did they even feed you?" I ask, my eyes taking in the sores on his wrists from the chafing of the rope.

"The King has had other priorities today."

I eye my former guard, searching for dishonesty I know I won't see. Not because it isn't there, but because he'd never let me know it was. "Plain answers only. If I untie you, will you run?"

He looks me in the eye. "No."

"Will you hurt me?"

"No."

"Will you give me any reason to regret doing so?"

No hesitation. "No."

"I believe you." I retrieve cheese and bread from the always-present basket and a jug of water and thunk them down beside Caspian. Then I untie his hands.

"Thank you." He rubs the sores and winces. "Your kindness is appreciated."

I lower myself to the ground, close enough to be present but far enough away that I can escape if he makes any sudden moves. He notices but doesn't comment. As he tackles the water, I let my eyes trace the shape of the face I know so well. The smooth, dark skin, the laughing green eyes, the budding horns on his forehead that speak to his youth. The scar Danen gave him for his betrayal. It is a face I once trusted completely. A face I couldn't get out of my mind, that had me thinking and feeling things I'd never thought or felt before.

I sigh and lean back against the log. "How did we get to this place?"

One glance and he knows I'm not talking about Hellequin Wood. The question is largely rhetorical, but he considers it anyway. "I had no choice. I know that sounds trite, but the General laid claim to my blood the moment I entered this world. Just as he did my father before me."

"So your Fomorian lineage is your father's?"

"Yes."

"Did your mother know?"

He pauses. "I feel like she must have. I never met him, but I do know his appearance was too Fomorian to risk placing him at court. I never asked her, though, and she never volunteered."

The frank conversation with Caspian is unusual but not unwelcome. I don't want it to turn into some kind of interrogation, but as long as he keeps answering questions, I'll keep asking them. "How much did she know of your mission?"

"Nothing." I look at him sharply. "It's true. The two of us never discussed my Fomorian blood, nor my connection to the General. He never visited me when she was present, and as you know, he laid commands on me to bind my tongue. Mother opposed my decision to take service in the royal guard and refused to speak to me about the matter."

"Then what was her problem?" The question is more for myself than Caspian, but he answers anyway.

"She hated you. Because she planned to take Summer House from Hanathen and restore it to its former glory, and your arrival stole that opportunity."

## Chapter Forty-Three

It seems everybody hated me. Vogelein hated me because he loved my mother and I reminded him too much of her. Ailie hated me because she envied my crown. Now I learn that Crysta hated me, too.

"What do you mean, return Summer House to its former glory? Summer House had plenty of glory."

"But under the crown, we also had restrictions. Conduct agreed to by all parties necessary to form a unified body. Mother's ancestors made concessions she objected to."

My eyelids threaten to close, but I fight against them. Now that I'm at rest my body is giving up, but I really want to hear this. "What concessions?"

"At its core, final authority in ruling matters. Your ancestors rarely intervened in House affairs, but knowing they could chafed at Mother. The burden of tributes and taxes and warriors caused her no end of grief. But Hanathen was the last straw. Do you recall the old human stories of ignorant travelers stumbling upon a gathering of Fae? Being lured into a Fae dance, perhaps, or tricked into eating something disgusting disguised as a delicacy?"

I nod. "Summer House likes to play tricks on humans."

"Indeed. In her later years, Hanathen limited Fae travel between the Realm and the human world. No more revels. No more tricks. She told no one her true purpose in hiding you, but swathed these new rules in vaguery and misdirection. So, Mother began her plans. She would secede from the unification of the Realm and return Summer House to an independent entity."

"Then Hanathen died." My words are barely a

mumble, my thoughts difficult to hang on to.

"And you arrived. And Summer House's priorities were once again placed on hold."

"It didn't have to be this way." I wobble my head back and forth in a weak imitation of a shake. "We could have been allies, Crysta and me. I value Summer House's strength. Compromises could have been reached."

"If you knew my mother, you would understand. She is through with compromises."

I have no answer for that. The pause between us stretches. But I still need one more answer and my coherent time is quickly running out. "You told me Halasuwa died."

"I saw him die."

"If he is alive, how are you free from his commands?"

Now it's Caspian's turn to stretch the silence, and I nearly fall asleep listening to the chirp of the crickets. When he finally answers his voice is barely audible. "I do not know."

Much as I want to, I can't grasp onto a fully formed thought. The coolness of the night breeze makes me shiver, and a second later another body presses against my side.

"Rest, My Lady," Caspian's voice whispers in my ear. "I'll not let any harm come to you."

I don't have the energy to not trust him. I've pushed too hard for too long. I let myself slip into sleep with the smell of rain and fireflies lingering in my nostrils.

****

I wake too soon to a gentle hand shaking my shoulder. "Eve, wake up. I need to speak with you."

Consciousness returns slowly. I blink open heavy eyes to find Morgan kneeling beside me, predawn light spilling around her halo of hair. Her voice is low and urgent, cast for my ears only.

I disentangle myself from Caspian, who had slumped over in his own sleep and ended up with his head resting on top of mine.

"You two look snuggly."

"Not intentionally." I follow Morgan across the plateau, stretching and working the kinks out. My night with Caspian was unexpected, to say the least. And unwise. But he held to his word and no harm came to me. *But then, physical attack was never the main threat. It was always his words that couldn't be trusted.* "How is Oberon?" I ask, effectively turning the conversation away from me and Caspian.

Morgan checks all directions before answering. "He still sleeps. But this sleep is not natural."

"We already knew that much."

She shakes her head. "No, I don't think you do. There is another presence inside his head preventing him from waking."

That *is* news.

Morgan isn't done. "Tell me everything that happened when you found him. Every detail matters."

I tell the story as the sun comes up. My brain is still fighting fuzz, but the event is so ingrained in my memory I have no difficulty recalling it. Finding Oberon in the hidden room. The desiccated condition of his body. The words he said to me. The treacherous swim to the surface and the explosion of Oberon's magic that saved our lives. Eredin Glas expelling the water from his lungs and his slip into unconsciousness.

Morgan's eyes grow darker the longer I talk, and by the time I finish her own storm clouds are roiling inside. "Do you trust Eredin Glas to deal truly with you?"

My answer is instant. "No. Not when his own

interests are at stake."

"And he wants your magic?"

"He has been clear on that point. He wishes Fae magic to be under his control, and will not be swayed."

"Then, Eve, I believe it is Eredin Glas who keeps Oberon asleep. The mark of power on him is strong, and mind magic is not an easy thing to accomplish. No novice holds him, and none other has motivation to do so."

The remaining cobwebs fly out of my head and I feel too stupid to be angry. Of course Eredin Glas did it. I've seen his mind magic at work, so I know he's capable. If Oberon were awake, he could help me, and then I may not need the King anymore. No way he was taking that risk. "Can you wake him?"

"I could, but I do not have what I need here."

"I'll get it for you." It doesn't matter where I have to go, I'll get her whatever she needs. The vow passes my lips without a thought.

"It is not that simple. The herb I require is not in my possession. I have only found it growing wild once before, many years ago. You have not the time nor the ability to search the worlds for it. Even if you did, the King is neither ignorant nor stupid. He knows my purpose here and will not grant you access to his mounts again."

"Please, Morgan." My chest constricts and I lose the careful control I keep over my voice. "Tell me what you need. Let me figure out the way."

She sighs heavily and glances across the plateau at my palafito. "It is called Bacopa Rosea. It is a tufted yellow flower with rigid, waxy leaves. And it isn't for Oberon, it is for me. Eredin Glas's block is too strong, and I will not be able to break it without augmentation."

*Bacopa Rosea...*

"I know where to find it." The memory comes

crashing in. Following the Hunt down a narrow game trail to what Lella affectionately dubbed 'the wild', where the vegetation could dwarf mountains and beasts I've never seen before lurk.

"It grows here in Hellequin Wood."

"Yes."

"He won't let you go after it."

"I won't be the one he's hunting." The plan forms in an instant. I'm not surprised to find Caspian awake when I look at him. He probably noticed the moment my body left his and hasn't taken his eyes off me since.

"I'll do it," he whispers, exaggerating the words so I can read his lips.

I walk back over and kneel beside him. "You don't know what I want from you."

"Does it matter? It will wake Oberon, and I do not fault you for choosing his life over mine."

I raise my eyebrows at him. "I didn't tell you about Oberon."

"Nothing on this plateau is a secret. I can read you, remember? Whatever you need me to do, I will likely die for it. But if we succeed, Oberon will wake, and you will restore Fae magic. It is an easy decision."

It is an easy decision, but not for the reason he thinks. No matter his sins, Caspian remains important to me. I can't change the memories I have of him or the way he made me feel. But if sacrificing him means saving my people, I won't do anything else. And he wouldn't expect me to.

"Morgan? What would you expect of Halasuwa's condition?"

"The treatment will have taken effect by now. It will close the wounds on his body, but only temporarily. His strength will not hold more than a day."

"A day is more than enough time." I touch

Caspian's wrist, avoiding the raw spots lingering there. No point in drawing this out. "I want you to break General Halasuwa from his guard and attempt to flee."

## Chapter Forty-Four

Caspian doesn't blink. "For you, My Lady, I will do it." And with that vow his fate is sealed.

We all know he could die. Eredin Glas has so far stayed his hand at my request, but the moment Caspian acts like the traitor Eredin Glas believes him to be the King won't hesitate to kill him.

Caspian stands on shaky legs, weak from his forced inaction. He doesn't ask what I'll be doing in the meantime. He only has one question. "When?"

"Now." I swallow down a lump in my throat. *This is what being a queen means.* "Before anyone sees us conspiring like this."

Indeed, we have been conspiring in full sunlight on an open plateau. Eredin Glas is sequestered in his own palafito, though, and is not watching. If his eyes were on me, I would know. I would feel it.

"Where would the hunters have taken Halasuwa?" Morgan asks.

My mind goes blank. "I, uh, I don't know." My eyes search the cloudless sky for answers I can't see until finally I come up with an idea. "Find Danen among the hunters. They camp on the beach and along the edge of the woods. He will tell you if he can."

"And if he tries to kill me instead?"

Danen's voice echoes in my head, replaying our last conversation. "Tell him my heart will always choose him. He'll know I sent you."

A shadow passes over Caspian's expression, gone before I can analyze it. "Yes, My Lady." With a quick check around the plateau, he gives me a short nod and takes off at a lope. I watch him until he vanishes down the path, then quickly turn away.

"Still toying with both boys' hearts, then?" Morgan clucks her tongue at me. "Good way to lose both of them."

"They are already lost to me. In the ways that matter, at least." I wrap my arms around Morgan in a surprise hug that she instantly returns. "I must go as well. Time is against us."

"Run fast," she whispers in my ear.

"I'll be back soon." Then I leave the plateau, too. My heart desires to run as fast as I can, but that kind of pace is not sustainable and I don't want to wear myself out too quickly. Especially not on little sleep and no breakfast. My first stop, though, as always, is the meadow.

Gent seems to know I'm coming. He's at the edge of the woods, some distance from the rest of the herd.

"Hey, boy." I scratch the nose he shoves into my chest. "Want to go for a run?"

He snorts and tosses his head, stepping back from my touch.

Dread pools in my gut. *He's not my horse. He belongs to someone else.* I raise my eyes to see Morhogg standing on his hill, watching over his domain. I keep my body behind Gent's, doing my best to hide myself from the stallion's view.

"You can't come with me, can you? The King ordered you not to bear me anymore, didn't he?"

Gent pushes his head into my chest and huffs. If he could speak, he couldn't have said it any plainer.

"I still love you." I whisper the words into his ear, letting my own sadness fill the space between us. "You're a wonderful mount, and I'm hopeful we will ride together yet again." I drop a kiss between his ears and step back. Two more steps, then I turn and re-enter the trees. I scrub at my eyes, set my spine, and turn toward the wild part of the island.

It's slow going. I'm starting at a different place than last time, and finding the right game trail proves to be a difficult task. *Oh, Gent. I miss you already. You would know the right way.*

"Lost, Eve?"

I close my eyes and take a breath. "Hail, Lella. Did the King send you?" I ask, turning to find the tall, dark-skinned hunter staring me down. If Eredin Glas sent her to retrieve me it's all over.

"Should he have?" she counters, leveraging her body off the tree she was leaning against.

"No, he should not have. But he might have done it anyway."

She barks a laugh. "Fair enough. I have not spoken with my liege yet this day, but I have been following you. Something is amiss, and I was hoping you would see fit to confide in me."

"Out here, where there are no witnesses?" I don't like suspecting Lella of treachery, but I've known from the beginning my friendship with her had its limits. She is loyal to the King.

"Out here, where there is no one to overhear the sensitive information you are keeping inside. Your actions have not gone unnoticed among the Hunt, though we are not keen to involve ourselves in outside matters. Fae business is not our business. But I do know that you travel without the King's leave, you bring strangers to the Wood, and you harbor new animosity toward the King."

I freeze in place, focusing on my body. If she moves, I'll run. I have to at least try.

"Fae business is not my business. But, as your friend, your business could be my business, if you would see fit to share it with me."

"And if my business goes counter to the wishes of

your King?"

"My liege has given me no commands concerning you. I have no obligations to him in this moment."

I ponder her words. *Is it possible she really has no ulterior motive?* "I want to trust you, Lella. I consider you a friend as well. But I fear, if I tell you my errand, you will feel differently about helping me."

"I watched you leave the plateau." She steps closer, hands coming out to her sides and showing me she holds no weapon. "Moments after the traitor Fae left the plateau. Yet I raised no alarm. Please, trust me."

As the words leave her mouth a shout echoes behind us. A second shout follows, then many more, until the woods ring with the sound of the uproar. Lella raises her eyebrows at me.

I make my decision. "Caspian is distracting the King while I retrieve a Bacopa Rosea bloom from the wild."

She nods. "Then you need to go this way." Without further conversation, Lella takes the lead, steering me through a break in the underbrush I didn't even notice. Before too long we're on the game trail I was looking for, walking quickly to put distance behind us.

We don't speak. I keep an ear out for sounds of pursuit, but only the natural sound of the woods can be heard. I can't help wondering if Caspian has succeeded in distracting the King, or if I was wrong and he doesn't care that I'm out here at all. *Is it possible I sent Caspian to his death for nothing?* Surely not. My instincts can't be that off the mark, not after everything I've been through. I don't let myself dwell on Caspian's fate. I can't afford the tears those thoughts would draw.

I realize I've let my mind wander when my feet splash down into freezing water. My legs already ache and sweat is pouring down my back. My stomach rumbles loud enough for Lella to hear, making her laugh.

"Hungry, Your Majesty?"

"I skipped breakfast." I force the words out between pants, bending down a bit and resting my hands on my knees. "My body gets stronger every day, but is still far from where it needs to be." *Not to mention how I've been abusing it lately.*

"Over here." On the far bank Lella snags the branch of a bush hanging low with bulbous purple berries. "These are safe to eat. They won't fill much, but they'll take the edge off."

"Thank you." I don't hesitate to pop one in my mouth. If Lella wanted to harm me she would have done it before dragging me all the way out here.

We don't rest long. Lella waits patiently while I catch my breath, refilling both of our water skins and double-checking the placement of various knives on her person.

"Okay. Let's go."

Lella chooses our path and heads off into the trees. The moment we leave the creek everything gets much, much bigger. Having seen this place already does nothing to diminish the pure joy that springs up inside.

"Watch yourself, Eve. We're entering the wild. You need your wits about you."

"You told me there were no predators here."

"No predators, but only the King himself has traveled every inch of the Wood. Wander too far from me, and you'll end up so lost he'll be the only one who can find you."

A shiver passes through my body and I hurry to catch up to Lella. No more distractions. I keep my eyes open and my head swiveling, searching for the puff of yellow that will signal my prize.

"Do you recall where you saw this flower?" Lella asks over her shoulder, keeping her eyes straight ahead.

"In the tunnels." I close my eyes, letting my mind conjure up the image. "You showed them to me when we were hunting the stag."

"I remember. The tunnels?"

"Yes. The trees shedding bark. The shavings look like tunnels strewn across the ground. The Bacopa Rosea grew along the inside of the bark."

"Gotcha. Looking for bark."

Lella switches trails, taking us closer to the giant shedding trees. Still, we walk another hour before sighting any of the curled-up strips. The first one comes up empty. So do the next six. My stomach reminds me that berries are far from sufficient sustenance and a headache takes up residence in my forehead.

"Eve! Over here! This one has flowers!"

I hurry to Lella's side and gasp. The bark coils like a spring, rivers of yellow blooms twirling along the grains in kaleidoscope. "You've found it."

## Chapter Forty-Five

"You need rest, Eve."

"I have to get back." Our argument is at an impasse. My pockets are bursting with freshly picked plants, roots intact as Morgan instructed, and my heart yearns for my grandfather. But it's a long walk back and my body is already struggling.

"It doesn't matter how many flowers you have if you don't make it back."

"I would make it back. You wouldn't leave me out here to die."

"I am not throwing you over my shoulder like a sack of potatoes. If you collapse, I will build a fire, catch some fish, and wait for you to wake up." There's no humor in her eyes. She may not be Fae, but she means every word coming out of her mouth. I believe she'll do it.

And she'd be right. If I'm stupid enough to knowingly push myself past the breaking point, then I should suffer the consequences of that decision. I study the sky. It's impossible to see the sun beyond the canopy, but based on the amount of light and how long we walked it should be sometime mid-afternoon. "Two hours. Wake me in two hours, not a minute more."

"Yes, Your Majesty." Lella gives me a mock bow and drops her pack to the ground. She rummages around inside while I make myself comfortable in a patch of fuzzy green stuff.

If I weren't so exhausted I wouldn't have a chance at sleeping. I'm too close. Everything is falling into place, and once Oberon is awake, he'll be able to tell me how to fix everything. As it is, I've barely closed my eyes when Lella is shaking me awake.

"Two hours, Eve. On the dot."

Everything hurts. I'm sore from the hike, sore from sleeping curled up on the ground, sore in general from the pace I've been keeping the last few days. Still, I bolt up from my weedy bed as adrenaline courses through me once again.

Lella hasn't been idle. True to her word, the embers from a small cookfire smoke beneath the water she poured on it and the smell of fish lingers in the air.

"Here," she says, thrusting a warm, folded-up cloth into my hands. "Walk and eat."

Inside the package are delicate pieces of white fish. I scarf them down as my feet get moving, my stomach happy while my achy muscles protest at being on the move once again. The fish is gone in minutes, and Lella tosses me another package filled with a collection of berries and flower petals. "I assumed, being Fae, you wouldn't mind eating the bounties the earth provides."

Indeed not. I enjoyed many edible flowers in Emain Ablach, most often while exploring with Danen. He was adamant that I understand my world and my place in it. As always, thinking of Danen twinges a pang in my heart.

"Lella?"

"Hmm?"

"Do you know of any way to free a hunter from the Hunt?"

Her pace slows for a step, but her voice is normal when she answers. "Why would a hunter wish to leave the Hunt?"

"That's a very Fae answer."

"But a true one. Our life here is good. The lives we left behind no longer exist. Even if we wished to leave, where would we go?"

"That may be true for you, and for most of the

other hunters as well, and I would not dream of taking this life from you. But please do not play coy with me. Fae business may not be your business, but you are neither stupid nor incompetent. You know why I'm asking, and which Hunter concerns me."

Lella sighs. "Danen is beyond your reach, Eve. He made the same oaths I did. To serve the King. To spend eternity riding the skies in pursuit of magic. Even if these oaths could yield, his word as a Fae could not."

I huff and let myself fall back a few steps. This conversation is getting me nowhere. I understand Danen's oaths, I do. That's the problem. I can't simply run off with him and expect nothing to happen. *One thing at a time.* Magic first. Then I can turn the full power of my ancestors toward freeing Danen.

It takes longer for us to get back to the meadow than it did to get all the way out into the wild. My fault. The longer we hiked the slower I unwillingly got.

Lella leaves me with an apology once we hit familiar paths. "I do not know how the King will feel about me accompanying you today. I have no wish to draw his ire."

"It's okay. I can take it from here." I grab her hand as she turns around. "Thank you, Lella Ult Chikat. You saved me today, and in doing so have saved all of my people. I will not forget your kindness."

Lella pulls her hand away. "Enough of the fancy talk. Go, give those flowers to Morgan."

I hurry away without further words. Lella may balk at the formality, but despite our friendship I'm still a queen. Sometimes I have to act like it.

The sun sits low on the horizon when I finally regain the plateau. If I'd hoped to sneak back quietly, though, I was wrong.

"Welcome back, Eve." Eredin Glas sits at the fire,

a setting so familiar and once comforting, but there's nothing comforting about it now. His posture is relaxed in the same way a cat's would be, when they know their prey is trapped and they can devour it at their leisure. He holds an apple in one hand, casually slicing pieces off with the knife in the other. "Did you have a nice walk?"

"You know."

"I know everything that happens in my Wood. I thought you understood that." Eredin Glas stands. Gracefully. Dangerously. He holds out a hand. "Well? Let's see it."

Figures appear in my peripheral vision. Morgan, Rosalyn, and Tupi all spill from my palafito as the King's words command the attention of the entire plateau. Hunters melt from the shadows, more than I bother to count, faces I recognize appearing in the darkness. Jarild. Yaikhaa. Farooq. Nes-Unnefer. Lella.

"Lella?"

"Do not blame her. You know where her loyalty lies."

"You've been playing me all day, then?" I should have learned not to be surprised, but I am. I actually thought we were a step ahead of him this time. I thought I could win. "Why bother?"

"You needed protecting."

I can't deny it. Without Lella, I'd still be out there, wandering around in the dark, lost and starving. Her betrayal still hurts, though.

"Eve?"

I sigh and pull a flower from my pocket. The sheer number I picked seems outrageous now. He'll grind them to dust and that will be the end of it.

The King lifts the wilted yellow blossom to his nose and breathes it in. "Ahh. So sweet. Bacopa Rosea has always been a favorite of mine."

My fatigue makes keeping my frustration and impatience at bay difficult, and his dawdling makes my blood boil. "What of Caspian?"

"What of him?"

"If you knew it was a ruse, where is he?"

"He is dead."

My heart stops, and I can't stop it from showing on my face.

Eredin Glas laughs. "Yes, that is the face I expected to see. You do still harbor affection for the traitor. Set your mind at ease, Eve. The traitor lives." With a wave of his hand fire roars to life around us, revealing a large, lumpy bag hanging from a nearby tree. "He is contained, where he can cause no further trouble. Though I cannot confirm he is whole. My hunters, after all, did not know his effort to free the Fomorian general was not sincere."

*He's trying to get under my skin.* It's working, but I can't let it show. The hunters surrounding us stand silent. Not even a breath of movement, menacing in their very presence. *Where is Danen?* "What now, then?"

The King twirls the blossom between his fingers. "You tell me. You toiled all day for this flower. Don't you want to know if it works?"

*Huh?*

He smiles, a toothy, predatory smile. "Call your human witch. Wake the old man. Let's see what he has to say. Just remember that this is the path you chose."

I watch Eredin Glas, breath held, waiting for the back end. He can't be serious. Whatever game he's playing I can't see the end of it. *Unless he knows Oberon won't tell me what I need to know. But then, why would he keep him under in the first place?* None of it makes any sense, but I see no other choice.

"Morgan?"

She appears at my side in an instant. She doesn't speak, though, just meets my eyes with an intense gaze of her own. I can almost hear her asking me if I really want to be doing this.

"Can you do it?" I ask, passing over a handful of flowers.

She takes the offering and leans forward, resting her forehead against mine. "I can do it."

## Chapter Forty-Six

I go with Morgan. So does Eredin Glas. Tupi and Rosalyn stay close, hovering within earshot but staying out of the crowded palafito. A rustling behind us means the hunters are finally moving, and I get a distinct feeling the noose around me is tightening. I don't have to see them to know they've closed ranks around my palafito, ready to jump at their King's least command. The eyes I feel on my back, though, are anything but hostile. *Danen.* It's a relief to know he's there, even if he's out of reach at the moment. A handful of candles burn at the corners of the platform, casting us occupants in dim light and making us stand out like a beacon on the plateau.

Morgan, for her part, is the picture of calm. She kneels beside Oberon and lights a stick that smells like peppermint. She breathes deeply of the smoke, then wafts the stick over Oberon's sleeping face. With steady hands she lifts a perfect Bacopa Rosea plant, examining it for imperfections before stuffing the entire thing whole into her mouth. She closes her eyes as she swallows, not even chewing, gulping several times to get the plant down. Then she takes several deep breaths and lays her hands on Oberon's head.

She doesn't say anything. Her body goes deathly still, not even seeming to breathe. Time slows. The King and I stand there in silence, not looking at each other, the tension between us building with every passing minute.

Finally, Morgan stirs. She sits back on her heels and lets out a long, slow breath. When she opens her eyes, they're glassed over and reflecting some kind of silver light. "The block is gone. If enough of him remains, he will wake."

"How long?" I whisper.

"I don't know."

We wait. The night ticks by, the darkness above us growing deeper. Clouds cover the stars tonight. In all of my nights here I've only seen perfect skies. A reflection of the King, then? It wouldn't surprise me to know he dictates the weather in his own world.

Oberon groans. I drop to my knees in an instant, and as I hit the cushion his eyelids flutter open. "Titania?" he gasps, his voice dry and raspy.

I grab his hand. "Grandfather, it's me."

"Eve?"

"Yes." Movement sounds behind me as Eredin Glas shifts in place, but I ignore him.

"Here." Morgan lifts a cup smelling faintly of flowers to Oberon's lips and helps him take an unsteady drink.

When she lowers it, I see something solid bobbing on the surface but can't make it out in the shadows.

"Morgan," he says, and smiles. "I have missed you, my friend."

"And I, you."

"Grandfather," I say, drawing his eyes back to me. "A lot has happened since you fell asleep. Do you remember when I found you?"

"Of course I remember, child," he says, looking slightly offended. "I was waiting for you. Took you long enough to come."

I give him a smile. "I am sorry for that. You were waiting to tell me something, right? Something about the magic?"

A light goes on in Oberon's eyes, one I haven't seen since those first days I met him in Emain Ablach. Before his mind started to fail in earnest and he was weak in body but strong in spirit. I exchange glances with Morgan and she nods at the cup. "Ask your questions quickly," she murmurs. "I don't know how long the effects will last."

Oberon needs no prodding, though. Spurred on by whatever herb Morgan drugged him with the words come spilling out of his mouth. "Yes, the magic. You broke it, Eve. You didn't mean to, but you did. Your mother foresaw this."

"No." I shake my head. It doesn't matter that Halasuwa told me the same thing. I know the magic's failure was my fault, but being directly responsible? It can't be true. "No, I didn't. I chose to fight. I drowned Emain Ablach rather than risk my people for Hanathen's visions."

"Do you remember the disasters, Eve? The sinkhole? The earthquake? The fire? The storms?"

"Of course I do."

"What caused those things?"

I don't have to think. "I did. My indecision, my inner conflict threw the entire Realm into chaos. But I made my peace with that," I can't help protesting. "I accepted my role and my legacy. I calmed the Realm and channeled the tsunami building in the lake as a weapon against the Fomorians."

"And when that weapon fired, the magic broke." Oberon's voice is gentle. Patient. Teaching.

Meanwhile, I'm growing more and more frustrated. "But it shouldn't have!"

"But you believed that it would."

That stops me in my tracks. My mind races, pondering his words. Caspian told me the Fomorian plan was for me to break Fae magic. It wasn't something I could be coerced into; I had to choose it. How that would be accomplished we never got around to discussing before I had him arrested and ran off to fight a war. Oberon's words, though, make it sink in. "I did this?"

"You never fully understood your connection to the Realm. To the Fae. Your ancestors built that land. They bled for our people. That connection lives still in your blood. You are in control of far more than you know. If you had grown up there, you would have appreciated that responsibility. You couldn't have known how closely tied you are to every facet of the Fae people."

My blood pounds in my ears. *I did this*. My lungs suddenly feel too heavy, the air too thick to breathe. I squeeze Oberon's hand tighter and tighter, desperate to keep myself from flying off the face of the earth.

Then a cool hand lands on my forehead and a weight settles against my side. "Eve, be still." Tupi's gentle voice croons in my ear. "You cannot change what is past. Focus on what comes next."

*What comes next.* Breathing comes next. With conscious thought I slow my breaths, forcing my body to hold onto them an extra beat before releasing them. I'm aware of the eyes on me, every person present fixated on how I am reacting to this news. *I broke Fae magic. I feared that it would happen, and so it did. My people died because of me.*

Those thoughts won't help right now. Focus on what comes next. Behind me, I hear Danen moving closer, his steps familiar and comforting.

I raise my eyes back to Oberon's. "How do I fix it?"

He smiles. "With magic."

I don't react. The words bounce off me like I'm a brick wall.

His smile falters, like he's misunderstood something important. "You can turn Fae magic back on, Eve, the same way you turned it off. With your will."

It can't be that easy. Then again...

Even after Emain Ablach fell, remnants of Fae magic remained. My chain and medallion. The bond of my words. My inability to lie. Things I believed to be so ingrained in my Fae nature that I never questioned their veracity. Do those things still work because I believed they would?

"But I don't have the magic to do that." I slam my hand down as my overwhelming emotions bubble to the surface. "I am powerless, don't you see? Even if I try to will Fae magic back, it won't work!"

Oberon doesn't recoil. Instead, he uses his spindly arms to shove himself into a wobbly, upright position. Then he grabs my chin and forces his face in front of mine. "You don't have magic. But I do."

Suddenly, his actions make perfect sense. "You knew the hidden room would shield you?"

"I believed it would. It holds a special place in your heart, and I could not see you allowing it to be destroyed."

"But you couldn't have known it would happen that way."

He pats my cheek. "Your mother was never wrong, my dear. If she were leading us, she would have held fast, but her own magic was not what it once was. She was destined to falter, and when she did, the Realm would have fallen with her."

"The Realm fell with me."

"The Realm survived with you. Your bloodline survived, and with it, the hope that our people may yet rise again."

Hope blooms in my chest. "What do I do?"

Oberon's voice is as steady as I've ever heard it. "You take my magic, and you fix what has been broken. Only Fae magic can right this wrong, and you are the only one who can wield it."

"Take … your magic?" My eyes search his, desperate to understand. "How does that even work?"

"It is less a taking, and more a giving. I will feed my magic into you, and you will choose to restore all of Fae magic." His voice drops to a whisper. "It is that simple."

*That simple. Could it really be?* There's only way to find out. "What about you, Grandfather? Will you be hurt?"

"Saving you will be the best thing I have done in this life."

"That's a very Fae answer."

"Those are the only answers I can give. Are you ready, child?"

My adrenaline spikes. "Now?"

"Is there a better time?"

"No. No, there isn't."

"Then take my hand, child, and do not fret. Saving our people is what you were born to do."

I clasp both of Oberon's hands in mine and look deep into his eyes. His hands grow warm, and the hush surrounding us deepens until not a sound can be heard through all of Hellequin Wood.

I didn't see Eredin Glas move. I was too focused on Oberon's eyes, on the fire he was stoking with every word out of his mouth. I should have been paying attention. Silent and deadly, the King takes one step forward and rams his scythe straight through Oberon's heart.

## Chapter Forty-Seven

A strangled yell forces its way out of my throat. Oberon's blood sprays, soaking my entire front. His body falls forward, the sudden weight catching me off guard and toppling me over backward. The connection that was building between us dies, the warmth fading from his hands as the light fades in his eyes.

Around us, chaos erupts. Tupi and Rosalyn scream and flee into the trees. Morgan, perpetually unfazed, throws some kind of powder in Eredin Glas's direction and leaps to her feet, holding a dagger. He knocks her aside easily, though, and she tumbles to the ground outside. Hunters swarm the platform, claiming each of my friends and holding them fast.

There's still one friend left, though. With a bellow, Danen charges up the steps and launches himself at the King.

I squirm out from underneath Oberon's body in time to see the two of them collide and topple over the edge. I follow, slipping on blood but not stopping to let myself dwell on it. I have to see what's happening.

Down on the ground, Danen and Eredin Glas regain their feet.

Eredin Glas laughs, a mocking, derisive laugh. "Come on, then. Show me what you've got."

With a blade in his hand, Danen is poetry in motion. He doesn't hesitate to advance on Eredin Glas, attacking immediately. As Eredin Glas lifts his arm to parry, I catch sight of a small dagger buried to the hilt under his ribs, blood leaking down his side. Danen's opening shot as they collided. It won't be enough.

Fury builds inside as I watch the two of them dance. Their blows leave no room for recovery or breath.

I look down at my hands, covered in Oberon's blood, the knowledge that his body lies on the floor behind me setting my insides ablaze. Oberon wasn't just my last chance to save the Fae on my own; he was my blood. My family. My only connection to the queens who came before me. My own dagger lives in my boot; an instant later it's in my hand. I wait for an opening, then launch myself off the platform.

My aim is true. I land on Eredin Glas's back, my dagger slicing through his ear and driving down into the side of his neck. He howls, reaches behind with one massive hand, and flings me to the ground.

I hit hard, bouncing once before sliding through the dirt to a stop.

"Enough!" Eredin Glas screams, raising one hand to the sky. Light fills the plateau as the full moon above us bursts out of the clouds.

Danen doesn't listen. He charges in, sword aimed for a killing blow. His enemy is injured and weakened; now is the time. The warrior in him can't make any other choice.

Eredin Glas doesn't flinch. "I said, enough." He closes his fist and a pulse blows out in all directions.

Danen is knocked off his feet, spinning through the air to land beside me. He tries to rise, but a massive weight lands on us, pinning us to the ground.

"Now, stay down." The words are superfluous. Neither of us could move if we tried. Some magic of the King's keeps us here, and here we'll stay until he decides to release us. The King advances on us, the expression on his face cold enough to make even Winter House tremble. He pulls Danen's dagger first, letting it fall to the ground as the wound beneath it immediately starts to close.

He winces as he pulls mine, which seems to be stuck in the bone. "This one was close, Eve. Nice aim."

He tosses it aside as his body heals. When he kneels down beside us, the King's fire burns in his eyes. His entire face is cast in shadow, his teeth eerily white against the darkness. The power rolling off him makes my stomach turn.

"Danen. You betrayed your King." His voice is low and dangerous, yet resounding like the surf crashing against the rocks. "Did you think I would let that go unpunished?"

The King snaps his fingers and Danen vanishes.

"No!"

His eyes turn to me. "And you. I am surprised you tried to kill me. I didn't think you had it in you."

"Where is Danen?"

The King waves his hand. "Far, far away, and no longer your concern." He stands, and the weight holding me down lifts.

I stand. "You killed Oberon."

"Of course I did. How does that surprise you? I thought we understood each other, Eve. You want more than anything to save your people. And I, more than anything, want your magic at my disposal. And I will do anything I must to get it."

He raises his eyes to my palafito. "I tried to keep Oberon out of this. I put him to sleep so he couldn't interfere. If you had left him that way, he would still be alive."

"Don't you dare put this on me," I hiss, trembling all over. The urge to finish what Danen started washes over me, but attacking Eredin Glas now is pointless. I don't have a hope of killing him single-handedly. The fantasy of vengeance is sweet, but the lesser, rational part of me knows that Eredin Glas is now my only option for restoring Fae magic.

He knows it, too. So, while I rage and seethe, he

returns to that same predator calm he projected sitting at the fire earlier. He walks forward until we're nearly touching, his head so far over mine I have to crane my neck to meet his eyes. And meet his eyes I do, because even now I will not quail before him.

When he speaks, his voice is hard and cold, the same he used when he banished Danen, but his words are for my ears alone. "You see now what I have known all along. I am the only way you can save your people. You are hurting, but remember this. I gave you one more day, and I am a man of my word. Sunrise, Eve, and your time is up."

Like I need to be reminded. He doesn't insult me further by restating his threat, but neither does he back away, leaving me to be the first to turn. I'd rather not show myself the weaker party, but I'm not certain how much longer my legs can hold my weight. After Oberon, and now Danen, it's all too much. I have to get out of here before I either break down, which is unacceptable, or have to flee, which is also unacceptable. So, with as much dignity as I can muster, I step around Eredin Glas, strut over to where my dagger still lies in the grass, and pick it up. No one stops me.

All eyes are on me as I evaluate my options. The hunters, loyal to their king, are not indifferent to my pain. I've gotten to know several of them, and their expressions hold varying degrees of pity and compassion. Still, none of them will lift a finger to help me. Not when their King has set himself so strongly against me. My eyes seek out Lella amid the congregation. Obvious pain shows in her eyes, but she stands as still as the rest. I believe she truly cares for me, but sometimes that isn't enough.

Morgan, Rosalyn, and Tupi are no longer restrained, but neither are they free. They sit under guard, shielded by hunters I don't know with hard looks on their faces. It's a clear message that I am not allowed to have my friends back. Eredin Glas wants me to feel every bit of this. Alone. Desperate. Weak.

I start walking, not sure where I'm going until I stop in front of a tree. The sack dangling from it is still, and I have to believe that's because the occupant doesn't know what's going on out here rather than the alternatives. Dagger in hand, I seize the rope connecting the bag to the branch above and begin sawing at it.

Footsteps crunch behind me and a shadow blocks the moonlight over my shoulder. I don't pause. "Touch me and I'll kill you," I murmur, meaning every word. The intruder doesn't move, but neither do they stop me. The rope snaps and the bag drops, a hiss of pain sounding as it strikes the ground.

Caspian worms his way out of the bag, rubbing his head but looking otherwise whole. He takes in the scene, his face filling with concern at the sight of me covered in blood and the plateau behind me crawling with hunters.

"Eredin Glas killed Oberon," I say before he can ask.

His gaze hardens and his eyes shift behind me. "And your shadow?"

"Won't interfere if they know what's good for them." The shadow behind me is not Eredin Glas. That much I know. I don't know which hunter followed me over here or exactly what their intentions were, and I don't plan on turning around to find out.

I start walking again, straight past Caspian, knowing he'll follow. The hunter stays behind, letting us go. Caspian doesn't say anything, but he grabs my hand and I let him. Hand in hand, we follow the path that will lead us off the plateau.

# JESSICA GOEKEN

## Chapter Forty-Eight

Caspian doesn't push me for words. His innate ability to read my face is a moot skill, though. I'm broadcasting everything I'm feeling for all the world to see. And I don't care. Halfway down the path my legs finally give up, buckling under my weight and sending me crashing forward. Caspian's arms are there, though, catching me before I hit the ground. Without a word he threads a hand beneath my knees and scoops me into his arms.

I rest my head on his shoulder and let myself forget. Forget the hurt and the betrayal, forget that he sold me out to my enemies, forget that he orchestrated the deaths of my human parents. Forget that I can't trust him, and just let myself breathe in his familiar scent of rain and fireflies and feel safe in his presence again.

We walk far away from the plateau and the hunters who are no longer my friends. Past the camps and the trees and along the beach until the gentle pulse of the waves lulls me into a half-doze. It won't matter how far we walk, though. Eredin Glas will always know where we are. He will always be able to find us. That thought isn't warm or snuggly, though, so I shove it away and bury my nose into Caspian's neck. His chest rises and falls with his breath, slightly labored under the extra effort, but his arms never falter. And finally, finally, I sleep.

"My Lady." Caspian's voice is soft in my ear, his breath tickling the little hairs along my temple.

"Hmm?" Sleep refuses to recede, and I have no desire to make it. My whole body feels heavy, my head pounding with the worst headache I've ever had.

"You can go back to sleep soon, My Lady, but

you should wash the blood off first."

The word blood drags my consciousness kicking and screaming back to the forefront. My eyes snap open to find Caspian's face in front of mine. With a strangled yelp, I push him away and tumble down into the sand. I crouch there on my hands and knees, heaving and gasping, my lungs refusing to work right. *This is Oberon's blood.* My grandfather is dead. My hope for saving the Fae is dead. I have nothing left.

No. I have Caspian. He's still where I left him, a couple steps behind me waiting silently for me to need him again. I can't seem to stop needing Caspian, even when all sense and logic tells me to stay far away from him. I squeeze my eyes shut, letting burning tears fall, begging the world to be different when I open them again.

It's not. The moon is still high in the sky, meaning the night is still early. After all that's happened, I feel like entire days should have passed, but it's good that they haven't. The sun will rise soon enough, and I will have to decide how I wish to lose my people: fail to save our magic and live amongst them as a pariah, or restore their magic and abandon them forever. It's an impossible decision.

My body still feels too heavy to move, but I finally stand. When I turn to face Caspian, his expression is drawn and full of sorrow. Some sorrow for Oberon, but mostly sorrow for me. My pain is his pain. I can't deny the strength of his feelings for me, regardless of his actions.

"The blood, My Lady."

It still coats my front. I feel it on my face, my neck, my chest. I see it on my hands and on my clothes. Caspian wears it now, too, like an ominous stain foretelling the future of the Fae.

We've stopped where the sea moves inland to form a sheltered lagoon. Sweeping trees line the banks, hiding the forest beyond and creating an isolated atmosphere. The moon rests atop the water, a perfect replica of the one shining overhead. The water is calm and shallow, which must be why Caspian picked it.

I still don't address Caspian, but I do wade into the water. Step by step, farther and farther until it begins to cover my face. Still, I wade deeper, holding my breath and letting the water close over me. The water pushes in from all sides, wrapping itself around me in the embrace I so desperately need. I let it hold me until my chest burns, then I push with my feet and let my head crest the surface. That's when it really hits me that I'm covered in Oberon's blood, and I begin scrubbing furiously. My skin. My clothes. My hair. I can't see the blood, but I know it's there. The saltwater stings my skin as I rub it raw, chokes my throat as I suck it in and spit it back out through my teeth. No matter what I do, it will never be enough, I will never be clean, never—

"Easy, My Lady, that's enough. That's enough." Caspian's arms wind around me and drag me backward through the water. I fight against him, thrashing and kicking, but it's no use. He's always been stronger than me, and I'm running on essentially no sleep and little food. The adrenaline that pushed me into attacking Eredin Glas is spent. Nothing remains inside.

Caspian scoops me up again and carries me across the sand and into the tree line. I fall still as the trees close in overhead, blocking out all but the most stubborn of moonbeams. The darkness here is gentle and comforting, so different from the darkness I've grown accustomed to over the past year. Night creatures chatter in our wake, unperturbed by our presence. Everything about Hellequin Wood that reminds me of the Realm is right here.

Choosing his spot carefully, Caspian sinks down into the bowels of a great willow tree, the ground below carpeted in velvety leaves. He settles me in his lap, tucking my head under his chin, and reclines the both of us against the trunk.

"It's okay. You are safe with me, My Lady."

That's all it takes to open the floodgates. I'm too exhausted to even try to stem the flow of emotion, but I find I don't want to anyway. Everything hurts, and trying to pretend it doesn't would be a great disservice to the ones I have lost. Diminish them, somehow. So, I cry. I sob and sputter and hack and do all manner of unqueenly things, hidden here in the trees with only Caspian to see. Caspian, who doesn't judge me for caring about things or for showing emotion. The scene is all too reminiscent of a similar night long ago, when he held me in the dark as I lost control and mourned the loss of my parents. Tonight's pain is every bit as raw and destructive as that pain, the ghosts of which will haunt me for the rest of my days. Some things you never get over.

Caspian says nothing as I spend the remainder of my energy venting all of my pain, anger, and hopelessness. His arms stay strong around me, his cheek stays pressed against me, and his heartbeat stays steady in my ear. And, when I have nothing left to give, he still holds me tight as I pass back into oblivion.

I rouse of my own accord next time. I'm far from rested, but even in oblivion I am aware that I can't stay here. "How long?" I croak at Caspian.

"Six hours, give or take." With one hand, he sweeps the dried, crusty hair from my forehead. "How are you feeling?"

I uncurl myself from his embrace, stretching out the aches and the kinks, and pull myself to my feet. Ignoring his question, I walk back and forth, swinging my arms and trying to get my blood flowing. "How long until sunrise?"

"If I were to guess, three or four hours." Caspian's eyes follow me as I pace. "What happens at sunrise?"

"All of this ends. One way or another." I can't fault Caspian for his confusion. I haven't kept him in my confidences. Still, articulating the words isn't easy. I walk him through all of it, both the promises and the threats Eredin Glas has made.

"According to Oberon, I need an infusion of Fae magic to be able to use it and turn all of Fae magic back on. That's why he concealed himself in the hidden room."

"Yet the King claims he can perform this function?"

"He's never explicitly said." I mull over the King's words, searching for any grains of truth I may have overlooked.

"Is he in possession of Fae magic?"

Understanding dawns. "He is. The Wild Hunt pursues magic users. When they find their quarry, the King absorbs their magic. It's like he sucks it out of their bodies. I've seen him do it."

"So, if he has hunted Fae, and we must assume he has, then he has absorbed Fae magic."

"And he can channel that into me just like Oberon could." I've missed this between the two of us. "The problem is convincing him to do it without selling him myself."

"My Lady," Caspian says, his eyes lighting with mischief. "We're Fae. We'll trick him."

## Chapter Forty-Nine

"You can't trick the King of the Wild Hunt. I've tried."

"*Well…*" Caspian draws out the word. "You've only been a Fae in practice for a year, and you have little tricking experience. Luckily, tricking humans is Summer House expertise."

"Eredin Glas isn't a human."

"He used to be."

That one throws me. "Really?"

"He hasn't been in a long, long time, but his core is still very human. He shields himself in power and mystery, but he is not without weakness. Exploit that weakness, and he will fall." Weighted silence falls between us until Caspian gives me a nudge. "You know him better than I, My Lady. What are his weaknesses?"

*Eredin Glas doesn't have weaknesses.* I can't say that. It doesn't solve the problem and will be less than useless. *Think! Think! Think!* I start pacing again, running my hands through my hair and pulling at the tangles. *Tupi will be so mad at me for this.*

My stomach growls, distracting me from my thoughts. "Ignore it," I tell Caspian as he gets to his feet.

"I cannot, My Lady. I hunger as well, so while you ponder the King, I will find us something to eat."

I don't argue. Nor do I give guidance. We have no supplies, so we'll be eating whatever plants he can scavenge. It won't be the first time. Again, my memories fly back, this time to Caspian feeding me in the desert when I was broken from missing the window to get back to the Realm. Just like when he comforted me after losing my parents. Even though he orchestrated those events my feelings from that time were very real. And still are. I know Caspian has done awful things, but so many of my memories of him are good that the two sides prove difficult to reconcile.

When Caspian returns, I think I have an answer to our conundrum. As I expected, his tied-up shirt contains a variety of scavenged foodstuffs, from flowers to nuts to roots dug out of the ground. "This land is overflowing with life, My Lady," he says in excitement. "It feels nearly like home."

"I know what you mean," I say softly, banishing the reminiscences that have been plaguing me. "But it's not home. It will never be my home."

Caspian reads my tone and the smile falls from his face. "Have you uncovered any insights into the King?"

"I think I have. He projects arrogance and bravado, and I do not think that is a falsehood. Yet he responds harshly and decisively when that image is threatened."

"So we play to his ego?"

"Yes. Build him up. Make him think he has won."

"While sealing his own fall. The right wording will be essential. However, he knows you're with me, so he'll be anticipating a trick."

"So we need a decoy trick. A big one, so that when he sees through it, he will think I'm beaten." Easier said than done. Coming up with one way to trick Eredin Glas is difficult enough. Two tricks feels impossible.

"Not impossible." Caspian lays his hand on mine. My gaze shoots to that hand and he quickly withdraws it, but an intimate expression stays etched on his face. "I need you to trust me in this, My Lady." He takes a deep breath, then plows on, his voice growing heavier with each word. "I do not say this to hurt you. But, I spent all of my time with you layering tricks and misdirections, and you never saw them coming. I fooled every Fae at court. I fooled Vogelein, and Danen, so do not think the King of the Wild Hunt is beyond my abilities. I am the best option for getting you out of this mess."

"I know you are." I drop my eyes to the ground. "But I don't know if that's a good thing."

Silence falls between us, heavy and tense. It's easy to fall back into the camaraderie Caspian and I shared, but that isn't who either of us are anymore. Caspian may very well be who I need right now, but if we succeed? What do I do with him then?

**\*\*\*\***

The sun rests just below the horizon when I ascend the plateau. Freshly scrubbed, wearing clean clothes pilfered from the hunters' tents and my silver hair braided back, I look as ready for battle as I can. Lumps on the ground indicate where the hunters bedded down for the night, choosing to close ranks around their King rather than seek their own camps. I walk quietly among them, but not quietly enough. Trained hunters that they are, they wake at my passing and straggle behind me until I've garnered quite the following.

I find Eredin Glas at the fire, right where I expected him to be. His eyes tell me I'm right where he expected me to be, too. They take in the various blades tucked into my boots and the short sword strapped across my back. "Have you come to kill me, Eve?" he asks, brushing his hands on his pants and standing up to his full, imposing height.

"After our last encounter it would be foolish not to be prepared for the possibility." Every single word I say matters. The delivery, the inflection, the pauses, all have been carefully scripted by my own professional liar.

He waves at the weapons. "I see you took advantage of our conclave last night."

"I did. Your hunters have excellent taste."

"That they do. They will be expecting their items returned, of course, once you are done with them."

"I will return them once I have received back what is mine. Speaking of, where are my friends? I do not see them here."

"The humans and the pixie reside comfortably in my quarters at the moment. I did not require them, as I chose to wait here for you."

There's the transition. I don't take it, though, choosing silence instead. If Eredin Glas wants to force this issue he will be the one to do so.

It doesn't take long. The sun crests the horizon, spilling pink light across the ground. "The time is expired, Eve. Have you reached a decision?"

*Here we go.* I meet Eredin Glas's gaze with all the authority I can summon into my own. "I am not ready to abandon my people to their fate."

On cue, Caspian flies over the far end of the plateau, his Fomorian magic on display. And he's not alone. A hulking beast with curling ram's horns lands heavily beside him, shaking the ground and sending unwitting hunters to their knees. General Halasuwa bellows a challenge, then lowers his head and rushes Eredin Glas.

My mouth drops open as I witness the speed Halasuwa puts on. He snorts like a bull and charges like a freight train.

Eredin Glas shoots me a furious look, then whips his attention back to the rampaging Fomorian. He bellows in response, hoisting his scythe and striding into the open to meet his opponent. As the King moves, the ground trembles in his wake. The fresh dawn darkens with wicked storm clouds, and a vicious wind slices through my clothes.

The hunters spring into action, fanning out to back up their King. It quickly becomes apparent, though, that Eredin Glas doesn't want their help. The two larger-than-life figures crash into each other with enough force to split the ground beneath them.

Caspian catches my eye and winks, and I race toward the fray.

Halasuwa's injuries won't let him stand against Eredin Glas for long. The Fomorian rears back and head-butts Eredin Glas, shattering his nose, then catches him around the throat with his remaining massive hand. The Fomorian hoists the King into the air, but Eredin Glas has only begun fighting. Here, at the pinnacle of his land, surrounded by his hunters, his power is immeasurable. Bolts of lightning shoot from the sky and strike Halasuwa, over and over.

Halasuwa roars but is otherwise unfazed, and then brings his own magic to bear.

*Come on, come on.* It feels profoundly wrong to be rooting for my enemy. Still…

Eredin Glas's face tells me the exact moment he feels Halasuwa's magic. Fomorian magic isn't strong, but it's sneaky, and the tendrils weaving themselves inside Eredin Glas in search of Fae magic can't feel pleasant. Halasuwa finds what he's looking for, though, his own face tightening under the strain.

"Where's the girl?" Halasuwa grinds out, forcing the words out between clenched teeth.

"I'm here." I dodge Eredin Glas's swinging arms to wrap my hands around Halasuwa's stump. The moment I connect with him I feel the Fae magic thrumming under my fingertips. My heart races as my hands warm, just like when I was holding Oberon's. *Maybe this will work after all…*

Eredin Glas thrashes, wedging a foot against

Halasuwa's chest and shoving. A knife appears in his hand and slices for the hand holding his throat. History repeats itself as Halasuwa loses his second hand, screaming in pain and reeling backward. He doesn't have long to dwell on the loss, though. Eredin Glas hits the ground, swings his scythe around, and buries it in Halasuwa's chest.

Halasuwa's eyes meet mine at the impact. For once, I don't see hatred behind them. Not now, not at the resolution of our bargain. I chose the time and manner of his death, and he met his end locked in battle with an enemy. It's the closest we could ever have gotten to friendship. He falls away from me and I lose my balance, tears springing to my eyes as the connection to my magic is severed once again. The dying bray of Halasuwa resounds in my ears, sending a harsh ringing through my brain. I shake my head and push myself to my knees as a shadow falls over me.

## Chapter Fifty

Eredin Glas stands black against the morning sunlight, now released from the clouds his fury created. His chest still heaves from exertion, but the eyes he trains on me are alien and full of fire.

"Is that the best you can do?" he growls, grabbing me by the hair and hauling me into the air. "This puny attempt at a coup is all you've got?" He thrusts his face into mine and gives me a shake. "Is this the bargain you struck with the Fomorian? To kill me? I expected better from the Queen of the Fae."

His head suddenly snaps to the side. "Don't think I've forgotten about you." With a wave of his hand a blast of air hits Caspian and knocks him across the ground. Eredin Glas keeps pushing until Caspian reaches the edge of the plateau and tumbles off.

"You'll kill him!" I shriek, thrashing my arms and legs. I can't reach the King, though, and only succeed in ripping out chunks of my hair.

"When will you understand? You can't win." Eredin Glas throws me to the ground and kneels down beside me. His voice lowers. "This is your last chance, Eve. Submit to me. You know you have no other choice if you ever want your people to have their magic back. Are you going to be the queen they need, or not?"

He knows just how to cut through me. I sniffle. My body protests when I force myself to my knees. I keep my eyes trained on the ground, letting the pain pulsing through my head show in my every expression. My arms and legs tremble, and I let my voice tremble with it. "I am the queen they need," I whisper.

"Excuse me? I can't hear you."

"I said, I *am* the queen they need."

Eredin Glas shifts his weight, crushing the grass beneath his heavy boots. "And?"

"Please, give me my magic back."

He barks a laugh. "Finally. You are a tough nut to crack, Your Majesty. It isn't that simple, though, is it?"

*No, it isn't.* "Tell me what you want."

He leans in closer. "You know what I want." I do know, but I need him to say it. Fortunately, he doesn't need further prompting. "I want you to join with me. Accept your place as my queen and ride at my side for the rest of your days."

*Perfect.* I raise my eyes and meet his gaze. I let all of my sorrow and regret fill my expression as I make my vow. "I will be your queen. I swear it. Give me my magic, and allow me to restore my people, and I will be your queen for the rest of my days."

"Agreed." Eredin Glas's grin splits his face, and he holds out a hand to help me to my feet. Around us, the tension on the plateau palpably eases at the sudden change in the King's bearing. The early sun shines brightly in a cloudless sky, and a gentle breeze rustles the treetops in a comforting whisper.

Once I'm standing, Eredin Glas plants his feet in front of me and grasps my hands like Oberon did. "This is a good thing, Eve. You made the right decision."

"Yes, I did." Our eyes remain locked on one another as his hands grow warm. My body responds to the proximity of Fae magic, reaching for it with every fiber of my being. Twice now I've been so close only to have it ripped away. I hunger for it, and as it flows into me, I throw my head back and close my eyes in bliss.

Magic fills up every empty space I didn't know I had. The half-existence I've been living for the past year explodes into sensation and color, the very air suddenly tingling and overstimulating against my skin. My body comes alive, thrumming with energy and awareness and purpose. I *feel* everything. The leaves on the trees, the waves against the beach, the worms crawling in the dirt beneath my boots. I could stay like this forever, blissfully lost in my own personal euphoria.

I don't notice when Eredin Glas releases my hands. I suck in sun-soaked breaths until his voice finally breaks through. "Eve!" From his tone, it's not the first time he's said my name.

"Hmm?" I slowly open my eyes, squinting against the influx of light.

"It's time you come down and fulfill your end of the bargain."

*Come down?* I look at the ground only to find it several feet below where I expected it to be. I'm floating in the air, arms spread out as if I've been bobbing on the ocean's waves. Flowers have exploded out of the dirt in all directions. Daisies, lilies, passion flowers, lotuses, jacarandas, amaryllises. A rainbow of color spreading across the plateau.

He's right. I can't keep this feeling to myself forever. And I don't want to. This magic is the first step to healing my people. It's time for them to have it back.

With a thought, I drift back down until my feet once again stand firmly planted.

Eredin Glas gives me a look that says he's not impressed, but I can see the impatience behind it. He wants me to get on with it so we can move on to the being-under-his-control-forever part. He won't be too pleased with how that turns out, but I do take his admonition to hurry to heart.

With a breath, I draw my mind inside myself. Ailie struggled so hard to teach me how to do this, but I wasn't ready then. I know myself better now. I'm not afraid of what I'm going to find in here. *Just do it. Will*

*Fae magic back.*

I feel it. The second I decide to do it, warmth suffuses my body. It builds to a fiery crescendo, then bursts outward in all directions. I feel like a volcano, spewing magic into the atmosphere. More than that, I can feel my people. Spread as they are across the human world, I see them like points of light, flaring in brilliance as their magic takes hold. First their surprise, then their joy, rushes through me. It builds, and builds, until it suddenly becomes too much and I hit my knees, wrapping my arms around my head. I pull back, withdrawing from our connection, letting my people celebrate in peace.

My awareness returns into my own body, and as my mind becomes my own again, I raise my face back up to the sky. *I am whole.* I scream, unleashing all of my pent-up angst and fatigue in that one primal noise. The sky responds, churning with black clouds and thundering loud enough to shake the ground. The temperature plummets, instantly freezing over the flowers I just grew and stopping the breath in my lungs.

"Eeeee!" The squeal reaches my ears from across the plateau as Tupi explodes from her captivity in Eredin Glas's palafito and zooms toward me. Her wings flap so fast I can't even see them, and a second later her body barrels into mine without even slowing. The two of us tumble across the ground, her warm Spring magic colliding with my display of Winter magic and spawning a chilly day with sprinkling showers. We lay on the grass and laugh, our legs tangled around each other, sending bursts of flower petals raining out of the clouds above.

Until a familiar shadow falls over both of us.

Eredin Glas does not look amused at our antics. I couldn't care less, and I send a burst of flower petals raining down over him to prove it.

"Is this how a queen behaves, Eve?"

"Yes," I giggle. "Yes, it is."

With a wave, Eredin Glas disperses my clouds and returns the temperature to normal. "I understand your elation, but your celebration is premature. Our bargain is not yet concluded."

I sober instantly. I untangle myself from Tupi and get to my feet with as much dignity as I can muster. "You're right. We still have business to attend to."

# JESSICA GOEKEN

## Chapter Fifty-One

Eredin Glas stares at me expectantly. I take a few steps forward, moving into his personal space while shielding Tupi behind me. I throw one hand out to the side, palm out, indicating to Tupi that she should stay where she is. She knows me well enough to not ask questions, especially as the air on the plateau once again fills with tension. She is quickly joined by Morgan and Rosalyn, drawn forth by my apparent victory.

"I expect you to honor our agreement," Eredin Glas says, "now that I have fulfilled my obligation. Fae magic is yours once again."

"Yes, it is. Thank you. I will accept your fealty whenever you are ready to give it."

Confusion flickers across Eredin Glas's face but vanishes just as quickly. "You seem to be mistaken. It is you who owes me fealty."

"Not according to our bargain—"

"I laid out the terms of our bargain," Eredin Glas says, interrupting me. "You join me. Become my queen. Ride with the Hunt."

"Those were your stated desires, yet I set the terms upon which we agreed. Our bargain states that I will be your queen for the rest of my days. I will become your queen once you swear fealty to me."

It only takes a moment for Eredin Glas to work through the nuance of the words that passed between us. His face turns murderous as he realizes I'm right. "You evil, deceitful—"

"Fae?" I supply helpfully. I take another step closer, nearly brushing against him, and lower my voice the same way he does to me. "What did you expect? You struck a bargain with the Queen of the Fae. And you believed you would prevail?"

Eredin Glas's eyes flame and he gnashes his teeth. "You will not get away with this. I will never swear fealty to you. You are no match for me, and you know it." The sky darkens again and his thunder rumbles.

"I *was* no match for you. When I was weak, vulnerable, and susceptible to your manipulation. I did not desire to force you into this. If you had treated with me fairly from the beginning, and not held my people's magic hostage against my own servitude, then we could have ended this on better terms. However, a deal struck with a Fae is binding. You know this better than anyone. You can try to think your way out of it, try to out-clever me, but the end has already come. You *will* swear fealty to me, because you already vowed to do so."

Eredin Glas fumes, but he keeps his mouth shut. I feel the hunters behind me before I hear them, and I use a blast of wind to knock them off their feet just like Eredin Glas did to Caspian. I allow one to remain standing. "Hail, Jarild. Please, join us."

The King's lieutenant edges cautiously into view, hand on the hilt of his sword. "My liege?" More hunters approach but stay cautiously at a distance, waiting for a sign telling them what to do.

"The King is in no immediate danger from me. However, I do believe he is contemplating trying to kill me. That is an option, but I am no longer the harmless waif I once was." I emphasize this statement with a sharp bolt of lightning that strikes the ground at Jarild's feet, causing him to yelp and jump back. "How many hunters is my death worth?"

"My liege?" Jarild repeats, his voice strong despite the threat looming in front of him. The Wild Hunt spends their existence hunting magic. I must seem no different than their usual quarry.

Eredin Glas pauses long enough to make me think he's actually going to do it. Part of me hopes he will. The one time our magics clashed I emerged the victor. *How would it turn out now?*

Then, he says, "Stand down."

"Wise choice."

Eredin Glas straightens his shoulders. "This is not the end, Eve. I will find a way out of this, I swear it, even if it takes me until the end of my days."

"You would not be the King I know if you didn't. Now, kneel."

Eredin Glas hesitates and I send the ground rumbling. Still, he stands a moment longer, asserting one last act of defiance, before stepping forward and slowly lowering one knee to the ground. His eyes burn down to coals, and I know for a certainty I will never see his warm, chocolate eyes again. This act cements us as enemies. There is no going back.

I wave my fingers, and the surrounding hunters move in closer. "You will all want to hear this," I say.

"Eve La Stella, Queen of the Fae, I hereby pledge my fealty, and the fealty of the Wild Hunt under my command, to you. I accept you as my queen, and will serve you in whatsoever way you see fit, until the end of your days." The hunters circling us fall utterly silent, and I work to keep my breaths calm and even.

"I accept your fealty, Eredin Glas, King of the Wild Hunt. Rise."

Eredin Glas gains his feet and stands staring down at me. The sudden shift in our relationship is discomfiting, but I don't let it show. I can never show weakness in front of him again. He'll tear me apart.

His voice is heavy with disdain as he asks, "What do you wish of me, My Queen?"

I am now responsible for the fate of two peoples,

and the weight of that responsibility lands heavily on my shoulders. "I do not wish to interfere in the conduct of the Hunt. You, Eredin Glas, will retain your autonomy in leadership, answerable to me as I see fit. When I contact you, you will answer, and when I summon you, you will come."

Eredin Glas gives a mock bow. "As you will, My Queen." He turns and stalks away, the hunters falling into place behind him. I let them go. They have much to discuss, and it is time to turn my attention homeward.

With the departure of the hunters, Tupi, Morgan, and Rosalyn cluster around me, varying degrees of elation and apprehension on their faces.

"Do you think it wise to leash the King of the Wild Hunt?" Morgan asks, jumping right into it.

"No," I answer honestly, "but it was the only viable option left to me."

"He will not take this lying down. He will thwart you at every turn, and he will devote his life to making you pay."

"I know he will, but I will handle Eredin Glas in due time."

I lock eyes with Tupi. She, of the three of them, is the only one who fully understands what I'm feeling right now.

"You did it, Your Majesty." Her eyes brim with tears and her wings buzz uncontrollably.

"*We* did it, Tupi. Fae magic is restored. Our people will once again be whole."

"What will you do now, Eve? I mean, Your Majesty?" Rosalyn stands plastered to Morgan's side, and while her eyes skirt mine I can read the discomfort on her face. I never ceased to be a queen, but my newfound display of power has obviously unsettled the girl. Thankfully, we have plenty of time ahead of us to grow comfortable with each other.

"I will rebuild. I will cleanse the Realm of the darkness that has taken hold in my absence, and I will bring the Fae back into their rightful land. But, first…"

When I was still drenched in the awareness of my people, I saw two lights indicating Fae in Hellequin Wood. Tupi, who now stands with me, and Caspian, who still lays at the bottom of the cliff where Eredin Glas threw him. With a burst of wind, I lift his broken body and guide it to the ground in front of me.

"Is he…"

"He lives," I whisper, before resting my hand on his chest. The healing Spring magic comes easily, and Rosalyn gasps as she sees his body knit itself back together in front of her eyes.

Caspian groans and flutters his eyes open. "I told you to let him kill me," he wheezes.

"I'm not ready for you to die yet."

He gives me a weak smile.

"But, neither can I keep you at my side."

Caspian sighs. "I know."

"Your betrayal led to the downfall of the Realm and the slaughter of our people. My position requires me to pass judgment, and I will do that now. The punishment for treason is death. However, your aid today was pivotal in securing the return of our magic, and that cannot go ignored. You doomed our people, yet you have also saved them. I do not sentence you to death, Caspian, but I do sentence you to banishment. Your life is your own, but you will never step foot in the Realm again."

The lighthearted atmosphere of a moment before vanishes in a breath.

Caspian gets slowly to his feet, ignoring everyone else but stepping in close to me. "I do not fault you for this decision, My Lady." His next words are for my ears alone. "My heart sorrows with all I have lost, and I know for a certainty that I have lost you. I will always belong to you, My Lady, no matter through which world my feet travel." He kisses me on the cheek, then walks away, disappearing into the trees without a backward glance.

"Your Majesty?" Tupi touches my shoulder, pulling me from my churning thoughts. Her face wars with both hope and uncertainty, looking to me for guidance.

I shake off the fog that Caspian's words cast over me. I look at Tupi, Morgan, and Rosalyn each in turn, setting my expression into one of determination. "We will leave Hellequin Wood as soon as we are able. We will travel to the human world and connect with our people. Then, we will lead them home."

# Epilogue

"How does it feel?"

I look over my shoulder at Reif, King of Atlantis, and find his eyes cast far out to sea. "How does what feel? The sun? The sea air?" It's an inane question. Of course he's not talking about the sun or the sea air.

His eyes shift to mine, those sea green orbs the exact color of the waves sloshing against my feet. "Power. Freedom. Having your life back."

I shake my head slowly. "I do have my magic returned, but I would not say I have my life back. My people remain scattered and hostile to reconciliation, and my land has been overrun with creatures of darkness. It is this that prompted my visit here, in fact."

King Reif is no dummy. I have not divulged the details of my victory over Eredin Glas, but the authority in my bearing is unmistakable. He can see I am no longer under the thumb of the King of the Wild Hunt. Yet, I'm obviously here for something. "I am no master of Fae politics, Your Majesty. I fear I am unqualified to counsel you in the restoration of your kingdom."

I wave the words away with my hand. "I can handle the people." I hesitate for only a breath before plowing forward, choosing to trust this near stranger with just how precarious the Fae situation is. "But our numbers are heavily diminished, and our strength is weak. I will unite our people once again, but we do not yet have a home to return to.

"On my last visit you told me how your ancestors once aided Queen Peony with, in your words, 'an incursion of sea monsters into the Realm'."

A knowing look comes into King Reif's eyes. "You wish for my help to expel the creatures currently occupying the Realm?"

*Now or never.* "I do. I do not know if the Fae are up to the magnitude of the task before us. Therefore, I wish to resurrect the old alliance between the Fae and Atlantis. Come to our aid, and we will be beholden to come to yours."

It's a risky promise, but it's also the only one I can make right now. Indebting the Fae with an unspecified favor to an untested ally could prove our downfall. But we cannot do this alone. It is up to me to choose who to trust, and I have a good feeling about choosing Atlantis.

King Reif considers. "Forgive me, Your Majesty, but I would be unwise in rushing into a bargain with a Fae, even one so transparent as yourself."

"No forgiveness needed. I well understand your responsibility to your city and to your people. Bargaining with a Fae has historically been an unwise move. But, if our ancestors could find common ground, I choose to believe that we are capable of such feats as well."

"You possess the silver tongue of your ancestors, Your Majesty."

"Eve, please."

"Eve." He nods. "I must bring your proposal before the Chamber. I will need their support if I am to enter into an alliance with your people."

"I understand," I say, masking the sinking of my heart. I do understand, but I had hoped that I would be leaving here today with the promise of aid. Nevertheless, I will retake the Realm, with the support of Atlantis or not.

King Reif starts talking again before I can make my exit. He's several words in before I realize just what it is he's telling me, but when I do, my heart thuds heavily against my ribcage.

"Before you go, as a gesture of good will between our two peoples regardless of any formal alliance, I have come into possession of something that I would like to return to you."

He opens his mouth just a sliver and a shrill whistle comes floating out. The sound floats hauntingly across the open water like it has a specific destination in mind. Almost immediately, it's answered by a whinny I recognize instantly.

"They came to me when the borders of the Realm fell, seeking sanctuary. Atlantis has always been a safe place for their kind."

Now I can see them, the flash of their multicolored scales sending rainbows of sunlight in all directions. Their feet barely touch the water, racing every bit as fast as a mount of the Wild Hunt. At their head, black dragon face held high and antlers standing tall, rides the one who holds a piece of my heart. She whinnies again when she sees me, putting on enough speed to outdistance the rest of the herd.

I can't contain myself. I rush forward, plunging into the water, ignoring the way the waves pull at my legs. I strain against the swell to reach her, but she doesn't need my help. She plants her feet and slides to a stop in front of me, pulling up short a mere hair's breadth from my face. She's so close I can barely see her, but I don't need to. She slams her head into mine as I throw my arms around her neck.

"Keshi!"

**The End**

**JESSICA GOEKEN**

**Evernight Teen ®**

**www.evernightteen.com**